Second

Chances

A Novel

By

K. L. McKee

K.L. McKee

Cameo Mountain Press

Palisade, CO 81526

Copyright ©2021 by Karen Lea McKee

Front Cover Photo—Mount Lamborn

Back Cover Photo—Peach Blossoms

Photographer K. L. McKee

First Edition

North Fork Series Book #3

"Be kind and compassionate to one another, forgiving each other, just as in Christ God forgave you." Ephesians 4:32

Dedication

To the orchardists who battle the elements 24/7, 365 days a year to bring delicious fruit to our tables.

K.L. McKee

Notes and Acknowledgments

None of the characters in *Second Chances* exist except in my imagination and bear no resemblance to people living or dead or any relation to persons of the same name.

Some geographic locations in the book are real. Although the North Fork Valley is an actual location in Western Colorado, the town of North Fork does not exist. It is here that I took liberties with geography, creating the fictional town of North Fork, set against the West Elk Mountain Range and the Castle Range. Mount Lamborn, Grand Mesa, Ragged Mountain, Marcellina, West Beckwith, Gunnison, and the Rubies mentioned in *Second Chances,* are real with elevations ranging from 11,000 feet to over 12,000 feet. Kebler Pass and Lost Lake Slough are also locations in the North Fork area.

Growing up in a community surrounded by fruit orchards—cherries, apples, peaches, pears, and apricots—I have a special affection for the growers. Growing fruit is one of the most unpredictable of all types of farming. The growers battle the elements throughout the year in order to provide quality fruit for our enjoyment. The orchardists have my deepest respect.

As with all projects, numerous individuals contributed to the writing of this book. Many thanks to orchardists John and Doris Butler and their work establishing the Mesa Land Trust, Marti Fuller of Fuller Orchards, and Jan Pomrenke, for their input on fruit growing. Without these individuals, my story would not be authentic. The author takes full responsibility for any errors or misunderstandings concerning fruit growing and land trusts.

Every writer needs a support group. Patti Hill, Lucinda Stein, Pamela Larson, Joyce Anderson, Donna Bettencourt, and Penny Shiel became my friends, my best critics, and my cheering section. They kindly but firmly put me on the right track to make the words of my story come alive. My biggest supporter is my husband, Steve. I am forever grateful for his understanding and continued support of my passion for writing.

Second Chances

A NOVEL

CHAPTER 1

Denver, Colorado—June 16, 2003

Marco Rodriguez, exhilarated and reckless, pressed harder on the gas pedal, his foot stretching to reach it. The silver Chevy Tahoe surged along the near empty street. He laughed and yelled at the same time. The speedometer inched to sixty miles per hour. Marco peered through the steering wheel as the SUV raced along the street, weaving in and out of the sparse traffic. He saw the light turn red at Lincoln and East Alameda too late to stop, so he gunned the vehicle. This time of night what would it matter anyway if he ran the light? Too late he caught the blur of red to his right. The blare of the horn, the screech of tires, and the crunch of metal against metal were the last sounds he heard.

~

Alex Lambert sat in the courtroom and fought the anger welling inside. The last few days he'd lived a nightmare—in his dreams when he could sleep during the long hours of each day, and in the unbearable loneliness of the nights when he couldn't sleep. He moved through his life in slow motion, wondering what if . . . What if he'd gone with Amy to visit her mother? What if she and Alex Jr. had left Fort Collins an hour earlier as planned? What if some punk hadn't driven drunk? The "what if's" drove him crazy.

The bailiff intoned "Please rise. District Court of Denver City and County, Juvenile Division, is now in session, the Honorable William Hastings presiding."

The judge entered the courtroom. "Be seated," he said to the few people in attendance. He turned to the bailiff. "Call the first case."

"The City and County of Denver versus Marco Rodriguez."

Hate filling his heart, Alex waited to see the monster who had stolen everything he loved and held dear. Instead, a small, thin boy, no older than nine or ten, was ushered into the court, his red, puffy eyes darting around the room. Scratches and bruises covered his face and a bandage hid his right eye. The public defender held the boy's arm as he faced the judge. He sat in an oversized chair, his head and eyes downcast. Alex had expected a teenage punk with tattoos and an attitude. The last thing he expected was a diminutive boy who slumped under the weight of the world. He couldn't take his eyes off the scene before him.

The judge addressed the public defender. "Ms. Crawford, your client is charged with driving without a license, driving while intoxicated, running a red light, speeding, reckless endangerment, and involuntary manslaughter in the deaths of Amy Lambert, her four-year-old son, Alex, and her unborn child. Mr. Rodriguez, please stand."

The small boy stood on shaky legs, his head hung, refusing to look at the judge.

"Mr. Rodriguez, look at me," the judge ordered. The boy lifted his head, his eyes blank. "Do you understand the charges?" A slight nod came from the defendant. "Please answer out loud," the judge ordered.

"Yes, your honor," he answered, barely above a whisper. Tears rushed down his cheeks.

"How do you plead?" the judge asked.

He looked at the Public Defender. She nodded. "No c-contest." He choked on an escaping sob.

"Very well. Sentencing will be a week from today. Until then, Mr. Rodriguez, you are remanded to the custody of youth services." He tapped his gavel. "Next case."

Alex slipped out of the courtroom. He was shaking and unable to absorb what he had just witnessed. A child. Not a teenager. A child. Why? What was he doing driving . . . and drunk? The arrest documents had him at .12 blood alcohol level. He wasn't tall enough to see over the top of the steering wheel, yet he'd been driving at sixty miles per hour on a semi-deserted street in the middle of Denver. Where was his mother? His father? Earlier, Alex had glanced around the courtroom and hadn't seen anyone who appeared to be related to the boy.

Barbara Crawford, a woman he had dealt with involving other cases, strode down the hall toward him. He stood and caught her eye. "Barbara, may I talk to you a moment?"

She stopped and offered her hand. "I'm so sorry for your loss, Alex. I can't imagine how you're coping. Unfortunately, my turn came up and this case landed in my lap. I'd give anything not to have to deal with it. How are you holding up?"

Alex ignored her question. "How old is he, Barbara?"

"Ten. He was celebrating his birthday the night of the accident."

Alex looked away. "Ten," he said to himself.

"Sad, isn't it? I couldn't believe it myself. So young to screw up his life. Considering everything, I'm sure your department will throw the book at him. He's in for the maximum, and probably not much of a future beyond that."

Alex ignored Barbara's reference to the District Attorney's office where he served as a Deputy D.A. He didn't know what to say. He still reeled from the realization that a ten-year-old had taken his family from him.

"Thanks, Barbara."

"If there's anything I can do . . ." followed him as he walked away.

~

Near Rangely, Colorado—November 6th, 2003

Clay Ryan chewed his lip as he guided the gas truck around a curve. A year ago, he'd seen the backroom dice game as a quick way to make money. Backroom gambling was illegal in Colorado, but if you knew the right people, you could always find a game and a way around the betting limit. The buy-in was high, but so was the payoff. Over the next few months, he'd gotten himself in too deep, and continuing with the game was the only way to dig out.

The night before he was on his way to riches when his rotten luck kicked in. He'd been raking in the dough until the last throw of the dice. The pot had built to a huge amount, and he decided to let it ride for one more roll. Luck had followed him all night. He couldn't lose. But he did, and he owed the casino not just the one hundred grand he already had on the books, but an additional three hundred grand. He'd have been up two hundred grand. Three hundred grand in winnings to owing four hundred grand he didn't have—at least not in cash. He never seemed to get a break. He'd been forced to turn over the signed papers. He had no choice.

He thought of Trish and the kids. She'd be livid when she found out what he'd done. But then she was always on his case about something. She needed more help with the fruit orchards, the house needed repairs, and she hated that he drove a gas truck. Why didn't he find something safer to do in North Fork instead of being on the road so much? He was sick of her nagging.

Too bad he'd gotten her pregnant and been forced to

marry her. And then she lost the baby. Of course, a little over a year later they had Scott. Should have stopped there. Their daughter, Meghan, was okay, but girls were girls. At least he could take ten-year-old Scott fishing and teach him sports.

Clay needed a way out of debt—and his marriage. He was tired of being tied down. There had to be a way to start over. Several weeks ago he'd pondered the idea of faking his death, but rejected it when he couldn't figure how to get away with it. That was when he was only one hundred grand in debt. But desperate times required desperate planning.

He couldn't go home. Maybe he could figure a way to wreck the gas truck and make everyone think he'd been burned up in the crash. If he was dead, he wouldn't have to face Trish. His measly $50,000 life insurance policy would tide her over for a few months. He could start life over, and if he was found out, he'd claim amnesia. He'd be free of the responsibilities that were weighing him down. His perfect plan had one flaw; he needed a body to insure he'd burned in the wreckage.

While stopped for lunch in Rangely, Clay continued to ponder the idea of "dying" in a fiery crash. He'd done some research on burned bodies. He still couldn't figure out how the authorities would explain the absence of charred human remains. No matter how he staged the accident, he still needed a body. As he left the diner, the snow that started when he took his lunch break had increased with a vengeance. Ordinarily, he would find a motel and wait it out, but the weather provided perfect conditions for an accident. It would ruin his flawless driving record, but no harm, since he'd be "dead." The problem of a body, however, still remained. He shrugged his shoulders, paid his check, and headed for his truck.

"Hey mister! You going to Vernal?"

His hand on the cab door, Clay looked up to see a man about his age and height walking toward him.

"Could I get a ride with you? I'm headed to Utah."

Clay smiled. He loved when a plan came together. Maybe his luck hadn't run out. "Actually, I'm going south to Fruita. Climb in. You'll probably have better luck hitching a ride to Utah from there than from Rangely. Unless, of course, Vernal is your destination."

"Nope. Headed to Salt Lake." The stranger climbed into the cab and settled onto the passenger seat. "Thanks, mister. You're a life saver."

"Happy to oblige. Call me Clay."

~

North Fork, Colorado, November 7th, 2003

Insistent pounding on the door awoke Trish Ryan from a restless sleep. She and Clay hadn't been getting along lately, and he left on his last run without as much as a goodbye kiss. They'd argued again over his being gone more than he was home. He volunteered for extra shifts whenever he had the chance. That kept him from having to work in the orchards, which he hated. And, she was sure, kept him from having to spend time with her.

The pounding came again, and she glanced at the clock. 3:35 a.m. She slipped on her robe, combed her fingers through her hair, and hurried down the stairs, her heart racing. When she flicked on the porch light, she saw Kale Morgan waiting. Her heart plummeted to her stomach, and she said a quick prayer for Clay. A deputy sheriff didn't knock on your door in the middle of the night unless he had bad news.

She flung the door open. "Is it Clay?" She stared at her childhood friend, numbness engulfing her.

Kale shook his head. "I'm sorry, Trish. I wish I didn't have to be here."

Trish sucked in air and froze. After a few moments, she found her voice. "Come in out of the snow, Kale. What happened?"

"Mom? What's going on?"

Trish turned toward the stairs. "Go back to bed, Scott. Nothing to worry about." She waited until she heard Scott's door close, then turned to Kale. "Would you like some coffee?" Unwilling to hear what Kale had to say, she busied herself with the coffee pot. "What hospital is he in?" she asked as she filled the pot with water.

"No coffee for me, Trish. I need to get back on the road. Several people have found the ditch tonight. Roads are slick as grease."

Trish turned off the water and waited.

"I think you should sit down," Kale said to her back.

She turned from the sink and slipped onto a kitchen chair. Kale pulled another chair out and sat opposite her, taking her hands in his.

"Clay lost control of the truck on Douglas Pass. The road was snow-packed and icy. He missed a curve and . . . and the truck burst into flames and blew up. I'm really sorry, Trish. Clay was burned beyond recognition. We could do some DNA testing, but since it was his truck . . . ."

Trish had known Kale all her life. They'd even dated a few times in high school. His gaze never wavered as he told her what happened, but she saw tears forming in his eyes.

Kale exhaled and looked away. "I hate this part of my job." When he turned back to Trish, he asked, "Is there someone I can call for you?"

Trish shook her head. "No." She blinked back tears. "There's no one."

K.L. McKee

10

CHAPTER 2

North Fork, Colorado—November 26, 2003

Trish shoved stuffing into the cavity of the turkey, slammed the lid on the roaster, and banged the oven door closed. Less than a week ago, her world had fallen apart for the second time that month. Only two days after burying Clay's burned remains, two men had knocked on her door and demanded she pay Clay's debts or turn over her home and orchards.

"What debts?" she asked.

"His gambling debts," the shorter man answered, "for $400,000 dollars plus interest. That comes to around $500,000. He used this property as collateral."

"You must be mistaken," Trish countered. "Clay

couldn't use this property as collateral without my signature."

"We have the papers right here." The man held up an envelope. "May we come in?"

Trish faltered and nearly invited them in. She fisted her hands. "Talk to my lawyer."

"And who would that be?" the taller of the two asked.

"Jess Atkins. He has an office in town." She slammed the door and shoved the deadbolt in place.

She had called Jess immediately, told him what happened, and made an appointment to see him the following day, convinced the men were trying to con her. The next afternoon in Jess's office, the reality of Clay's shortcomings came to roost. Jess confirmed he'd met with the gentlemen, but they told him nothing about gambling debts. When he challenged them about the gambling, they feigned ignorance, insisting the debt was a short-term loan from a Nevada bank, and the note was due.

Panic tightened her throat. "Jess, I don't have that kind of money." When she and Clay had married, her parents had retired and turned the running of the orchards over to Trish. They were killed in an auto accident three years later in Arizona. Trish was the sole beneficiary. Everything—house, orchards, equipment—was in her name only. She ran the orchards and made a decent profit—enough to live on comfortably and pay the property taxes every year. Clay's job had been supplemental income. He wasn't interested in the orchards, grudgingly helping her when necessary.

Trish blinked back tears. "I don't understand. I never

would have signed over the deed to Clay or anyone else. The orchards are my life. Why would I—"

"Is this your handwriting?" Jess asked. He pointed to her signatures on copies of the papers he'd been given. "Because if it isn't or you can prove it isn't, then these people don't have a claim. Unfortunately, we can't prove Clay was gambling illegally, even though we know that's what they told you. I think they were trying to intimidate you, thinking you'd cave and let them have the property. They probably figured a woman wouldn't care about fruit orchards. The paperwork is from a bank in Nevada—a loan on your property. Nothing else."

Trish stared at the signatures on the paperwork. "It's my handwriting," she admitted, "but you *know* I would *never* do this."

"Did Clay have you sign any papers in the last few months? For anything?"

Trish swallowed to push down the fear rising inside. "I co-signed on the papers for a pickup. The old one needed replacing, and Clay found a newer used one." She remembered the day clearly. Last August he'd purchased the pickup. She was in the middle of peach harvest and rather than go to the bank to sign the papers, Clay had brought them to her. She hadn't paid much attention to what she was signing, even though she signed numerous times. She had pickers to attend to, the packing shed to oversee, and customers to deal with, so she signed where Clay indicated. And he knew where I kept the title to the house and orchards, she thought.

"I questioned why there were so many papers, but Clay assured me that's the way the banks were. At the time, I trusted Clay. An obvious mistake." Tears spilled onto her cheeks as she explained to Jess what she thought happened. "I don't suppose there's anything we can do, is there?"

"We can try to fight it, but it's going to be difficult to prove you were duped. I'll do what I can, but our case is pretty thin without Clay here to confront. It's going to be difficult to prove you didn't know what you were signing."

"Any suggestions?" she asked as her tears flowed.

"Talk to Bob at the bank. He knows you and knows your credit is good. See if he will lend you the money against your house and orchards to pay off the Nevada bank. Maybe we can negotiate a little and get the amount down." Jess shook his head. "I'm sorry, Trish. I wish I had better advice."

With a heavy heart, Trish had done as Jess had suggested. She'd had no other choice. Jess had managed to knock $100,000 off the amount, but she still owed $400,000.

At a time when she should be thankful for her blessings, she found herself in debt to the bank, not only for the pickup, but for property she had once owned free and clear. She stared at the oven and the baking turkey. She hated Clay. Hated herself for marrying him and for trusting him. She crumpled to the floor and sobbed, unable to even pray. Lately, she and God weren't on speaking terms.

~

Denver, Colorado—June, 16, 2004

Alex Lambert stared at the headstone, three names etched on the gray granite. *Amy. Alex Jr. Molly.* He never had the chance to know Molly—still in her mother's womb when she died. What would she have been like? Raven-haired and blue-eyed like her mother, or dark blond and green-eyed like him? Alex Jr. was a pistol. Energy and sweetness wrapped up in a perfect package. On the one-year anniversary of their deaths, the ache in Alex's heart had only multiplied, not lessened. When would the pain go away? And as the ache of loss worsened, so did the hate that ate at him.

"Oh, Amy, I miss you so much. What am I supposed to do?" Alex crumpled to his knees. "I miss you and little Alex. Life is empty without you. I didn't get the chance to even know Molly. Some days I can't bear the loneliness. How can I go on?" A tear trickled down his cheek. "You were my life. You meant everything to me." Another tear escaped, followed by another, and then another until sobs wracked his body.

Alex crumpled onto his back, his arm over his eyes. He cried until he had no more tears. He couldn't stop thinking about the rotten juvie that had caused such deep pain. His pastor had encouraged him to forgive and move on, but he hadn't been able to do that. The judge had given Marco Rodriguez the maximum sentence allowed under the law, but five years was inadequate for stealing three lives. In four more years, Marco Rodriguez would have his life back, unless he messed up again. In four more years, Alex would still be grieving.

It was dusk when he drove out of the cemetery toward home. But instead of going home, he drove aimlessly through the city. He knew he couldn't continue to function with pain and hate living inside him, but he had no idea how to purge them. When he pulled into his driveway at midnight, he resolved to move forward. Once inside the empty house, he dropped to his knees and prayed.

~

Alex stared at the manicured grounds and plain brown buildings of the Mount Evans Youth Services Center. He was crazy for coming here. Even crazier for putting his job on the line. When filling out the request for visitation, he'd used the excuse that the District Attorney's office was following up on youth offenders, and he'd been assigned one Marco Rodriguez. A blatant lie. He'd never lied *about* his job or *for* his job, until now. Mouth dry, he closed his eyes and said a quick prayer. Before he could change his mind, he stepped from the car and entered the brown gatehouse, the U.S. and Colorado flags billowing in the breeze at the front.

While the guard checked his credentials, he passed through the metal detector, then waited for approval to enter the facility. His nerves tingled as he contemplated his first encounter with the Rodriguez boy since the sentencing. What would he say? *Hi. I'm the man whose family you killed. I came to see how you're doing.* That would go over like a bowling ball on a soccer field.

Once Alex decided he needed to face the boy who ruined his life, he looked into how Marco Rodriguez was handling incarceration. What he found surprised him. Rodriguez was a model resident. He attended church services every Sunday, worked as a service dog trainer throughout the year, and did some gardening in the summer. An avid reader, his grades in school were exemplary, and he showed promise on the basketball court. He kept to himself as much as possible, interacting with the other youth only when necessary. Counselors and teachers couldn't say enough about how well he was doing. They even commented that he was far more mature than his eleven years. Alex had expected rebellion, not achievement.

~

One of the guards informed Marco Rodriguez he had a visitor. He'd been here a year and nobody had come to see him, which was fine. Three meals a day and a clean place to sleep was more than he'd had his entire life. He didn't need anybody. He never knew his father, his mother his only family. When he'd been sentenced to five years at Mount Evans, she hadn't bothered to appear in court. In fact, he hadn't seen his mother since the night of the accident. For all he knew, she could have overdosed or been beaten to death by her pimp, or one of her johns, or her drug dealer. He'd stopped caring a few months after he'd arrived at the facility. He didn't need her or her troubles.

When he entered the large visitation room, a tall dark-blond man built like a linebacker waited. A cop? Maybe, but why a cop? He approached the man with trepidation. If this didn't go well, he'd return to his room immediately. He had that choice.

Marco spent his days trying to improve his situation. He'd never be able to forget what he'd done, although he'd tried. Occasional nightmares about that night wouldn't let him forget. He had only himself to answer to, and he had demanded a lot of himself since he'd arrived at the facility. The teachers and minister had taught him that only he could change his future. He sure as hell didn't want to be like his mother. Or his so-called friends, for that matter. They had abandoned him, too.

As he approached, the man turned. He looked vaguely familiar, but Marco couldn't remember where he'd seen him. *Here goes. Let's see what the dude wants.*

~

Alex watched as Marco Rodriguez walked toward him. He had grown taller and filled out since Alex last saw him. Alex had attended the sentencing, but refused to speak when given the chance. He saw no reason to pour out his pain to a kid who already pleaded guilty and expressed remorse over his actions. A remorse that had done little to appease Alex. Instead, here he stood, a year later, still looking for answers.

"Hello, Mr. Rodriguez. Or may I call you Marco?" Alex tried to sound natural, but he shook inside. He tamped down the urge to yell at the kid and demand why he had killed his family. That wasn't why he'd come. He'd come at the urging of his pastor to hear Marco's story, hoping, somehow, that it would help him understand and move on.

"Do I know you?" Marco asked.

His jaw set, Alex cleared his throat. "My name is Alex Lambert. My family was in the car you hit." He paused to let that revelation sink in and watched as first shock and then fear traveled over Marco's face.

"Look, man, I'm really sorry . . ." Tears clouded his eyes. "I didn't mean . . . Forget it, man, I don't *need* this." Marco turned to go.

Alex put a hand on Marco's shoulder, and stopped him from leaving. "Please stay and hear me out. I don't know exactly why I'm here, but I need . . . need . . ." *What do I need?*

Marco shook off Alex's hand and turned toward him. Alex blinked at the confusion on the young man's face. As the boy turned his head away, Alex watched him fight back tears.

"I need," Alex continued, "to hear your side of the story. Maybe that will help me understand. I'm angry one day with no desire to see you or ask you why. The next day I find myself wondering why a ten-year-old boy was driving drunk. Most of all, I can't get the image of you standing before the judge out of my mind.

"I need to know why. I need closure, because the pain is eating me alive." He fought his own tears and waited. When Marco said nothing, Alex added, "You aren't obligated to talk to me, I know that, but *please* help me. I can't go on like this anymore, and maybe you can't either."

Marco turned his head to look at Alex. He lowered his

19

eyes and shook his head. "Man, I don't need this. I'm sorry."

As he walked away, Alex's shoulders drooped. He'd tried. He left for home, his question still unanswered.

Three days later, Alex received a call from Mount Evans Youth Services. Marco Rodriguez had asked to see him.

The next afternoon, Alex stood in the same spot in the visitation room he'd occupied when Marco refused to talk. After a few minutes, he saw Marco move slowly toward him. Alex held his breath.

The young man stopped a few feet short of where Alex stood. He frowned and then uttered, "I don't know why." Tears brightened his eyes.

"I know this is hard, but you know how, and maybe that's as good. Are you willing to tell me that much?" Alex didn't understand what was happening to him, but he found himself wanting to know more about Marco Rodriguez. There had to be a reason a ten-year-old kid was drunk and driving a vehicle he was too young and too short to drive.

Marco shrugged his shoulders. "Okay."

"Let's sit down." Alex motioned toward a table behind him. After they were settled opposite each other, Alex spoke again. "I'm in no hurry. Take your time."

Marco, in halting words, told his story. The more he talked, the more Alex found himself hating Marco's situation, not Marco.

Marco explained he was celebrating his tenth birthday that night, and he was old enough to join a gang. But he had to do something crazy and daring in order to join. It was decided he should steal a car and drive it through Denver without getting caught. "Piece of cake," he'd told the leader. "Just watch me."

To get his nerve up, he raided his mother's refrigerator while she was with a john and drank several beers. When he was "feeling no pain," he swiped the john's keys and took his SUV for a ride. What could it hurt? It was the middle of the night, not a lot of traffic where he planned to go, and once he'd driven a friend's car around the block several times. He knew what he was doing.

His mother didn't care about him. She called him a thorn in her side and a few other choice phrases. Told him more than once she'd be a lot better off if he just disappeared. What better way than to join a gang and be taken care of by his friends? He hadn't seen the red car until it was too late. He'd blown through the red light, and here he was.

By the time he finished his story, tears streamed down Marco's cheeks. "I wish I hadn't done what I did, but I can't take it back. I *can* make it . . . me better. Reverend Moss says I can. He says Jesus has forgiven me, because I asked. Do you think that's true?"

Alex swallowed the lump in his throat. "Yes, that's true." Before him sat a young boy of eleven, going on eighteen, who needed forgiveness from the man he'd wronged. Jesus could forgive, but Alex wasn't sure he could forgive. Not today, anyway. "Has your mother been to see you?" he asked instead.

"No, and I hope she doesn't. I don't need her. She'll only cause me trouble. For all I know, she's dead anyway." He sniffed and wiped his nose and eyes on his sleeve. Alex

21

handed him a handkerchief.

Without thinking it through, Alex asked, "Would you mind if I came to visit you next week? Maybe we can work through this together." His life had been empty and meaningless without his family. He needed something to fill the void. Seeing Marco might help him move forward.

Marco stared at him. "Seriously?"

Alex smiled for the first time since he'd entered the facility. "Seriously," he said, surprising himself.

Marco shrugged his shoulders. "No hay bronca." At Alex's bewildered look, he said, "No problem, man, if you want to."

"I think I want to." Alex offered his hand to Marco.

~

Alex stood in front of his boss, wincing at the fury in the words the District Attorney threw at him.

"I can't believe you took it upon yourself to go visit that boy. You lied to the director of the facility as to why you were there. That doesn't reflect well on this office. We're supposed to uphold the law, not break it."

"All due respect, John, I didn't exactly break the law. You didn't assign me the job of seeing Marco, but I didn't lie about who I was."

"That doesn't matter one iota! It's a conflict of interest, if nothing else. You're not to see him again, understand?"

"I'm sorry, but I've scheduled another visit next Wednesday, and if that goes well, I'll go again on Sunday, and I'll go every week until I feel I don't need to go anymore.

If Marco doesn't want to see me, all he has to do is say so."
Alex held his breath and waited.

John scowled. "Why is this so important? The kid killed
your family. Shouldn't you be moving on?"

"I can't. Not till I find out why," Alex stated simply.
"And not until I can forgive him. I *need* to forgive him. My
life is in shambles right now. This was the only way I could
think of to move on." Alex took a deep breath. "This kid
never had a chance at a decent life before the accident, but
now he has a chance to redeem himself, and he's doing his
best to do that. I don't have all the answers, and I don't know
if this is the right thing to do, but I think I need to be a part
of his redemption. I might just gain my own at the same time.
He needs to know I can forgive him. *I* need to know I can
forgive him."

"And can you?" John asked.

"I don't know, but I have to try."

John shook his head. "I must be crazy to overlook
something like this. If I think this is going nowhere or
becoming a problem, you *will* stop the visits. Understood?"

"Absolutely."

"If I have to address this again, you're out of a job. Now
get out of here."

Relief flooded over Alex as he left John's office. His
boss was right. Alex had broken the rules and put his job on
the line. For the moment, he'd sidestepped losing his job. He
wouldn't be so lucky the next time. Yet he couldn't stop
himself from visiting Marco. He had to see where it would
lead. He had to expel the poison killing his soul.

K.L. McKee

CHAPTER 3

North Fork, Colorado—January 2007

Trish slammed the front door behind her and trudged through the half-foot of snow that had fallen the night before. She had hoped to put Manuel and his crew to work pruning the peaches today, but the snow—and it was still snowing—changed her plans. Clear skies and mid-thirties temperatures were predicted the next few days, which would give the pruners access to the orchards. Until two years ago, she would have been in the orchards working, but thanks to Clay—she squelched the anger boiling inside—she had to mortgage her house and land in order to pay off Clay's debt to the so-called bank. That meant getting a job.

To complicate matters, her bottom line had dwindled the

last two years. One major freeze after another in the spring of 2004 forced her to run the wind machines too many nights, and the cost of propane had steadily risen each year. She'd had to borrow more money from the bank to tide her over until harvest. Rainy weather and hail during the harvest season in 2004 delayed picking and damaged the peaches and apples. Her regular buyers looked elsewhere. In January of 2005, the unseasonably cold winter damaged some of the trees.

By spring of 2005, however, her hopes rose. She had a bumper crop in all her orchards, including the apricots and cherries. Unfortunately, so did everyone else, and the price bottomed out. Most of her proceeds from the sale of the fruit went to taxes, labor, and other expenses, such as sprays, packing and shipping costs, and fuel, to mention only a few. She had very little profit to put toward the mortgage.

The bank was willing to work with her, but she wasn't willing to add more to her already mounting debt. That left the choice of selling her heritage, or going to work. Neither option appealed to her, but she had no choice. Her parents insisting she get a college degree turned out to be the only bright spot in the whole scenario.

Clay had grumbled about her "getting educated" while he worked, but she ignored his protests and honored her parents' wishes. After earning her undergraduate degree at Mesa State College, she and Clay and their two small children had moved back to North Fork. There she completed her Master of Library Science degree through an online course. When she finished, she stuffed her degrees in a drawer and worked the land—something she loved above everything. Something Clay hated. But then he had hated everything.

Trish backed the pickup out of the garage and turned toward town. She enjoyed her job at the library, putting her degree to good use. A full-time librarian position opened in November of 2005. Her friend, Sarah Morgan, the North Fork Regional Library Director, hired her when she needed a job. The only problem with the job was that it kept her from being in the orchards as much as she wanted. The paycheck, however, covered living expenses, so she could put what little profit she'd made on the fruit toward paying off the debt.

She hoped 2007 would prove to be a good year for the orchards. She'd lost money the last three years on her apricots, cherries and peaches. Only the apples had proven to be a profitable crop. Her Rome Beauties and Old-Fashioned Red Delicious that her father and grandfather had planted when she was six were in high demand by specialized retailers. She wished she had more of them. The trees were old, but healthy. Unfortunately, five acres out of eighty-five wasn't enough to compensate for the loss on the other crops. And Washington state apples were beginning to take over the market.

Trish gritted her teeth and cursed Clay under her breath. She'd made a decent living on the orchards before Clay gambled them away. If he hadn't died in the accident, she would have killed him herself for tricking her. At least the constant bickering disappeared with his death. She had considered divorce before the accident. Neither of them was happy, and she wanted out.

Clay's meager life insurance policy had been enough to pay off the pickup and cover his funeral expenses, but little else. Another example of Clay's lack of responsibility and foresight where his family was concerned. She couldn't sue the gas company for anything, as the accident was deemed driver error. The gas company argued Clay should have waited out the storm in a motel instead of driving on slick roads in a major snowstorm.

Trish turned into the library staff parking area. She had to put away her hateful thoughts and face the day. Sarah would pick up on Trish's dark mood and want to know what was wrong. Trish didn't want to get into another discussion with Sarah about forgiveness and letting go. She didn't need the lecture.

In spite of her best effort, testiness followed her throughout the day. She snapped at adults asking stupid questions and admonished kids unnecessarily. She either ignored other staff members or criticized the job they were doing. Her thirteen-year-old son, Scott, added to her already irksome day. He and her ten-year-old daughter, Meghan, walked to the library every day after school to wait for a ride home.

"Hey, Mom," Scott approached the Reference Desk. "You got a minute?"

Trish frowned. Every time she looked at Scott, she saw Clay—same brown eyes, same dark hair, same disarming smile, same disposition, and the same look Clay had when he wanted to talk her into something. And she always caved. Well, not this time. "What do you want?"

"A bunch of the kids are going sledding up Dry Gulch. Can I go?"

"No."

"Aw, come on, Mom. Everybody's going."

"I'm sure 'everybody' is not going. You have chores to do at home, which you've put off every day this week."

"I'll do them tomorrow. *Please* let me go. They're going to roast marshmallows, hot dogs, and everything."

"No."

"But Mom—"

"I said no and that's final."

"You don't let me do anything." Scott whined. "I *hate* you."

Trish glanced around to see if anyone had heard the exchange. She was thankful very few people were in the library. "Keep talking like that and you'll be grounded for a month. Where's your sister?"

"She's in the kid's room looking for books."

"Go find her and tell her we're leaving in ten minutes."

Scott spun around and stomped toward the Children's Center.

Sarah approached the desk. "You should let him go, Trish. It would be good for him."

Of all people, she hated that Sarah had overheard. "He hasn't earned the right," Trish said. "He's neglecting his chores." She gritted her teeth and narrowed her eyes. "He's just like his no-good dad."

"*Trish.*" Sarah shook her head. "Don't let Scott hear you say that. If you're going to compare him to his dad, at least make it positive. Otherwise, he's going to rebel. Big time. He's a talented athlete like Clay. Build on that."

"I'll handle Scott the way I see fit."

"Danny's going sledding, and Cam is supervising, along with some of the other parents. Scott will be fine."

"No, Sarah." Trish resented Sarah's advice about her bitterness toward Clay. Sarah had the perfect life. Trish didn't. "I'm not changing my mind. Scott has to learn some responsibility."

"All work and no play . . ."

"Sarah, just let it go. Scott's not going and that's final."

Sarah shrugged her shoulders. "Okay. By the way, haven't seen you at church lately. Will you be there Sunday?"

"That's another thing. Stop trying to save my soul." She spoke through her teeth so only Sarah could hear. "I won't be at church Sunday or any Sunday after that. God and I aren't on the best of terms. He's abandoned me, so I'm ignoring him."

"Oh, Trish. God hasn't abandoned you. Please let me help. This bitterness you're harboring is going to eat you alive. And it's going to affect Scott and Meghan if you don't let it go."

"This *bitterness* is what keeps me going." Trish glared at Sarah. "And my kids are *my* business." Trish scooted her chair away from the desk and stood. "I'll see you Monday. Have a good weekend." Trish pivoted on her heels and headed for the Children's Center to gather her kids and go home.

Trish spent a miserable weekend. Scott's constant complaining about chores and missing out on sledding with his friends grated on her. She was actually relieved when Monday arrived. The kids returned to school, and she returned to work. The relief lasted only a few hours. At two in the afternoon, she received a call from the school. The principal wanted to see her.

~

Trish eyed the clock on the school office wall. She'd been waiting over fifteen minutes. She could only imagine what kind of trouble Scott had caused. Why couldn't he be more like Meghan—even-tempered and sweet? He had too much of his dad in him. She startled when the principal spoke her name.

Trish settled in the chair across from Principal Blake's desk. She could barely get a breath as she waited for the bad news. She was tired of hearing negative comments about her son. And she was tired of dealing with him by herself. Another reason to resent Clay.

After greeting Trish, Principal Blake sat and leaned forward, settling his arms on the desk.

"Why am I here, Jim?"

"Scott is becoming a discipline problem. He's continually disruptive in class and has taken to bullying one of the other eighth-grade boys who is a bit on the heavy side. I don't tolerate either one of these behaviors."

31

"Of course not. I understand." Fury built inside Trish, and she fought to stay calm. "I'll have a talk with him when I get home. He'll definitely be grounded."

"I don't think that's the answer, Trish. Scott needs counseling and a little more positive reinforcement at home."

Offended at what he was implying, Trish fired back. "Are you saying I don't know how to handle my own son?"

"Not at all." Principal Blake leaned back in his chair. "What I'm saying is he's having difficulty dealing with his father's death. I know that was a little over three years ago, but he's showing classic signs of grief. I'd like him to see Cam Morgan, the high school counselor, for evaluation and help. Cam is a board certified child and adolescent psychologist and—"

"I'm well aware of Cam's credentials. He's married to my boss."

"Well, I think he could do Scott some good, but we need your permission. Best take care of it now before Scott enters high school next year."

Trish stared at Principal Blake and fought back tears of anger, frustration, and worry that word would get around town. "He's a lot like his father—irresponsible, rebellious, and lazy. Lately, I've had trouble getting him to listen to me."

"I'm sorry to hear you say that. At any rate, do we have your permission to schedule time with Cam? He'll be discreet."

She sighed. "It looks like I don't have much of a choice.

Scott doesn't listen to me anymore."

"This is a positive step, Trish. Stop by my secretary's desk on your way out. She'll have the necessary forms for you to sign." He stood and offered his hand.

Trish left the office without acknowledging the gesture. She and Scott would have a serious conversation after supper.

~

Trish stared across the kitchen table at her son. Silence stretched a chasm between them. How could she get through to him? He didn't seem to care that his behavior was unacceptable. Just like his dad, he had a jock's attitude that he was better than anyone else because he was good at sports. Why had that attracted her to Clay in the first place? She should have known better. Clay's macho demeanor was irresistible when she was seventeen and believed he would conquer the world. Instead, he got her pregnant. She should have refused to marry him, although she thought she could change him. And in a small town, pregnant and unmarried…

Scott glared at her. "Can I go?"

"Not until you understand it's not okay to disrupt class or bully someone. Your teacher and other kids deserve your respect."

"My teacher's stupid. He doesn't know anything about current events. He had the cabinet guys wrong because the book had the old names in it. That's just stupid. Doesn't he know they changed clear back in 2004? And Mike eats like a pig and looks like one!"

33

"Scott! You don't have any idea why Mike is heavy. Maybe there are medical circumstances or problems at home. Leave him be. It's none of your business." She fought to control her temper. "As for your teacher, you can point out his mistake without causing a disruption. Talk to him after class."

Scott rolled his eyes.

"Don't take that attitude with me," Trish fumed. "You are now grounded for the next two months. No after school activities, no hanging out at Dairy King with your friends. Once home, you'll do your assignments. No television or video games. And you *will* work in the orchards on the weekends."

"Dad never worked in the orchards. Why should I?"

"Because this fruit ranch is your future. You need to learn how to take care of it. As for your dad, you'd do well not to be like him."

Scott's eyes radiated pure hatred. "Is that all?"

"No. You'll see Mr. Morgan, the school counselor, after school on Wednesdays."

"No way."

"Either you meet with him, or I won't sign your permission slip for little league baseball this summer. Your choice."

"That's not fair!"

"That's the way it is."

Scott jumped up and dumped his chair onto the floor. "I hate you! I wish you'd died instead of Dad!" He fled the kitchen and raced upstairs to his room.

She stared after him, tears blurring her vision. How could he wish her dead instead of Clay? She had done her best the last three years to be mother and father to him. Why was he still so angry? Meghan didn't feel that way, did she?

Tears trickled down her cheeks. He was definitely Clay's son, and she didn't want him to be like Clay. She wanted him to be better. Trish couldn't shake the gloom that hovered, threatening to undo her world.

K.L. McKee

CHAPTER 4

North Fork, Colorado—October 2007

Trish stared at the bills sitting on her kitchen table. No matter what, she couldn't get ahead. She'd relied so much on learning the fruit business from her dad, and at the moment, could use his advice. He'd died much too soon. Looking at the figures again, she sighed. The fruit would make a little profit this year, but not enough to make a much of a dent in her debt.

She'd lost her apricots and half of her cherry crop to an early spring freeze. Thankfully, the peaches had survived. The low temperatures did a decent job of thinning the crop. That saved her some labor costs, as the need for thinning was minimal. Between the peaches and a good apple crop, she'd kept her head above water. Barely.

She wanted to cry. Why had so many bad years happened one after the other? And Scott. He was showing some signs of improving, but he still had a long way to go. She butted heads with him regularly, but at least he'd stopped the bullying. His little league baseball season had proved helpful. He pitched for the team, and they won their division. Cam Morgan was right, Scott definitely had his father's athletic ability. As a freshman this fall, he'd made the varsity football team as backup quarterback. She had taken Cam's advice and praised him for inheriting his father's natural ability for sports.

Cam had asked to talk with her the previous April about the counseling sessions he'd had with Scott. The last thing she expected was Cam telling her she needed to change. Trish had settled across the desk from Cam, holding her breath and waiting to hear his revelations about Scott. Cam's advice about approaching Scott in a more positive way had rankled her.

"How's Scott doing?" Trish wasn't sure she wanted to hear the answer, but she asked, as it seemed the thing to do. "He doesn't say much at home, and I haven't noticed a big change in him."

"We've had some interesting sessions. I think he's beginning to see how his behavior affects others, but he won't make a huge change until things are different at home."

"What's that supposed to mean?" Trish scowled. "Scott needs an attitude change. It's as simple as that."

"That's not entirely true, Trish. I've come to believe you could do some changing, too."

Anger threatened to explode. First the principal in January, and Sarah continually after her about her bitterness and treatment of Scott. She hadn't expected Cam to dump on her, too. Trish tamped down the words she wanted to say. "I'm not the one who needs counseling, Cam."

"On the contrary, I think you need to re-evaluate your attitude." All pretenses of pleasantness vanished. Before Trish could verbally object, Cam continued. "You have developed a hatred for Clay because of what he did to you. And you've telegraphed that hatred to Scott. I wouldn't be discussing this with you, but Scott gave me permission to talk to you about how he feels at home. He believes you hate him because Clay was his father."

"I don't hate Scott." She swallowed the lump in her throat. "I just don't want him to be like Clay."

"That's the problem. He remembers Clay as the father who showed him how to fish, taught him to throw a football, and hit a baseball. He knows what an outstanding athlete Clay was in high school. He wants to be like him."

"Clay was a liar and a cheat, lazy and full of himself. Scott is better than that."

"Scott doesn't know that side of Clay. He doesn't know about the debt Clay left, resulting in you having to borrow money against the house and orchards. He only knows him as the father who loved him and did things with him."

"You know about the debt?"

"Sarah told me."

"She had no right." Trish looked away from Cam and fought to keep herself calm. She'd never told the kids why she had to go to work except that without Clay's salary, they needed the money. She believed they weren't old enough to understand about his gambling and the mortgage. But for Cam to know. *How humiliating. How many other people in town know?*

Cam continued. "Scott has some serious self-esteem issues." He paused for a moment, then continued. "He tells me you keep saying he's just like his father—lazy, irresponsible, and rebellious. Those are not positive reinforcement words. Scott needs to know he has some good qualities. His Dad's good qualities. You're the most important person in his life. He's craving to hear positive things from you—sooner rather than later." Cam leaned back in his chair. "I think Scott reminds you of Clay because he looks so much like him. I see a lot of Clay's mannerisms in him, too."

Trish closed her eyes for a moment. Cam was right. Scott was a perfect remake of his dad. If she hadn't given birth to him, she'd have wondered if he belonged to her.

"Clay and I weren't getting along very well before he died. I was considering filing for divorce. I never told the kids. And I never told them he had a gambling problem. When he died, it didn't seem important. Maybe I should have said something. I didn't think Scott would understand."

"Scott would understand honesty. And you need to tell him how much he's like the positive side of Clay. You might explain why you fell in love with Clay in the first place. Scott is fourteen years old. You don't need to go into details, but give him an idea of why you and Clay were together. It may take him a while to come around, but being honest will go a long way in changing the path he's on right now."

Tears stung Trish's eyes. "I don't know how to start. I've resented Clay and hated him for so long for what he did. I don't know how honest I can be." A sob escaped her.

"You can. You're a strong woman, Trish. Scott will probably ask some uncomfortable questions, but you need to answer him as best you can. If you don't, I'm afraid you're in for a lot of heartache where Scott is concerned."

"Should I include Meghan?"

"If you want. She probably needs to know, too. That might make it a little less uncomfortable for Scott."

Trish fished a Kleenex from her pocket and wiped her nose and eyes. She stood and offered her hand to Cam. "Thanks, Cam. I'll try."

Cam shook her hand. "You'll be fine. I'm sorry if I was hard on you today, but I thought you needed to hear how Scott feels."

As Trish reached for the door handle, Cam said, "Scott's a good kid. You should be proud of him."

"I am." Trish sniffled and turned toward Cam. "Guess he needs to know that."

Trish had driven home that afternoon dreading her ultimate encounter with Scott. It was cowardly, but she decided to wait a few days in order to think things through. Throwing herself on her bed, she cried . . . and cried. When the tears subsided, she dried her eyes and noticed the Bible lying on the bottom shelf of her nightstand, a fine layer of dust dulling its leather cover. Perhaps it would give her some direction.

She'd taken her anger out on God and Clay, blaming them for all her problems. Maybe, just maybe, her anger was misdirected, at least where God was concerned. Wiping the dust off, Trish opened it to Psalms. The Bible hadn't been opened since the day she learned of Clay's deceit. She'd felt abandoned and betrayed by everyone she loved, and more especially God.

She'd had a strong faith before she met Clay, but he didn't like church and refused to go with her. To keep peace, she had attended church less and less, particularly following her parents' deaths. After her conversation with Cam, something clicked inside. Three different people had told her the same thing. Three people couldn't be completely wrong. She needed help. Scott needed help.

Alone in her bedroom, Trish reached out to God. As she prayed for guidance, some of the weight of the last few years lightened. She still had plenty of worries—finances, how to keep her land, and dealing with Scott—but she had to start facing those worries and do something positive about them instead of blaming them on a dead man. It wouldn't be easy, but then the last three, almost four, years hadn't been easy, either.

After praying, she felt a little better, but she wasn't ready to forgive Clay. And she wasn't ready to let God off the hook, either. However, she had to try something. What she'd been doing wasn't working.

Sunday evening, after the Broncos game, Trish had approached Scott and Meghan. The Broncos had won, so Scott was in a good mood.

"Meet me in the kitchen for ice cream sundaes. There's something I want to talk to you about."

"Do I *have* to?" Scott asked. "I have homework."

"This is important. Homework will wait."

Scott stared at her like she'd turned into an alien.

"It won't take a long time. By the time we've eaten the sundaes, you'll be free to do your homework."

They settled around the kitchen table, bowls of ice cream with caramel, chocolate, nuts and whipped cream waiting to be devoured.

"So what's up?" Scott asked.

"Yeah, Mom, how come you let us have sundaes before supper?"

"Well . . ." Trish took a deep breath. "I wanted to talk to you about your dad." She watched Scott for a reaction.

His spoon clanked on the edge of the bowl, and his jaw clenched. "If this is about how rotten he was, I don't want to hear it."

Trish's heart lurched. Had she really been that negative about Clay? Of course she had. She knew it, and so did Scott.

"Scott, that's not nice," said Meghan.

"That's all we hear when she talks about Dad."

"I'm sorry, Scott." Trish grimaced. "I've been unfair to both of you about your dad." Her natural defenses kicked in before she could stop. "But you have to understand he put me—us—in a very difficult situation."

43

"He died!" Scott spat. "How's that bad for *you*?"

Trish fought back tears. She had to stay calm. "He was my husband, your father, and we did love each other once."

Scott rolled his eyes.

"Please be patient and listen to what I have to say. Then you can ask whatever you want." She took a deep breath. "When I started dating Clay, he was a senior and I was a junior. He was handsome, fun, and a star athlete." She smiled at the memory of never experiencing a dull moment while dating Clay.

"I thought the sun rose and set in him. He was always willing to help others, which made him very popular. He struggled with keeping his grades up so he could stay eligible to play sports, but he managed. Your dad was named all-conference in football, basketball, and baseball, not just his senior year, but his sophomore and junior years, too. He was destined to get a scholarship to any Colorado college or university he wanted.

Unfortunately, he broke his leg in several places while playing in the state championship baseball game. The break was so bad it ended his hopes of a scholarship. He was devastated. I told him it didn't matter. He could still go to college. But he had no money for college. His dad had died in a coal mine accident when he was about four, and his mother struggled to make ends meet. I'm sorry you don't remember your Grandma Ryan. She was a wonderful person."

Trish sighed. "Anyway, he went to work in the mines. We were still dating my senior year, but I noticed a change in him. Sports had given him prestige, but in the mine he was just another strong back. He struggled every day with what that meant. I told him I still loved him and it didn't matter that he couldn't play, and that was the truth. But it still rankled him. He had dreams of becoming a major league baseball player. Still, he seemed to be content when we were together. When I graduated from high school, we got married."

"Because you had to."

Scott's comment surprised her. She hadn't realized he knew. She took a moment to recover.

"You're partly right, Scott. We got married because I was pregnant, but we were planning to get married anyway. Not long after we were married, I lost the baby." Trish took a deep breath and continued her story. "In spite of our loss, things were good between us. A few months later, I got pregnant with you, Scott. I had a scholarship to attend Mesa State College, so we moved to Grand Junction, and Clay got a job working for the city. Your grandpa and grandma wanted me to get my college degree, so they helped with expenses."

She smiled at Scott. "Clay was so excited when you were born. He talked incessantly about teaching you football and baseball, his favorite sports. He was a very attentive father and took care of you while I studied. I spent an extra two years getting my Master's Degree in Library Science, but I did it online after we'd moved back to North Fork."

"What about me?" Meghan asked. "Was Daddy happy when I was born?"

Trish hated lying, but Meghan didn't need to know that Clay wasn't thrilled about Meghan's birth. He considered having a daughter a black mark on his manhood. After Meghan's birth, they'd begun to grow apart. "He was happy when you were born. But you liked girly things, and your dad didn't do pink and lace very well, so he didn't spend as much time with you. But he loved you very much, and he used to play with you and tickle you until he got you to giggle."

Meghan smiled. She hadn't done a lot with her dad before he died but seemed fine with it. She and Trish did things together, which helped compensate for Clay's lack of interest.

Trish looked at Scott. "Do you remember the times he took you fishing, rabbit and pheasant hunting?"

"Yeah. That was great. I had fun throwing a football with him and playing baseball, too."

"You two spent a lot of time doing that. Anyway, when we moved back to North Fork and took over the fruit ranch, your dad changed a little. He didn't like working the fruit. It wasn't his thing. I started resenting his lack of interest. The orchards had been my life, and I couldn't understand why he didn't like them."

"Is that why he started driving the gas truck?"

"Yes. The extra money also helped with the bills. We were able to afford to do more things with his income."

"So why do you always tell me I'm lazy and irresponsible like him?" Scott glared at her.

"Because sometimes you are, Scott."

He slammed his spoon on the table and started to rise. She shouldn't have said that. Too late.

"Hold on. I'm not through."

He sat down and stared at the half-empty bowl in front of him.

"You tend to shirk your chores sometimes, and that makes me angry. But you also have a lot of your dad's good qualities. You're athletic and know how to have a good time. You offer to help other kids, and you get along well with people. Your dad was a people person. You're built like him and look like him. However, you're a better student than he was when you apply yourself."

"Then why do you hate him so much?" Scott's question was quiet but demanding.

"Because after he started driving for the gas company he changed even more. He discovered gambling, and he was addicted to it. I didn't know that right away. Every time he came home, he was hard to get along with. I think he must have been worrying about his gambling debts. He wouldn't confide in me, and we grew apart. I was focused on running the fruit ranch, and he felt ignored. He wouldn't help with the work and that drove more distance between us."

Trish watched Scott for a minute. His demeanor remained guarded. "After he died, some men came around to collect his debt. They told me it was a gambling debt, but when Jess Atkins confronted them, they said it was a bank loan and weren't responsible for how he'd used the money. I had no doubt it was a gambling debt. Your dad used the house and orchards as collateral for what he owed without

47

my knowledge."

"You're lying."

"No, I'm not." Trish closed her eyes and said a quick prayer. "I had to mortgage everything to pay off the debt. Before that, the ranch was free and clear. The current mortgage is huge, and it takes a great deal of money to make the monthly payment. Over the last three years, I've let my bitterness over what happened affect you and Meghan."

She swallowed her pride. "Your dad wasn't a bad person, just misguided. What he did was wrong, and we're paying for that. But you have some very good memories of your dad, and I don't want you to lose those. He loved you both very much, and for that, I'm grateful."

Trish covered Scott's hand with hers. "You have his good qualities. Be thankful for that and love him despite his faults." *And love me, too, despite my faults.*

Scott studied the tablecloth for a few moments. "Can I go, now? I need to get my homework done."

"You can go. Please think about what I've told you. If you have any questions—"

"Forget it." Scott scraped his chair back and fled to his room.

Trish sat frozen. Had she done the right thing by being so honest?

Meghan stood and threw her arms around Trish. "I'm sorry, Mom. Scott will be okay. I loved Daddy, but he was gone a lot. I don't miss him as much as Scott does."

"I know, honey. Thank you for understanding." Trish slipped her arms around Meghan and held tight. "I love you."

"Love you, too." Meghan slipped from Trish's grasp. "Got homework. Sorry," she said as she headed for her room.

Trish absently stirred the melted ice cream in her bowl. "Please God," she whispered. "Help Scott understand. And help me be more understanding."

Several days after her talk with the kids, Trish had visited Clay's grave for the first time since the funeral. Sitting by the mound of dirt and weeds, she asked God for forgiveness. She wouldn't forget what Clay had done, but she knew she had to stop the blame game. Cleaning away the weeds had a cleansing effect on her soul. Although her shoulders felt lighter when she left, she still had plenty of healing to get through. Too many years of bitterness had become a habit.

She shook her head and put aside the memory of the talk with Scott and Meghan. Scott hadn't said anything about what she'd told them, nor had he asked any questions. She could only hope he had listened enough to make a change.

Trish studied the bills in front of her for the umpteenth time. She would be able to put some extra money toward the mortgage, but it still wouldn't make much of a dent in the principle.

Crippling mortgage payments, the expense of saving for property taxes and paying house insurance, along with the normal monthly bills like food and utilities, not to mention the extra to raise two growing kids, took nearly everything she earned at the library. Sometimes, she didn't make enough on the fruit to cover the added expenses of labor and spray, which meant adding money to the mortgage. She fought the familiar anger toward Clay, but it did no good. She had finally figured that out. She'd always harbor anger at him for what he did. She couldn't help it.

Trish squelched the rising panic at losing her childhood home. "Guess it's time to consider listing the ranch," she muttered. Her options had dwindled until she had no other choice.

CHAPTER 5

Denver, Colorado—November 2007

Alex sat in the visitor's parking lot and gazed through the Expedition's windshield at the Mount Evans Youth Services Center. Closing his eyes, he inhaled deeply to calm his nerves. A light snow fell, each flake melting as it touched the ground. He watched the tiny flakes and reflected on the first time he'd visited the facility. He'd been looking for answers then, answers to why a ten-year-old boy would drive drunk, resulting in the accident that killed Alex's family.

Alex had ignored the rules when he visited the first time. As a Deputy District Attorney, he had no business confronting Marco, the boy responsible for so much pain in his life. It had been a selfish act on his part. He needed closure. What he'd discovered was not an angry irredeemable delinquent, but a scared boy with no home life, whose mother entertained men to pay for her alcohol and drugs, and with no idea who fathered him. Alex had discovered a lost soul. As lost as Alex without his family.

That first visit had turned into regular visits, sometimes as often as once or twice a week. In the past four and a half years, Alex had come to know a young man determined to change his life and his future. Marco had been an exemplary inmate, working to secure an education and skills that would serve him once he was released. If he kept out of trouble, his record would be forever sealed. Alex had found himself encouraging Marco, praying with him, and doing all he could to help Marco achieve his goals. They'd both come a long way since the accident, much to Alex's surprise.

Alex leaned against the headrest and whispered a prayer. "Lord, please let Marco be open to my offer. We've traveled a hard road together, and I've come to love him. He deserves every chance he can get. *Please*. This is the right thing to do, for both of us. Thank you, Father, for guiding me and bringing me to this decision. Amen."

Inside the facility, Alex studied Marco as he approached. He had filled out and grown taller, no longer the diminutive, frightened child he'd observed in the courtroom nearly four and a half years ago. His 5'7" frame carried 135 pounds of toned muscle from working out every day. Alex noted Marco carried something in his hand. He rose to meet him.

"Marco." Alex shook hands with him. "Is that a deck of

cards and a cribbage board I see in your other hand?"

Marco grinned. "I need a rematch. I can take you this time."

Alex smiled. "You're on, but no mercy."

"Don't need it or want it." Marco spread the cards on the table and each chose one. "Ha! Low card, my deal."

Alex watched Marco study the six cards in his hand, debating which to discard into the crib. One game, and then he would disclose his idea. Better for both to be relaxed before discussing serious business.

Alex discarded his two cards to the crib and cut the deck. "How's the dog training going?"

"Pretty good." Marco turned up a jack and pegged two points. "I've got a stubborn one this time—a golden lab. She's a sweet dog, but she doesn't want to pay attention. Too easily distracted. Once she settles down, though, she'll make a great service dog."

Alex admired the success Marco had with service dogs. Learning to train dogs brought out the best in the boy and the dogs. Along with the training, Marco also worked in the center's garden during the summer. He was seldom idle. That kept his mind off his troubles.

"She's in good hands with you."

"Thanks, man. I love working with the dogs." Marco's hand pegged sixteen points, and the crib netted eight points.

So much for trying to distract him, Alex thought. He had pegged a measly four points.

They played two games, each winning one, before Alex worked up the nerve to broach his idea.

"So, Marco, have you made plans for when you're released? You have until next August, but I'm guessing you've been giving it serious thought."

Marco stopped shuffling and set the cards aside. "Yeah, I've been thinking a lot about it. It scares me . . . the outside. This is the best home I've ever had." He shrugged his shoulders. "I can't plan too much until I know what foster home I'll be living in and what school I'll be going to. All I know is I want to finish high school and then figure out what's next."

"Have you thought about college?"

Marco stared at the table between them. "Thought about it, but probably can't afford it."

"You could train dogs to help with expenses."

"I guess. I'd like that, but when people find out... "

"Keep your nose clean and your record is sealed."

"Yeah, but I have to be honest if they ask."

"Probably won't know to ask, but if they do, be honest. Most people are willing to give youth offenders a second chance. They'll recognize your skill with dogs and be willing to pay for your expertise."

"Easy for you to say, man. Look at you. You had all the advantages."

"The only advantage I had was a stable family. I worked hard to get where I am. My grades and my baseball skills gave me a good college scholarship, but I also worked two jobs to pay for my education. My parents couldn't help a whole lot." Alex watched Marco. "If you want it enough, you'll make it work."

Marco's mouth twitched. "I want it. I'd like to be a teacher and help other kids like me."

"Then you'll find a way." Alex took a deep breath and exhaled slowly. It was now or never.

"I've decided to quit my job at the DA's office. It's no longer what I want."

Marco frowned. "No way, man. Why?"

"Because I'm tired of the city. I want to get back to my roots."

"What roots?"

"Growing fruit. I was raised on a fruit ranch. When I graduated from high school, all I could think about was getting away from the small town I grew up in and the fruit orchards. Now I'd like to find a fruit ranch in a small town and become a farmer again." He paused, memories taking over. "I miss the smell of the orchards, the trees budding out, the beautiful pink and white blossoms, and watching the fruit as it matures."

"Never seen that." A sober expression of regret showed on Marco's face. Then he grinned. "Can't see you as a farmer."

"You find that funny? I have skills besides putting people in jail."

They both laughed, and Alex relaxed a little. Now for the bombshell. "I'd like to include you in my plans."

Marco stared at him. "In what way—cheap manual labor?" He raised an eyebrow.

"You know better than that." Alex realized Marco was still sensitive about his place in the world. "Just hear me out, okay? Don't say anything until I'm through."

Marco nodded and looked down at the table.

"I've been doing a lot of thinking and praying about this. It wasn't an easy decision, but putting it bluntly," Alex paused and then forged ahead, "I've come to care a great deal about you and your future."

Marco's head shot up.

Alex smiled. "I've come to think of you as my son. In fact, I'd like to adopt you. It will take a while to get approval, but I think I can use my position to pull some strings and move it along a little faster. Before you're released next August, I'm hoping I can legally call you my son." Alex had rushed through his practiced speech and held his breath, waiting for some reaction from Marco.

Marco leaned back against his chair and stared past Alex's head. Silence dominated their space. Alex barely breathed. Had he said it wrong?

Alex almost missed Marco's hushed comment. "I can't take the place of your son." Marco stood, gathered the cribbage board and cards, and pivoted to walk away.

"Marco, wait."

When he stopped and turned, Alex saw tears in his eyes.

Alex rose. "You're right. No one can do that. Ever. I'm asking you to be my *second* son. I love you, Marco. I'm proud of who you've become, and I'd like to think I had a small part in that. You've learned to walk away from trouble and set an example for the other boys. You befriended a scared young boy new to the facility and helped him adjust. I'm proud of the young man who tries to beat me at cribbage every week. You make me proud when you ace your tests and make A's on your papers. You make me want to say to people, 'That's my son.'"

Alex waited through far more heartbeats than he thought he could endure. Marco stared at the ground, tears slipping down his cheeks. He wiped them away with the back of his hand. Alex reached for Marco and embraced him.

"It's not *all* about what I can do for you. You lift my heart and make me feel needed and whole again. I can give you the love you need. I'll say it again—I love you, son." Marco's shoulders heaved. "It's all right, Marco. Let it out."

After a while, Marco gently pushed away and sat down in the closest chair. "My mother never said that to me," he choked. "*Never.*"

Alex sat opposite him and rested his arms on his legs. "I *love* you."

Marco sat silent.

"I've tried to find your mother. She's moved since…at any rate, when I find her, I'm going to ask her to sign over her parental rights. From the way you've described her, I don't think that will be a problem."

"I don't understand why. Why you'd do this."

His comment reminded Alex that Marco had trouble trusting anyone—men or women.

"I didn't understand either when the idea first hit me. I'd been praying, thinking, soul-searching. The first thought of adopting you blew my mind. But the more I thought about it, the more it seemed right. I made a lot of phone calls and said a good many prayers. I know this is right. I can't promise I'll be a perfect father, but I'll try to be the best father I can. I had a good role model. My dad loved me through some tough times. I think I'm up to it."

Alex watched as Marco pondered his words. When he finally looked at Alex, his eyes brimmed again with tears.

"One other thing," Alex said. "I want to make our home a place for young men who are leaving youth services. I want to give them a chance to see life in a better light. You said you wanted to be a teacher so you could help boys like you. Being a role model to other boys is the first step in achieving that dream."

Alex waited.

"Can I think it over? I'd like to talk to Reverend Moss about it."

"Son, you take all the time you need. I'm in no hurry." Alex stood and clasped Marco on the shoulder. "I won't come back until you've made up your mind. It's not that I don't want to see you, but you need some space right now. This is a big step for both of us. Whatever you decide, it will not change how I feel about you."

Alex gave Marco's shoulder a squeeze and walked away.

Two weeks later, Reverend Moss visited Alex at his office. "Thank you for seeing me." Reverend Moss shook hands with Alex and took the chair he offered. "Marco Rodriguez has told me a great deal about you during the time he's been at Mount Evans. He looks up to you and admires your courage."

"Marco has turned into a fine young man. I couldn't be

prouder of him. He's worked hard to 'change his stars' as the saying goes."

"We've had many long talks. I can't tell you everything he's confided in me, but I will tell you he still carries around a lot of guilt over what happened. He knows God has forgiven him, and he believes you have, too, but he hasn't forgiven himself."

Alex nodded. "I understand that, and sometimes I see that in him. I try not to talk about it. Dwelling on the past serves no purpose."

"Marco told me you want to adopt him. He's having difficulty getting his head around that idea. He's afraid you're trying to make him a substitute for your dead son. He can't be that person."

"My son was four at the time of the accident. His personality was still developing. I have no idea what he would be like now. I'd like to think he'd be an intelligent, caring, fun-loving kid like he was then. He loved being outdoors, throwing a ball, and running. And he loved to give hugs." Alex felt the usual tears forming in his eyes when he thought about Alex Jr. "Those are the memories I have of my son.

"Marco is different. He's more reserved and unsure of himself, but he has such potential. I want to help him develop that potential—not as a bystander, but as his father. I love the young man he's become. It's as simple and as complicated as that."

"He's also afraid that if he agrees to let you adopt him, he will be a constant reminder of what happened to your family, and you'll come to resent him."

Alex thought about Reverend Moss's comment for a moment. Marco was far more mature than his fourteen years, and his concern was valid, however misguided. "If I were to resent him, it would have happened long before now." Alex closed his eyes, and then looked directly at Rev. Moss. "I've visited him regularly at the center. The Marco you and I both know is not the same person as the ten-year-old boy that caused the accident." He smiled. "He's won my heart. We both need a family. Right now, we're all we've got. We should take advantage of that, don't you agree?"

"What happens if you decide to marry?

Alex cocked his head. "No prospects right now. But if I did, she'd have to love and accept Marco. I wouldn't have it any other way."

Reverend Moss nodded. "Are you sure you're ready for this major change?"

"God and I have had a lot of conversations over the last six months about adopting Marco. It's what I want, and I hope Marco will come to feel the same."

"And if he doesn't?"

Alex smiled. "Then I'll keep in touch with him and help him in any way I can. I won't abandon him. He's had enough of that in his life."

Reverend Moss rose. "I appreciate you seeing me without an appointment. I needed to meet you and see if you were sincere. I'm a good judge of character—always had that second sense about people." He returned Alex's smile. "Now I see why Marco speaks so highly of you. He sees you as the father he never had, and he wants to be like you. I hope he decides to accept your offer."

"Thank you, Reverend Moss. You have to understand that my offer is a bit selfish. I can't imagine not having Marco in my life. I need him."

Reverend Moss smiled and offered his hand to Alex. "I don't know what he'll decide. Don't give up on him."

"That's the last thing I intend to do. Tell him I miss him."

~

The waiting was agony. Almost two months had passed since Alex had told Marco he wanted to adopt him. Alex had yet to hear from him. Any answer was better than the waiting. No word had worried Alex, but he hadn't changed his mind or his feelings. It took all his will power to keep from visiting the facility or calling Reverend Moss.

To Alex, Marco was his son. With the Christmas holiday quickly approaching, he had thought long and hard about what he wanted to give Marco for a gift.

Making his decision, Alex picked a Casio Men's Pro Trek solar digital sports watch. It was expensive, but the perfect gift for a fourteen-year-old son. He only hoped Marco would like it. While he waited for the clerk to wrap it, he prayed Marco would be in touch with him soon.

He'd spent some of the waiting time looking for property that would suit his needs. Property had come available in Palisade, his hometown, but he didn't want to be that close to his parents. He needed some autonomy. Nothing else had come on the market, but he believed the right property would become available when he was ready. He planned to formally resign his position at the DA's office after the first of the year, giving him the opportunity to concentrate on finding the right place to settle. The paperwork necessary to provide a halfway house for young offenders sat on his desk. He'd start the process as soon as he found a fruit ranch big enough for his needs.

On December 23rd, Alex received the call he'd been waiting for. Marco wanted to see him. With a great deal of trepidation and a little excitement, he drove to the youth services center. Unable to sit, he paced the visitor's area waiting for Marco to appear.

When Marco finally entered the visitor's room, Alex resisted the urge to rush forward. Marco's face betrayed nothing of the decision he'd made.

"Sorry it's taken me so long," Marco said. "Thanks for coming."

"Wild horses couldn't keep me away."

Marco set the cribbage board and cards on the table. "I've been practicing. I can take you. You up for it?"

Alex swallowed. This was not what he expected. He wanted an answer, and Marco wanted to play cribbage. *Humor him,* he heard his inner voice say.

Marco took the first game. As Alex dealt the cards to start the second game, Marco spoke, his voice quiet.

"I'd like to take you up on your offer," he said as he picked up his cards.

Alex set the deck on the table and watched Marco study

his cribbage hand. Alex closed his eyes and took a deep breath.

"You sure about this?"

Marco looked up. "Are you sure?"

Alex grinned. "More than ever."

Marco shrugged. "Then I'm sure, too."

Alex stood and gathered Marco into his arms and held him. Marco slipped his arms around Alex's back. "You won't be sorry, Marco. We're a family now."

Alex stepped back and held Marco at arm's length.

Marco grinned. "I'm still having trouble believing this, but if you say it will happen, then it will."

"It will." Alex picked up the package he'd set under the table. "An early Christmas present."

Marco hesitated.

"Go ahead. Open it."

Marco tore the paper away and opened the box. Tears filled his eyes as he stared at the watch. "I . . . I can't take this. It's too much."

"It's my gift to you, because I love you. I'd have given it to you no matter what your answer had been."

"Thanks." He swallowed hard. "Would you keep it until I get out? I don't trust some of the guys here."

"I'll keep it."

Marco handed the box to Alex. "I didn't get you anything."

"Marco, you just gave me the best present I've had in years. You said yes."

K.L. McKee

CHAPTER 6

North Fork, Colorado—January 7, 2008

Trish left the bank and hurried to her pickup. The temperature registered thirty degrees on the bank's marquee. She engaged the heater and felt a tear trickle down her cheek. She was definitely going to lose her heritage—the fruit trees her grandfather and father had planted, the house her grandparents built, and the only life she'd known. The life she loved. Familiar feelings of bitterness toward Clay surfaced, but she fought them down. She wasn't going there. Not today. Not any day.

She'd managed to hang on through the fall. The peach harvest had been decent, and the apple crop brought in good money, but not enough to pay the debt down to a reasonable amount. It had been building too long. She'd known since Thanksgiving she would put the orchards and house up for sale. Waiting until after the holidays seemed the best plan. She didn't want to upset Scott and Meghan, although she didn't think the loss would bother them as much as it did her. They wouldn't want to leave their home, but they'd adjust. She wasn't so sure about herself.

Trish had applied to the Brian Murcheson Fund for help, but her needs didn't fit their parameters. At least, Bob, her banker understood her predicament. They had set up monthly payments she could handle with a lump sum payment due after fruit harvest. Bob had worked with her through the good and bad years, the advantage of living in a small town—people were more understanding and aware of extenuating circumstances. They cared. Trish was thankful for that small consolation.

The time had come, however, for her to sell. As much as losing her heritage grieved her, her back was against the proverbial wall. With their meeting today, Bob had agreed to give her time to find a buyer. The interest would accumulate until everything sold, but she couldn't fault the bank for that.

Her next stop was to see Dale Thorndyke of Thorndyke Realty—"Specializing in farm and ranch properties" as his advertisements stated. She and Dale had discussed selling McBride Orchards several times over the last year.

Dale was more than a good friend. A couple of years ago, knowing she had to move on in her life, Trish had reluctantly agreed to a dinner date with him, which led to seeing him on a semi-regular basis. And that led to confiding in him. She wasn't ready for a serious relationship, but Dale provided safety and trust without pushing for more. It didn't hurt that he was easy to look at. Although not tall, a couple of inches taller than Trish, his dark hair and sleepy cobalt eyes added a touch of mystery to him. They enjoyed each other's company, and he took a genuine interest in Scott and Meghan. All pluses in her mind.

Trish pushed open the front door and greeted Dale's secretary, Becky, who motioned her to his office. Trish knocked and entered.

Dale rose from behind his desk. "This is a pleasant surprise. Aren't you working today?"

"I took the day off to take care of some business. Do you have a few minutes?"

He smiled. "I have all the time in the world for you. Sit down." He pulled a chair out for her. "So, what's going on?"

"I've..." Trish choked back a sob. "I've decided to list McBride Orchards and see what we can get." She had to pull herself together. Losing the orchards wasn't the end of the world, but that's how it felt.

Dale studied her a moment. "This is your final decision?"

"I have no other choice."

"I'm sorry it's come to this. I know how much you love the orchards." He returned to his chair. Pulling out a pad, he asked, "Do you know what you want to ask?"

"Enough to pay off the debt and buy another house to live in."

"Well then, let's see what we can do."

When they decided on an asking price, including land, the house, out-buildings and equipment, a myriad of emotions warred inside Trish. She felt a momentary tinge of relief that she'd finally made the decision to sell, but the regret at losing something she loved weighed on her. She wasn't ready to turn it loose, even though she knew selling was the only option.

Dale set down his pen. "Now that we've settled on an amount, sign here to make it legal for me to represent you." He pushed a paper across the desk.

Through tears clouding her eyes, Trish scrawled her signature on the line indicated.

"Let me take you to supper to celebrate." He slipped the paper into a folder.

Trish stared at him. She was fighting back tears, and he wanted to celebrate. What was wrong with him?

"Why would I celebrate losing my home? My life?"

Dale shrugged. "Maybe celebrate was the wrong choice of words."

"You *think*?" Trish's temper flared.

"Trish, I'm sorry. What I meant was, selling's the right thing to do, and you should be thankful you've finally made the decision. Buying you supper will give you a little time to get used to the idea and a chance to figure out how you'll tell the kids."

Trish didn't buy Dale's attempt at an apologetic look or his choice of words. Selling the ranch *would* be a celebration for him with the nice commission he'd earn.

She stood. "Thanks, but no thanks. I need to get home."

"Are you sure?"

"Another time, maybe." Maybe was the operative word, she thought. She didn't care for his lack of understanding. She expected more from him. Fighting tears, she drove home, forming in her mind the words she'd use to tell Scott and Meghan that the only home they had ever known would soon belong to someone else.

~

"But I *like* living here," Scott protested. "Why do we have to move?"

Trish sighed. She had expected Meghan to react negatively, not Scott. The only reaction from Meghan was to tap her foot and glance at the clock. Her favorite television show was due to start in a few minutes.

"Because we can't afford to stay here anymore. The debt is too much."

"Is it because of what Dad did?" Venom laced Scott's comment.

Trish was more than surprised at her son's question. Clay's actions hadn't been mentioned since she'd told the kids what happened.

"I'm sorry, Scott. He left me with a huge debt, and it's more than I can handle."

"What if I got a job?"

Where did that come from? "I appreciate the offer, but it wouldn't help that much, and a job would interfere with your studying and sports." She smiled at her son.

69

Scott stormed from the room. "I *hate* Dad for what he did."

Trish watched Scott's retreating back. She wished she had someone to help her figure out the mind and moods of a teenager. This was a side of him she hadn't expected. He worshipped his dad. She decided to wait a while and let Scott vent his anger before talking to him again.

~

Denver, Colorado—February 28, 2008

Alex put the finishing touches on his resignation letter. He was almost two months past the original goal for leaving the D.A.'s office. At the end of December, he'd been assigned a case he thought the Public Defender would be willing to plea out. He'd thought wrong. The accused refused to bargain, and it had taken until the first of February to convince both the defendant and the defense attorney the evidence was strong enough to lock him away for a long time. A plea deal was the only choice.

It took Alex the rest of the month to clear his desk. The letter made his resignation official in two weeks. The upside of the delay was finding a listing for McBride Orchards in North Fork, Colorado. Until that listing appeared, nothing had stood out to Alex as a viable purchase. As a kid growing up on a fruit farm only seventy-five miles from North Fork, he remembered the high quality of fruit that came from the McBride orchards. The listing was an answer to prayer. Of course, he hadn't seen the orchards yet, but the McBride reputation almost guaranteed that Alex had found what he wanted—a sizable fruit ranch in a small town. No price had been listed, but considering the acreage, house, and equipment, it would probably take most of his savings. The insurance settlement from the accident and Amy's insurance policy had been set aside for the future. Alex decided this was the future he wanted.

Marco's adoption had been set in motion. Alex was allowed to skip the adoption orientation because of his law degree. He did have to pass a background check, which had been done when he joined the D.A.'s office. That meant little about him had to be investigated. He enrolled in a required training program for adopting parents and submitted to an assessment by a caseworker. He'd spent days preparing his condo for the home visit and hired a professional cleaning service to put on the finishing touches. He passed with high marks.

Marco had filled out paperwork agreeing to the adoption. He "sweat blood," as he described it to Alex, over the questions, but with Reverend Moss's help, they managed to answer all that was asked. The interview with the caseworker caused more anxiety, but in the end, she seemed satisfied with Marco's answers. The final step was Juvenile Court, which was scheduled for mid-March.

Once Juvenile Court agreed to the adoption, Marco would have to live with Alex a year after he was released. If no problems surfaced during the probationary period, the adoption would be official. Alex and Marco both knew they would have some adjustments to make when they began living together. Nothing they couldn't handle. Alex knew the long adoption process was worth it, and he prayed it would be for Marco. Their unusual relationship might be cause for a judge to question Alex's motives, but he had confidence that he could convince the judge he was sincere.

With the resignation letter in hand, he walked to the D.A.'s office and handed the letter to John, his boss.

"You're sure you want to do this?"

"I'm sure."

"I was afraid of that. I'm losing my best prosecutor, you know."

"I appreciate the compliment, John, but I know this is the right thing."

"How's the adoption process going?"

"Nearly there. Juvenile Court and a year of probation after Marco is released, and then it will be final."

John slowly shook his head and smiled at Alex. "I thought you were crazy when I found out you'd gone to visit Marco. I'm still blown away by your relationship with him. It's truly inspirational."

Some days Alex had trouble believing it himself. "It's the work of God, John. He created love and respect between a couple of guys who needed it."

John fingered the letter. "Much as I hate to accept your resignation, I know I can't talk you out of it. I wish you the very best, Alex. You deserve it." He stood and offered his hand. "If it doesn't work out, come back to see me. I might consider hiring you back."

Alex chuckled. "I'll keep that in mind."

In his office, Alex pulled out his cell phone and dialed the number for Thorndyke Realty.

~

"Thorndyke Realty. Dale speaking."

"I'm interested in a property you have listed," the caller said. "McBride Orchards."

Dale frowned. No one had inquired about Trish's property since he listed it. He was hopeful he and his partners could get financing in place before someone expressed interest.

Dale cleared his throat. "McBride Orchards is one of our listings. What would you like to know?"

"Actually, I'd like to discuss it in person and see the property for myself. I thought we could set up a time to do that."

"Sure," he said, trying his best to sound pleased by the inquiry. Once he got off the phone, he'd have to do some scrambling to get things in place. He wondered how long he could stall the caller. "When did you want to look at it?"

"How about the first week in March, say Friday the seventh?"

Too soon. "I'm tied up that day and through the weekend. What about the following Friday?"

The caller hesitated. "I may be tied up then. Could we make it on Friday, the twenty-first?"

Dale waited to answer, making it appear he was checking his appointment book. He shuffled a few papers

73

loud enough to be heard over the phone and made note of the phone number. "I think that will work. What time?"

"I can be there at eleven."

"I'll see you then. And your name?"

"Alex Lambert."

Dale pondered the call for a few minutes, and then went to work researching Alex Lambert of Denver, which was the area code of the number he'd jotted down. He hadn't expected to find an Alex Lambert listed as a Deputy District Attorney. He would have to tread carefully while trying to out-maneuver a potential buyer and lawyer. Dale had other plans in mind for Trish and her property.

~

Alex had a strange feeling about the call he'd just made. Most realtors acted overanxious if they thought they could sell any property, especially one that would bring in a large commission. The realtor sounded as though he didn't want to meet with Alex. No realtor was that busy. Alex tapped his fingers on the desk. His prosecutor radar went active, although maybe he misunderstood. North Fork was a small town, and Thorndyke Realty was the only one listed. Still...

Logging onto the internet, Alex typed McBride Orchards into the search bar. His research revealed the owner was Trish McBride Ryan, thirty-four, widowed with two children. He also found she worked as a librarian at the North Fork Library. It certainly made sense that a widow with a job would want to sell the orchards. She wouldn't have time for both. Running that size an operation was a full-time job in itself.

He hated waiting three weeks to see the orchards. Now that he'd resigned his job, he was impatient to get on with the next phase of his life. The upside of waiting that long, however, was that he'd be done with Juvenile Court and his petition to adopt Marco. And he'd be free of the D.A.'s office.

The next day, Alex visited Marco. He grinned as the tall young man appeared in the visiting area with the cribbage board and deck of cards. Alex greeted him with a hug and they sat down. "When are you going to learn you can't beat me?" Alex teased.

Marco set the board down and spread the cards. "When are you going to admit I beat you as often as you beat me, old man?"

Alex drew the low card and shuffled the deck. As he dealt he looked at Marco and raised his eyebrows. "Old man? I can take you anytime. Arm wrestling, cribbage, you name it."

"No way. I'm going to take you to the bank today."

"Just try it." Alex discarded into the crib. "I called about a property today."

Marco threw his two cards into the crib and cut the deck. "Really? Where?"

"North Fork, Colorado. Small town on the Western Slope, about 5700 feet in elevation. It's surrounded by mountains, a perfect spot to grow fruit, and a great place to live. I think you'll like it."

"Sounds nice." Marco set his cards face down and

looked at Alex. "You really think Juvenile Court will approve the adoption?"

Alex smiled. "Marco, I think it's a matter of formality. There's no reason to turn us down."

"Wish I could believe that. I'm scared they'll say no."

Alex reached across the table and squeezed Marco's shoulder. "If they had any valid reasons to say no, they'd have done it by now. The Department of Human Services has approved the adoption. You've consented to it. I've passed the background check and home inspection. It's a done deal."

"Are they going to change their minds if you move?"

"No. They'll probably want to see the new home, but that's all."

"What if they question why you want to adopt the kid who ki—"

"Marco, we're not going there anymore. Understand? That's behind us. History. If the judge brings it up, we'll both be honest. Okay?"

Marco attempted a smile. "Okay." He picked up his cards and played the first one. "Seven."

Alex played an eight. "Fifteen for two."

Marco grinned. "Thought you had me, huh?" He played an eight. "Twenty-three for two."

"You're going to make this hard for me, aren't you?"
"You bet."

Alex watched moisture form in Marco's eyes. He couldn't remember exactly when it happened, but he loved this kid.

CHAPTER 7

North Fork, Colorado—March 21, 2008

Alex parked his Ford Expedition on the main street of North Fork and settled back in the driver's seat. He was early for his appointment with Dale Thorndyke. That gave him time to look around the town. Rather than get out of the vehicle, he decided to observe people as they walked by. The outside temperature gauge on the dash registered fifty degrees. Alex glanced at the sky. Clear and deep blue, something you seldom saw with Denver haze.

An age-old brick storefront, probably original to the town, faced him. Half of the building was the North Fork Drugstore, the other half a variety store. Other storefronts advertised a bicycle shop, a restaurant, an ice cream parlor, and a feed and supply store, all on the west side of the street. Thorndyke Realty, a theatre, a chiropractor's office and Granny's Café were some of the businesses that resided on the east side of the street. The town hall sat in the middle of the block on the west side. This was the kind of town he wanted to live in, the kind of town he'd grown up in—small, personable, and slower-paced. A perfect place for raising a son. Marco's life might have been different if his mother had lived here. She might have had a better chance, too.

Alex reflected on the turn of events over the last month. In early March, a woman was found dead in the Five Points region of Denver. Fingerprints identified her as Marco's mother. At least the hunt for her was behind them.

Alex remembered breaking the news to Marco. He had gone to the youth services center to tell him in person. Marco appreciated directness, so Alex didn't hold back.

"We found your mother," he said. "I'm sorry, Marco, but she's dead."

Marco showed no reaction.

"She was found in a dumpster by police, beaten to death. Probably by her pimp or drug supplier. I'm really sorry."

Marco looked away. "I'm not."

Alex waited. He'd hoped Marco would have some feeling of sadness, even if she wasn't a good mother.

After several minutes of silence, Marco looked at Alex. "You had to know her, man. She did nothing for me. I took care of myself. She wanted her next fix, not me." He heaved a breath. "I'm not sorry. She's found peace. That's what Reverend Moss would say."

Alex closed his eyes for a brief moment and nodded. The young boy that sat across from him had become wise beyond his years. "She is at rest, Marco. Maybe that is a blessing." Alex waited a few seconds, then broached the subject of a funeral. "Do you want to attend the graveside services? I think we can get you a special release from here for a few hours. With no relatives to claim the body, the county went ahead with the arrangements. She'll be buried day after tomorrow."

Marco pondered the offer, his fingers lazily tracing the tabletop. "No," he finally said. "Maybe Reverend Moss could say a few words at the service. Is that all right?"

"I'm sure it is." Alex rose. "I'll check with him. Anything else?"

Marco shrugged and stood. "Naw. Thanks for letting me know."

Alex nodded. "Let me know if you change your mind."

"'Kay."

Marco had walked away, his shoulders slightly hunched, and Alex had muttered a quick prayer for him.

Shaking off the memory, Alex stared through the windshield at the sidewalk in front of him. Two women met and chatted. An older man walked by and greeted them. *Awww, small towns. I love it.*

He smiled, remembering the adoption hearing in family court. Alex had worried that the judge would question his motives and deny the petition, but he made sure Marco didn't pick up on his anxiety. As expected, the judge had questioned Alex extensively as to why he wanted to adopt

Marco. Alex convinced him of the changes in Marco and himself and the feelings he had for the young man. His honesty about the past, how he had forgiven Marco, and what had changed in the ensuing years made a good case.

Alex swelled with pride when Marco had answered the Judge's questions clearly and with confidence. The judge commented that although theirs was an unusual case, he saw no impediment to granting the petition for adoption and wished them both well. Relief and joy had overwhelmed Alex at the decision. They had cleared one more hurdle.

Alex glanced at his watch and realized he had only a couple of minutes before meeting with the realtor. He locked the Ford Expedition and walked across the street to Thorndyke Realty.

~

Dale Thorndyke paced his office. He had to discourage the buyer he was scheduled to meet in a few minutes. Three weeks' delay hadn't been quite enough time to get everything in place. Another delay would make the interested party suspicious.

He needed Trish's property. He had plans for a subdivision with affordable homes for the residents of North Fork. Her property was perfect. Not too far out of town with a good view of the valley. Some financing and a builder had been arranged for the project, but he hadn't come up with the entire amount for the property. Loving Trish was a bonus. If he could convince her to marry him, then he would have access. He'd pay the loan down a little and convince her that there was more money in homes than in fruit. His partners wouldn't wait forever. She'd given up on the orchards anyway. Building homes would get her out of debt to a life of ease. They'd be able to travel and enjoy life.

His secretary interrupted his thoughts.

"Your eleven o'clock is here."

"Thanks, Becky. Give me a minute."

He had to come up with a plan and quick. *Think, Dale, think.* Trish didn't want to sell. She was doing it because she had no choice. He paced, his mind working overtime. He couldn't afford to have Alex Lambert make an offer. He would have to discourage him. Permanently. Get rid of the buyer, first, then figure out what to do next.

He met Alex in the outer office. "I'm Dale Thorndyke." Dale offered the tall blond man his hand. "You must be Alex Lambert. Welcome to North Fork." Dale ushered Alex to his office and offered him a chair.

"I'm afraid you've come for no reason. I'm very sorry, but the property you were interested in has just been pulled from the market."

"Really?" Alex Lambert looked skeptical.

"Afraid so. Mrs. Ryan, the owner, called me about an hour ago and told me she'd changed her mind. It was too late for me to get in touch with you."

"Any chance she might change her mind?"

"Doubt it. She sounded determined about not selling." It wasn't a complete lie, Dale told himself.

"I see." Alex inclined his head slightly. "I'm sorry, too. I was looking forward to seeing the property." He rose to go.

"I don't suppose you'd have another similar property available?"

"Wish I did." Dale stood and offered his hand. "I'm really sorry to have inconvenienced you."

They shook hands. "You will let me know if something comes on the market?"

"Absolutely. I have your number." Dale smiled.

"Thanks."

~

Alex sat in the Expedition, fighting down disappointment, while contemplating the meeting with Dale Thorndyke. Something wasn't right. His years of dealing with criminals made him a bit of a skeptic. He swore the realtor was lying. It was a gut feeling, but a strong one. On a whim, he asked for directions to McBride Orchards at the gas station. Even if the property was no longer for sale, he wanted to look at it.

He drove north and then west out of town. A graveled road led to a mesa with orchards all around. Peaches flanked the road on the north. The trees were pruned and ready to bud. Oh, how he loved this time of year. New life, new hopes, new starts. He passed a bunkhouse, and at the end of the road stood two-story house, a "For Sale" sign planted in the front yard. The house needed paint, but otherwise looked in good shape. Cherry trees grew on the west side of the property and a well-pruned apple orchard stretched behind the house.

A dirt road veered to the east, so he followed it for about

a quarter of a mile. A packing shed, an equipment barn, and a good half-acre of open ground—enough to build a house—welcomed him. Printed on the side and front of the shed was the name "McBride Orchards" in large black letters. An orchard truck—a flatbed truck with an open cab—sat idle against one of the buildings. Several ladders rested on the truck's bed along with a couple pairs of stilts used for pruning taller trees. He assumed the barn housed a spray machine, tractor, and other large equipment. Peach trees surrounded him on the north and east.

"Lord, this is exactly what I want." He still had a gut feeling something wasn't right, but he didn't know what to do about it short of accusing someone he didn't know of lying. Maybe his gut had taken up wishful thinking. He wanted the guy to be lying.

Time to regroup. There was still a place for sale in Palisade where he grew up, but he didn't want to be that close to his family, or be in direct competition with them. Seventy-five miles was a good distance. North Fork was higher in elevation than Palisade resulting in a two-week delay in fruit readiness. The delay gave Lambert Orchards a head start over McBride Orchards in market competition. Yet history proved they both did well.

Alex's heart quickened. He wanted this more than anything he'd wanted in a long time. His stomach growled, so he headed back to town to look for a place to eat, but not before taking a few photos with his digital camera.

~

"What can I get ya?" The waitress's nametag read "Wanda." She looked to be in her sixties, but the twinkle in her eyes said she stayed young at heart. Granny's Café had come highly recommended by the man at the gas station.

Alex glanced at the menu. "I'll have the North Fork Burger, fries and a Coke."

Wanda smiled. "Comin' right up."

When Wanda brought his Coke, he took a chance she might be willing to gossip a little. "What do you know about McBride Orchards?"

"Oh, lordy. Now there's a sad story. Trish Ryan owns it. She was a McBride, you know. Her deceased no-good husband left her owing a ton of money on it. She can't afford to keep it, so it's for sale. Had to take a job at the library. I feel real bad for her. Been in her family for generations." She started to say something else, but the bell over the door signaled new customers. "Sorry, duty calls. Howdy folks," she called and walked away.

Alex wanted to know more, but she said enough to make him question Thorndyke's comments. Things didn't add up.

When his hamburger arrived, he bit into it and closed his eyes in pure ecstasy. He hadn't eaten a hamburger so juicy and tasty for years. The French fries were homemade, thick, firm on the outside and soft in the middle. The menu boasted home-grown beef. It sure beat the fast-food chains. He was in heaven.

Alex didn't like defeat, so he contemplated his next move. His desire for the truth made him a good prosecutor, and he was determined to discover the truth.

Before traveling to North Fork, he had booked a room online in the Bross Hotel, a renovated hotel from the early days of North Fork. With no job calling him, he had plenty of time to take a few days and explore the area.

Over a piece of homemade apple pie á la mode, Alex came up with an idea. According to Wanda, Trish Ryan worked at the library. He could stop by and ask for help with a legal question—he did need to look at the county land codes—and then ask for Ms. Ryan and broach the subject of her land. He had nothing to lose. She might look at him like he was nuts. On the other hand, he might get an answer. Or at the very least, convince her to change her mind.

He belonged in North Fork. He knew it the minute he drove into town. The crisp, clean air, fields waiting to be disked and planted, irrigation ditches ready for cleaning and burning. Mountains to the east, tall and majestic, welcomed him like a long-lost son. Their rugged beauty took his breath away. He looked forward to exploring the lakes, rivers, and forests with Marco. Grand Mesa, with its lakes and hiking trails—a place he'd roamed often while growing up in Palisade—rimmed the north side of the valley, stretching miles to the west. This was home.

He drove to the library and entered the double glass doors. Several people milled around picking out books, others sat at tables reading, and some worked on computers along one wall. The reference desk was straight ahead. A cute redhead, who looked to be in her mid-thirties, sat at the desk helping a patron. Alex walked to the desk and glanced at the librarian's nametag. Could he be any luckier? Trish

Ryan, Librarian, smiled at him.

"I'll be with you in a moment," she said. Ms. Ryan rose from her chair.

Alex returned her dimpled smile. "Thanks," he said as he watched her lead the patron to a nearby section of books.

~

On her way back to the desk, Trish observed the tall man waiting for help. He was handsome and well-built, around her age, maybe a little older. She told herself she wasn't interested. Although she spent time with Dale, she wasn't ready for a serious relationship. She wasn't dead, however, and she still appreciated a good-looking man.

"Thanks for waiting. How may I help you?"

"I'm looking for the county land codes."

"This way." She stepped to a set of lower shelves marked "Reference" opposite her desk, pulled out a thick volume, and placed it on top of the shelves.

"Thanks."

Trish started to leave.

"Wait."

She turned back.

"I'm Alex Lambert." He offered his hand, but she ignored it. She knew a salesman when she saw one. "Are you the Trish Ryan who owns McBride Orchards?"

How would he know that? "I am. Why?"

"I'll be blunt. I understand you've decided not to sell."

Trish frowned. Not only was he blunt, he was wrong. "I don't understand. I've listed the orchards and house with

Thorndyke Realty. Have you talked with them?" At least someone was interested in her land. His was the first inquiry she was aware of.

"I have and was told you made a last-minute decision today not to sell."

Trish blinked. This guy was way off base. "I'm sure you misunderstood. The property is for sale."

Mr. Lambert smiled. "Pretty sure I'm not mistaken. Mr. Thorndyke himself told me you'd changed your mind. He seemed awfully anxious to get rid of me."

Trish studied the man. He didn't appear to be lying. She could usually spot a dishonest person a mile away. Except for Clay. But she'd been in love with him and gave him the benefit of the doubt. Unfortunately.

"Ms. Ryan?"

"Sorry. I think there's definitely been a misunderstanding. I'm not happy about selling, but I need to. I'm sure that's what he meant." She realized her comment sounded desperate. "My husband died several years ago, and working full time doesn't leave me enough extra hours for the orchards." She hoped that came across better and didn't sound as desperate.

An older woman walked up to the desk. "I need help," she announced loudly.

Trish turned. "I'm busy with a patron, Mrs. Decker, but I'll be happy to help you as soon as I can."

"Right now. I have an appointment in fifteen minutes and I don't want to be late."

"Mrs. Decker—"

"That's okay," Mr. Lambert said. "Maybe we can meet later over a cup of coffee. It looks like you're busy." He smiled. "I'm definitely interested in your property, so if you still want to sell . . . ." He pulled out a business card and scribbled a number on the back. "Call me."

"Well, I never!" Mrs. Decker said. "I don't like being ignored while you're trying to get a date."

Trish slipped the card in her pocket. Mr. Alex Lambert walked away, confidence in his stride, without using the land codes. She took a deep breath and turned her attention to Mrs. Decker, forcing a smile across her face. "Thank you for your patience. What may I help you with today?"

~

In his hotel room, Alex contemplated the meeting with Trish Ryan. He liked the looks of her. When he asked her about her decision not to sell the property, he thought he saw a spark of fire in her dark green eyes. She was definitely blindsided by his question. He took little satisfaction in knowing he'd been right about Thorndyke. He despised dishonest people, no matter how they might justify their actions.

He figured he'd opened a can of worms. Unless he misread her, he guessed Ms. Ryan would be confronting Thorndyke very soon. All he had to do was wait for a phone call—either from Ms. Ryan or Mr. Thorndyke.

He dialed a friend in the Denver DA's investigative department.

"Carol, Alex here. How are you?"

"Alex. Fine. Miss you already. You change your mind about quitting?"

"Nope. Need a favor."

"Name it. I owe you."

"I need you to check someone out for me." He gave her what he knew about Dale Thorndyke and disconnected. Maybe he was being a little underhanded, but the prosecutor in him didn't want Trish Ryan, or anyone else, duped by a dishonest realtor.

~

Trish sat in her boss's office and waited for Sarah to finish a phone call.

"What's up, Trish. Everything okay?"

"I need to take the rest of the afternoon off. Would that be a problem?"

"Scott okay?"

"Has nothing to do with Scott. I need to see Dale and then Jess Atkins."

"Has Dale found a buyer? That's great news."

"Maybe. Sarah, when did you know you could trust Cam?"

"I think I always knew I could. Home grown guy, good family with a good reputation. One of Rick's best friends. It's always hard to trust another person with your heart, whether you've had a good experience or a bad one.

"When Rick died, I didn't want to get involved with anyone. Then Cam moved in next door and stole my heart." She smiled. "I know things weren't great between you and

Clay, so trusting is a little harder. Give Dale a chance."

"That's just it. I think he's lied to me."

"Really?" Sarah frowned.

"I need to see him this afternoon. Find out what's going on."

"In that case, take the time. Not much going on this afternoon." Sarah frowned. "Care to elaborate? If you're going to see Jess, then you must think you need a lawyer."

Trish stiffened. "Depends on what Dale has to say."

CHAPTER 8

Becky wasn't at her desk at Thorndyke Realty, so Trish strode toward Dale's office. His raised voice drifted into the hall. She slowed when she realized he was on the phone. His words ignited anger and disbelief.

"I have things under control," she heard him say. "By this time next week I should have access to McBride Orchards." The urge to barge into his office was squelched by the need to hear the entire exchange.

"The legalities may take a few weeks," he said, "but it will get done. We should be able to start clearing trees no later than May and have several houses to sell by September." A pause and then, "She'll be ready, I guarantee it. Any later will dig into our profits and delay construction."

Another short pause. "I can handle her. She's between a

rock and a hard spot. She'll agree, especially when she sees how much money we can make by selling homes and lots."

Trish closed her eyes and clinched her fists. Dale wanted her property to build a subdivision. No way. Mr. Lambert had been right. Dale had lied to both of them.

Could she trust a stranger? What if Lambert wanted the same thing? He had asked about the county land codes when he came to the library. Was he planning to split her land into plots, too? Seeing her beloved orchards turned into a housing development would kill her. Bile rose in her throat.

Gritting her teeth, she backtracked a few steps and called out. "Dale. Are you still here?"

He met her in the hall. "Trish. What a pleasant surprise. I was just going to call you about dinner. What do you say?" He kissed her on the cheek and ushered her into his office.

She resisted the urge to wipe the kiss away, his pungent aftershave lingering. "Depends on your answer to a question."

"Fire away. I'm all yours for the rest of the day."

"Did you tell a Mr. Alex Lambert that I no longer wanted to sell?"

The smile disappeared from Dale's face, and Trish swore he paled a little.

"Why would you ask that?"

"Because he came to the library and asked me why I changed my mind about selling. He seemed very interested in buying."

Dale looked sheepish. "Okay, you caught me." He sat on the edge of his desk directly in front of Trish and took hold of her hand. She jerked it away.

He clasped his hands together. "Trish, I love you. We make a great couple. Let's get married. You won't have to worry about the bank loan. With my help, we can pay down the debt to a manageable level."

"Really?" She clinched her fists. "What size lots do you plan to put where the orchards are? Half acre? Three quarters? One acre?"

"I don't know what you mean."

"I overheard you talking about tearing out my orchards by May and building houses by September. Are you going to lie about that, too?"

Dale glanced away for a moment. He looked at Trish again and shrugged. "Okay. I planned to break it to you gently after we were married, but now you know. I'm sorry I didn't talk to you about it sooner. It's the most efficient and practical way to use your land. You won't have to work anymore. We'll make a lot of money. Be on easy street the rest of our lives."

Trish stood and glared at him. "*We*? There is no *we*. I don't want my orchards turned into a subdivision. The land is for growing fruit. Period. I don't care about living on 'easy street.' I *like* working—in the orchards and at the library. You can take your grand scheme and *shove* it. You're fired. I'll find someone else to represent my property."

"You can't fire me." Dale crossed his arms. "The contract you signed is irrevocable. If you don't want to do this with me, give me a few weeks. I'll come up with the money to buy the property outright. Better to sell to me than some stranger."

Trish's temper flared. "You don't have a few weeks. You have an interested party. Start there."

"How do you know he won't be building houses? He's a lawyer, not a farmer."

"I don't. At least he hasn't gone behind my back."

Dale wiped his hand over his face. "I'm really sorry, Trish, but just about any buyer is going to see the potential of your land for housing. Promise me you'll think about things once you've cooled down. I messed up. I should have been up front with you."

"Too late." Trish shot him a killer look. "As for the contract, I'm going to see Jess Atkins when I leave here. You'll hear from him." She fled the office, ignoring his pleas for her to talk things out.

A few minutes later, Trish sat in Jess Atkins' office, barely controlling the anger still simmering over Dale's betrayal. "I need to get out of my contract with Dale Thorndyke. He says it's irrevocable, but he's lied to me about his dealings."

"Sounds pretty serious. Why don't you explain?"

Trish told Jess in detail about the exchange with Alex Lambert and her confrontation with Dale and the contract she signed that he claimed was irrevocable.

"Is Mr. Lambert available?"

Trish pulled out his business card from her pocket and handed it to Jess. "He's still in town."

Jess copied the information. "Do you know why he wants your property?"

"No, but I intend to ask him."

"I can't promise anything, Trish. Real estate contracts are usually binding. Make an appointment for late morning or early afternoon on Monday. I'll see what I can do."

Trish left her lawyer's office with less assurance than she'd hoped.

~

Alex paced the hotel room. He'd hoped to hear from Trish Ryan by now. He glanced at his watch. 4:50. Maybe he'd misread her. He wasn't always 100 percent right about people. Best to consider alternate plans in case McBride Orchards had slipped his grasp. He'd learned over the last few years to always start with prayer. In his excitement about the McBride property, he hadn't done that.

"Lord, I've been so focused on wanting this property that I've failed to seek your guidance. I know what *I* want, but you know what's best. Your will, Lord, not mine."

He grabbed his jacket and walked the few blocks to Granny's Café. No sense starving, and the temptation of another juicy hamburger was more than he could resist. There goes my cholesterol count, he thought, but savored every bite of the juicy meal when it was delivered. While waiting for the bill, his cell phone rang.

Ending the call, he waved Wanda over. "I'm expecting a guest. How about a couple of pieces of hot apple pie à la mode and another cup of coffee, if that's what Trish Ryan drinks."

Wanda winked. "I know what she likes."

The wait seemed forever, yet only ten minutes passed before he saw Trish Ryan walk through the door. Tension showed in her face, her mouth drawn tight. She scooted to the middle of the bench seat across from him.

"Thanks for meeting me." She slipped out of her coat, closed her eyes and took a deep breath.

"I should be thanking you." Alex smiled. "I wasn't sure you'd call. Have you eaten?"

"No. Though the smell of Wanda's cooking gets my appetite going." She smiled.

Wanda delivered a steaming cup of coffee and two pieces of ice cream-topped pie.

"I didn't order pie," Trish said as Wanda walked away.

"I did. My treat. Guess I should have waited and let you order a meal."

"That's okay. I have kids at home that need to be fed."

Wanda returned and topped off Alex's coffee. "Anything else I can get you?"

"We're fine. Thanks," Alex said.

Trish ignored both her coffee and the pie. "Let's get right to the point, Mr. Lambert. Why do you want to buy McBride Orchards?"

Alex smiled. He liked her directness. That fire he'd seen earlier still highlighted her dark green eyes. "In a sentence— I want to grow fruit."

"*Really?*" She studied him a moment, then took a drink of her coffee, her eyes never leaving his.

"Really." He grinned.

"What do you know about growing fruit, Mr. Lambert?

96

Your card says you're a Deputy DA from Denver. I'm sure you didn't learn fruit crop production in law school."

"Where did you learn it?" he countered.

"I grew up with it."

"So did I. On a fruit ranch in Palisade. Farming is in my blood."

She frowned. "Lambert Orchards?"

"One and the same. My father and older brother run the orchards now. When I went to college, the last thing I wanted to do was grow fruit, so I became a lawyer."

Setting her cup down, she leaned back and studied him. "You want to give up a secure, well-paying career to grow fruit. Are you nuts? You know about spring freezes, peach borer, winter kill, and price instability, to name only a few problems."

"Crazy as it sounds, I can't wait to get started." He paused and then added, "And nothing in this life is secure."

She blinked at his comment. *So true.* "I'll be blunt, Mr. Lambert—"

"Alex."

She nodded. "Alex. I don't trust strangers, and I trust men even less. My late husband lied to me our entire marriage, and I just discovered Dale Thorndyke lied, so why should I believe you?"

Alex leaned back. Ms. Ryan definitely had trust issues, and he had no way of convincing her he wasn't lying. He looked directly into her eyes and without blinking simply said, "Because it's the truth."

A grunt of disbelief escaped her. "You were interested

in the county land codes when you came to the library, yet you left without using them. That says to me you already know what they are and are playing me. I'm guessing you're no different than Dale. You want to put houses in place of my orchards."

"Is that why he lied to me about you selling?" He shook his head, a frown creasing his brow. "That's low." He leaned forward and rested his arms on the table. "Mrs. Ryan—"

"Trish."

He smiled. "Trish. I'm interested in the county land codes because I want to put some of the property into a land trust so that it can't be used for anything but legal agricultural purposes—food crops, to be specific."

Trish's eyes grew wide. "You're serious?"

Alex nodded. "I'm serious."

"Then I'd want *that* in writing."

He took a bite of his pie, letting his idea sink in. The more he looked at Trish Ryan, the more intrigued he became. He wouldn't call her beautiful, but cute definitely fit. Her vibrant red hair brought to mind a fiery pixie. He liked her spunk, and noticed some of her tension had eased.

"I hate to tell you, but at the moment Dale still represents me for the sale of the property. You may have to deal with him, like it or not."

"Whatever it takes." Alex washed the bite of pie down with a sip of coffee. "Better eat your pie before the ice cream melts completely."

She took a bite. "I shouldn't be eating dessert before supper, and I should get home. My kids will be wondering where I am." She cut another bite. "Can't waste Wanda's pie, though."

Alex didn't want her to leave. He was enjoying her company. "I eventually want to add chickens and an apiary for pollination and sale of honey. It fits well with the fruit."

"I can see you're very passionate about this." She pushed her empty plate aside and signaled Wanda for a coffee refill. "Dale was sort of right," she admitted. "I don't want to sell, but I have little choice." Her eyes clouded, and she blinked. "Five generations of McBride's have lived on the property and four generations have produced fruit. It's difficult for me to let it go, and the last thing I want is for the orchards to become houses."

Alex felt a tug at his heart. He understood her difficult position. It would be as hard for his family to let go of their land. "I sympathize. Your place, however, is the first one I've found that's big enough to do what I want. You may think I'm crazy, but I believe God led me here."

He sugared the fresh coffee Wanda served and took a sip. "I took the liberty of driving out to look at your property this afternoon. It's perfect." He wanted to tell her more—his plans for helping troubled youth—but now was not the time.

"I appreciate your candidness." She grabbed her coat. "I really have to go."

Alex offered his hand. "Let's agree to work something out, even if we have to go through Deceitful Dale to do it." Trish's hand was strong and warm, and she smiled for the first time since she'd joined him.

"Agreed." She slid across the seat. "I'll be talking to my

lawyer Monday morning. I'll contact you after that." She stood, coat in hand. "Will you still be in town?"

Alex slipped from his bench seat and stood. "I have nowhere to go at the moment." He helped her into her coat. "I'll wait for your call."

Alex watched until she disappeared from sight. He liked the subtle swing to her hips. She had grit. He liked that. Grabbing his jacket, he stepped to the register to pay the bill.

~

Trish sat in her pickup and contemplated her meeting with Alex. Maybe she was crazy, but she liked him. For some unknown reason, she felt she could trust him. Perhaps it was his firm handshake, or the way he looked directly at her with his clear blue eyes. He seemed to have a strong faith, and she envied him. She liked his warm, friendly smile, too. It didn't hurt he was handsome—strong features, nice athletic build. Okay, that was actually a pitfall. She didn't trust handsome men. Clay and Dale for starters. Both were good-looking, both athletic, so that might be a mark against Mr. Alex Lambert. Anger welled in her at the thought of Clay and Dale.

She turned the key and backed out of the parking space. Tamping down her anger, she considered Alex's idea of chickens and especially bees. From the time she was ten, bees had fascinated her, but her father hadn't been interested. When she took over the business, the orchards occupied her time, the idea of bees set aside. Maybe Alex would teach her to be an apiarist.

"Stop that! You don't need a man messing up your life." She couldn't, however, get Alex or his smile out of her head during the drive home. Meghan nearly knocked her over when she walked in the back door.

"Mom, you got flowers! They're beautiful. Come see."

Trish hung her coat on a peg by the door and followed Meghan into the front room. On the coffee table sat a vase of baby's breath and at least two dozen red roses. She plucked the card from the holder.

Please forgive me, Trish. I didn't mean to keep you from knowing my plans. I just hadn't finalized them. I love you and want us to be a couple. I'm so sorry.

Love,
Dale

Trish threw the card on the table, picked up the roses and dumped them, vase first, in the kitchen trash.

"*Mom*, why'd you do that?"

"I don't want them."

"But Mom—"

"Meghan, don't argue. I don't like red roses."

"Can I have them?"

Trish sighed. Meghan was too young to understand the whys of her anger. "Take them to your room where I won't see them. Where's Scott?"

"In his room doing homework, I guess." Meghan rescued the roses from the trash and hurried to her room.

Trish sat on a kitchen chair and cradled her head in her

hands. No one had ever sent her flowers, not even Clay. He was too cheap. Unfortunately, these were sent for all the wrong reasons. Roses or not, she wanted no part of Dale's apology. She scrubbed her face and decided to see what she could throw together for supper. The doorbell interrupted her. Dale stood on the porch holding pizza boxes.

"May I come in?"

"I'm in no mood for company. *Especially* yours."

"Did you get my flowers?" He peered past her into the living room.

"I did. Meghan rescued them from the trash. They're in her room."

"Trish, please—"

"Thanks for the pizza. Wasn't sure what I was going to do for supper." She took the boxes and slammed the door.

CHAPTER 9

Dale Thorndyke greeted Jess Atkins and directed him to a chair. "This is a pleasant surprise," he lied. Trish had followed through on her threat, which meant she was still mad. He thought the flowers would soften her anger, but he'd been wrong. And he was not only out the money for the roses, but two pizzas he didn't get to eat.

Jess took a seat. "You need to let Trish out of her contract. It's the decent thing to do."

Dale smiled. "Can't do that. She signed it, so no matter what she says, I still represent her property."

"According to Trish, you lied to a potential buyer. The law considers that a breach of contract."

"You only have Trish's word on that."

"Actually, I have the word of the prospective buyer.

He's willing to back her up."

Dale swallowed hard. He should have known better than to mess with a DA. "It was an honest mistake. I know Trish isn't thrilled about selling. I was trying to protect her."

Jess leaned forward. "Let's cut to the chase. You were trying to manipulate the sale for your own purposes. Not a good idea. Let Trish out of the contract. I've known you and your family for a long time, Dale. So far, you have a good reputation. I'd hate word to get around that you've been less than honest in your dealings. It's a small town."

Red darkened Dale's face. "You wouldn't dare."

Jess stood. "Try me." He walked to the door. "Think about it. You know my number."

"I have a right to the fee for the listing."

As he opened the door, Jess countered, "We might be able to come to a compromise about that. Your choice."

Dale sank onto his chair. His dreams of being independently wealthy just walked out the door. He despised lawyers.

~

Late Monday morning, Alex arrived at Jess Atkin's office. Trish was already there. A half hour earlier, Alex had received a call from her to meet. He was hopeful they had worked things out with Thorndyke Realty. Trish hadn't offered any details.

Alex sat in the empty chair next to her. "Mornin'."

Trish smiled. "Thanks for coming. Jess should be here in a minute."

On cue, Jess walked in. "I see we're all here. Let's get down to business." He sat in the Cordovan leather chair behind his desk and placed a thick folder on the desk top. "Mr. Lambert, as of this morning, Dale Thorndyke has agreed to let Trish out of her contract concerning the sale of her property. She is now open to negotiating with you concerning that property, provided you're still interested."

"I am, and please, I prefer Alex."

Jess nodded. "I've drawn up an agreement pertaining to the purchase." He handed Trish and Alex each a sheaf of papers. "The price Trish is asking for her house, orchards, equipment, and out-buildings, is at the top. This is by no means a final contract. Changes can be made by mutual consent of both parties, but it's a starting place."

Alex glanced at the asking price. A little more than he wanted to pay, but there was room for negotiation. "I'd like Trish to consider removing the house and the five acres of apples behind it from what she's willing to sell. That would leave about eighty acres of fruit, the outbuildings, and equipment. Will the county allow that kind of split?"

Trish stared at him. "You don't want the house?"

He shrugged. "I don't want to displace you from your family home, and I have plans for a house I want to build. I also got the distinct impression you love the orchards. It's a compromise that works for me. Hopefully, it will work for you."

"Why the five acres?" Trish asked.

Alex cleared his throat. "Most counties won't allow a land split for less than that. I've looked at the plat for the property and that would work well. You'll still be responsible for the Rome apples." Alex waited a moment. "I'd be willing to let you use the equipment and packing shed for a small fee."

Trish looked at Jess.

He raised his eyebrows. "It can be done, Trish, if that suits you."

She turned her gaze to Alex. "Y-yes, of course." Tears glistened in Trish's eyes. "Keeping the house and the Romes is more than I hoped for. I think it's doable."

"Good." Alex addressed Jess. "I'd also like to draw up a separate agreement between Trish and me for her paid consulting services. I'll need help getting started and becoming familiar with the orchards, the hired help, and the way the water rights work in this area." He settled back in his chair. "Be sure she keeps enough of the water rights for her five acres. From what I can tell, there's plenty to go around."

Trish frowned. "You want to hire me?"

"Who better than the previous owner? You game?"

Trish considered the offer a moment. "All right, you have yourself a consultant." She smiled, and Alex noted a distinct twinkle replacing the tears.

They spent the next two hours agreeing on a purchase price, how and when payment was to be made, surveying and land split fees, and the wording of the consulting contract. When they had both signed a preliminary agreement, Alex heaved a sigh of relief. *Thank you, God. It's a start.*

"I think that's everything," Jess commented. "Trish, if

you don't mind, I'd like to speak with Alex alone for a moment."

"I don't mind." She rose to leave.

"If you'll wait," Alex said to Trish, "I'd like a tour of the orchards this afternoon. I'll spring for lunch."

Trish nodded. "I'd like that. I'll wait in the outer office."

After Trish left, Jess studied Alex a moment. "You have quite a reputation as a Deputy DA. I have a lawyer friend in Denver who speaks very highly of you. Says you're tough but fair."

"Really? Who would that be?"

"Ken Larson of McCormack, White, and Larson."

"Ken said that, huh? He's a good man." Alex grinned. "He's bested me a few times, but I've turned the tables on him as often."

"He used to be my partner. Almost married my sister. When that didn't work out, he moved back to Denver, which brings me to why I wanted you to stay." He leaned forward in his chair and placed his arms on his desk. "I need a partner. I'm overworked, tired, and wanting to retire before I'm too old to enjoy it. I'd like my clients to be in good hands when that happens. Would you be interested?"

Alex cocked his head in a quick movement. "That's an interesting offer. You might have noticed I just agreed to buy an eighty-acre fruit ranch. I'm going to be pretty busy for a while building a house and working the fruit."

"I understand that. You would start part-time, which works well for me right now. You decide what you want to take on. I need someone I can trust. I do very little criminal work. It's mostly helping clients with wills, estate planning, tax problems. You could do a lot from home."

"I'm a little rusty in those areas."

"You'll pick it up in no time. What do you say?"

Alex pondered the offer for a moment. "Let me think about it. How soon would you like an answer?"

"Take your time. I'll be around for a few more years." He smiled and rose. "I appreciate what you're doing for Trish. Known her and her family a long time. This sale was difficult for her."

"She's done me a favor. I couldn't be happier." Alex stood. "You can do one more service for me." He handed Jess a folder. "I want to put the bulk of the land in a trust. The details of what I want are in the folder. I could do it, but you're probably more up to date on the land codes of this county, and having someone else do the legal work is probably a good idea."

"Interesting idea. I'll look these over and let you know if I have questions."

They shook hands. "My secretary will call to set up an appointment when the purchase papers are ready. Should be only a few days."

With his hand on the doorknob, Alex said, "I'll be around."

~

Alex forked a bite of chicken avocado salad. The North Fork Hamburger had been tempting, but he could see his cholesterol count rising.

"How long have you owned McBride Orchards?" His mouth watered as he watched Trish bite into the hamburger she'd ordered.

She swallowed. "It was homesteaded by my great-great grandfather in 1883. He raised sheep when he first came to the valley. My great-grandfather decided fruit would be a perfect crop for this area. He planted the original trees. Some have been replaced over the years, but the crops remain the same— a few cherries and apricots but mostly apples and peaches. My grandfather planted the Rome and Old-fashioned Delicious apples. With all the new hybrids, those varieties are hard to come by and bring a good price."

"So, like me, I'm guessing you've worked the fruit since you were old enough to climb a ladder."

She sighed and the hint of tears returned. "Mom was a teacher, so Dad took care of me during the day. He toted me into the orchards in a pack on his back when I was a baby. It's ingrained, like eating and sleeping."

Alex marveled at the emotions reflected in her eyes. "I remember running the packing house crew when I was ten," he said. "The women packing the fruit used to bring me cookies and candy. I loved it."

"When I was fourteen," Trish said, "I tried to tell some of the pickers how to do their job. The men didn't like a young girl telling them what to do." She smiled and the sparkle returned to her eyes. "It didn't take them long to learn I was orchard boss and knew what I was doing when they saw I could out-pick them."

"You really love the fruit. I thought maybe your

109

husband did the work and it became too much for you."

"Is that a sexist remark?" The smile disappeared, but the twinkle remained in her eyes.

He grinned. "Nope. Just didn't expect you to have such a passion for the fruit." Alex took a swallow of Coke. "May I ask why you *have* to sell, or is that none of my business."

Trish studied him a moment. "My late husband hated the fruit business. He was useless when it came to knowing what to do when. He used the property as collateral to cover his gambling debts."

Alex frowned. "Wouldn't he have needed your signature?"

The spark in her eyes turned lethal. "I was too trusting. Let's leave it at that."

"I apologize." Alex regretted asking. "It's really none of my business."

"Not your fault. I was stupid and gullible. It won't happen again." She grabbed a French fry and dabbed it in a dollop of ketchup. "Do you have a family?"

"I'm a widower. I have an adopted son who'll be joining me. He'll be fifteen in June."

"Oh. He's my son's age. Scott turned fifteen last October. Maybe they can be friends."

"That would be nice." Alex pushed his plate aside. "Do you want dessert?"

"I'm good. It's time I showed you around the place. Ready?"

Alex signaled for the check.

~

Warm sunshine and no breeze, unusual for March's unsettled weather, made a perfect afternoon. As Trish walked through the orchards with Alex, she marveled at his knowledge. He asked all the right questions, listened intently as she explained water rights, pruning, thinning, and spraying schedules. He checked the slightly swelling buds with the expertise of a seasoned fruit grower. The reality of not owning the orchards was slowly sinking in. She bit her lip.

It didn't help that Alex was the kind of man she could be attracted to. She definitely didn't need the complication. Forget that he was handsome, personable, and demonstrated the qualities she had wanted in Clay and Dale. They had disappointed. She had worked hard to be a good wife to Clay. She'd failed. She didn't need to fail again.

"You must have had a fairly warm February and March this year. The peach buds seem to be ahead of schedule."

"February was warmer than usual, and March has followed suit. If we're lucky, April will do the same. You know, however, that the odds are good we'll get a hard freeze or two in April. Never fails."

Alex smiled. "I know it all too well. In Palisade, we were lucky if it froze just enough to thin the apricots and peaches, but there were years when a hard freeze took all the apricots and most of the peaches. We'll hope and pray that doesn't happen this year."

"I hope your prayers are more effective than mine. The

111

previous three years have been killers on the peaches, apricots, and cherries."

"Speaking of cherries, I'm going to depend a lot on you for that crop. We didn't have cherries on our place."

"Like apricots, they're extra vulnerable to freezes and then the weather at harvest time. There have been years when it's been too rainy during picking season, and we've lost much of the crop to mold and rot. Or hail hits just before we pick and renders the cherries unmarketable." She sighed. "Sometimes I wonder why I love this business so much. If you don't winter kill, you spring freeze. If you have a good crop, so does everyone else and the price drops. You worry about rain and hail during harvest, and you still have to irrigate, prune, spray, and pay the workers their wages." She grinned. "Yet there's something special about watching the trees bud and produce fruit. I guess I'll never get tired of that."

Trish stopped walking, a faraway look in her eyes. "And the land—the rich soil and the distance between neighbors. I don't think I could live in town with the houses so close together. I need my space."

"I understand completely. The unpredictability of the business is why I didn't want to grow fruit. So I became a lawyer. But after dealing with crime for the last ten years, the fruit business started looking really good. I realized I needed to get back to nature and a less complicated life."

"And you think fruit is less complicated?"

"Maybe not less complicated." He thought a moment. "Maybe just more satisfying. Easier than dealing with criminals. And I know what you mean about neighbors."

Trish shook her head slowly. "You must be as crazy as I am. I can't get fruit farming out of my system. I love the library, but it's not nearly as satisfying as bringing in a crop."

Alex smiled. "Exactly."

As they approached the sheds, Trish broached the question of Alex's house. He outlined the area where he wanted to build. The open half acre of land provided plenty of space.

"The house will have five bedrooms—four upstairs with the master bedroom downstairs. Two bathrooms upstairs and two down."

"Four bathrooms? That's a lot."

"A Master bath and a ½ bath downstairs. The two full bathrooms upstairs will need to accommodate four or five kids."

Trish studied him. "I thought there was just you and your son. Or are you planning for more?"

"Well," he looked away, "I plan to open my home to troubled boys. I probably should have told you that up front. Just didn't find the right moment to say something."

"I see." He'd talked about chickens and bees but failed to mention troubled boys. At least that explained why he didn't want her house. She was unsure how she felt about this new development. He hadn't lied, but he hadn't been totally honest, either. She was right all along. Men couldn't be trusted.

"I want to do more than just grow fruit. In my job I see a lot of juveniles come through the system that have no place to go once they're out of youth services. No families to go home to, or families who don't want them or are negative influences on them. Too many end up back in the courts as adults because they weren't given the right opportunities. I hope to change that. I want to give them a place to learn how to work, take pride in accomplishing something, and earn money to go to school—college, technical training, or whatever. I want the boys to learn responsibility and provide them a good life-learning environment."

She could see the passion in him for helping young men. "Why North Fork instead of Palisade? You could have done this with your family."

"Palisade is too close to a larger city with all its temptations for troubled kids. I want them to experience a small town, learn to know and depend on their neighbors. My family earns enough to support two families. They don't need me and a bunch of kids taking up the profits. And I want this to be something I've done. It succeeds or fails with me and my partner—God."

The fact he hadn't told her about his plans up front rankled her. She didn't want Scott influenced by seasoned delinquents. He had his own troubles. And she didn't want to worry about Meghan, either. She wasn't sure how she felt about boys who'd been in trouble with the law living so close.

"What kind of trouble have these boys gotten into?"

Alex smiled. "No hard-core criminals. The boys will be carefully screened. We'll look for the ones who want to truly change their lives. And we'll have strict guidelines for staying here, including a contract they'll sign. They will be expected to work in the orchards and have household chores, too. This will be their second chance at a better life. They mess up once and they're gone."

"I'm not sure I'm comfortable with this. I have a fifteen-year-old son and a twelve-year-old daughter. I wish you'd said something in Jess's office."

Alex frowned. "You're saying you wouldn't have sold to me if you'd known." He stared at the peach trees behind the packing shed.

"I don't know."

"I don't understand you. You'd rather have Dale tear out your orchards and build houses than give a kid a chance to redeem himself. These kids need to learn a work ethic and good old-fashioned values."

Alex was clearly angry. Trish needed to explain herself.

"Look, my son Scott has had a rough time since the death of his father. He's discovered the man he idolized wasn't as great as he thought, and he's just beginning to get over the hurt. I've had some disciplinary issues with him. I don't want him influenced by some troubled boys."

Alex's jaw tightened. "Maybe your son could have a positive influence on these kids instead of the other way around. That's why I want them in a small town environment. To be around kids from strong families." Alex turned to look at Trish. "Just keep an open mind about this. It won't happen right away. My son and I need to get settled first. Then I'll embark on saving the world."

"I'm sorry." Trish looked down at the ground. "With all

that's happened the last few years, I tend to be a bit testy about things. And I'm not happy about losing my heritage, for any reason." A smile crept across her mouth. "But I'll try my best to keep an open mind while you're saving the world."

Alex returned her smile. "That's all I ask."

~

"Scott. Meghan. Downstairs now." Trish called up the stairs while Alex waited in the living room. At Trish's invitation, Alex agreed to stop by her house for coffee so they could talk fruit, and she could introduce him to Scott and Meghan. Within a minute, both kids bounded down the stairs.

Trish introduced everyone. "Mr. Lambert is buying McBride Orchards. We signed the preliminary papers this morning."

Meghan smiled at Alex. "Hope you like fruit farming."

"I think I will."

"*Great.* Just *great.*" Scott's angry comment took Trish by surprise. "Now I'll have to live in town. Just *great.*"

"Scott."

"I want to live in town," Meghan said.

"You would, so you can be close to your dorky friends."

Meghan stamped her foot. "They're not dorky!"

"Whatever." Scott turned to Alex. "Hope you'll *like* it here." His sarcasm dripped. He looked at Trish. "So, when is he kicking us out?"

"Scott, that's uncalled for."

"Screw it." He fled up the stairs, two at a time.

"Scott, come back here and apologize." She turned to Alex. "I'm really sorry. Scott had no right—"

"It's okay. I understand." He offered his hand to Meghan. "It was nice meeting you Meghan."

She shook his hand and smiled.

Turning back to Trish, Alex said, "I think I'll take a raincheck on that coffee. You need to explain things to Scott and Meghan. I'll be in touch."

"I really am sorry," Trish said.

"Nothing to be sorry about. Have a good evening." Alex closed the door behind him.

Trish sighed and glanced up the stairs. "Come on, Meghan. The three of us need to have a talk."

CHAPTER 10

Trish rapped on Scott's door. "Open up."

"Go away!"

"I'm not going anywhere until we talk."

"*Fine.*"

"You have five seconds to open up or you're grounded for two weeks."

The lock clicked and the door flung open. "Make it quick. I have homework." He glared at Meghan as she entered behind Trish. "What's she doing here? She's not allowed in my room."

"She is this time."

Meghan raised her eyebrows at Scott, a triumphant look on her face.

"What I have to say concerns all of us." Trish and

Meghan settled on Scott's unmade bed.

Scott sat backward in his desk chair. "So?" He drummed a pencil on the back of the chair.

"First, your treatment of Mr. Lambert was unacceptable. You have kitchen duty the next two weeks."

"No fair." He threw the pencil across the room.

"Make that three weeks."

"Crap." He gripped the wood chair back. "What's so important about Mr. Lambert? He's kicking us out."

"Mr. Lambert was an invited guest, and all guests in our home are treated with respect." Trish took a deep breath. Her impulse was to slap Scott for his belligerence, but she knew that would only escalate the situation. "Second, Mr. Lambert is *not* kicking us out."

"He bought the house and orchards, didn't he? That's what you said."

"If you'd stuck around long enough, you'd have learned he bought eighty acres, the out-buildings and equipment. He doesn't want the house. We're keeping it and five acres."

Scott stared at her. "Seriously?"

"We aren't moving to town?" Disappointment laced Meghan's question.

Trish wished, just once, that her kids would agree on something. Meghan wanted to move. Scott didn't. Well, she didn't either, so Meghan was outvoted.

"Mr. Lambert is going to build his own house near the packing shed. He was very understanding about my attachment to the house, and the orchards, too. We'll keep the Rome apples behind the house."

"So, do we still have to take care of those?"

"Yes, Scott, we do. And I'll need your help."

"Double crap." Scott said under his breath. "Why are we keeping five acres?"

"Because that's the deal I made with Mr. Lambert. Whether you're happy about the apples or not, I am." Trish stood. "Deal with it." She looked at Meghan. "Come on, Scott has studying to do."

"But I wanted to live in town so I'd be closer to Jessica. Geez, Mom, I hardly get to see her."

Meghan's whiney comment irritated Trish. She was in no mood for complaining. "You'll see her at school. Maybe we can invite her out for a sleepover sometime."

Meghan shrugged.

"You're both on your own for supper tonight. It's been a long day, and I'm tired."

At the door, Trish looked at Scott. "The next time you see Mr. Lambert, you owe him an apology, and I expect it to be sincere."

Scott muttered something unintelligible. Trish let it go.

In the hallway, Meghan asked, "Can Jessica come over this weekend?"

"I have to work Saturday. We'll figure out a time, but not this weekend, okay?"

Meghan's shoulders slumped. "'Kay."

Trish closed the door to her bedroom and settled on the bed. There were times she wished someone else would deal with her kids. Just when she thought she'd figured them out, they came up with new ways to irritate her. No matter what she did, it seemed wrong, and she had no one to support her decisions. When had Scott become so attached to the house?

To add to her frustration, she had mixed feelings about the agreement she and Alex had made. She still had her home and a much smaller debt, but she'd lost most of her heritage. What would her parents think? The life she loved was no longer hers. The loss was too much to bear. And she'd have to watch someone else manage her orchards. She buried her head in her pillow and sobbed.

~

Alex stared out the window of his hotel room and gazed at the night sky. He'd taken the first step to a new life, one he looked forward to. "Thank you, Lord. Now help me make this work." He thought about his wife, Amy, and his kids, Alex Jr., and Molly, the daughter he'd never met. His eyes clouded. Amy always wanted to live in the country, said it would be good for the kids. She never had the chance. But he did.

Marco will like it here, he thought. He still marveled at his relationship with the boy who had taken his family away. *God, you certainly work in mysterious ways.* Who'd have thought he and Marco would have a father/son relationship? It defied conventional wisdom, all odds, and every other cliché in the book.

Alex smiled. God had brought him to understand and love a lost boy, and that boy had become an amazing young man. Yes, God worked wonders no man could.

His encounter with Scott left him wondering how he

122

could help the angry young man. Scott needed a good male role model. Something that seemed to be absent in his life. Alex couldn't imagine what it would be like to lose your father at such an impressionable age and then discover he wasn't the man you idolized.

Alex didn't know all the details, but he'd gleaned enough from Wanda's tidbits, and Trish's comments to make it clear that her husband had been deceitful and reckless with money. He assumed Scott knew what happened. He'd seen the scenario too many times in his law career—marriages torn apart and families diminished because of selfish behavior. It was fairly evident that Scott's father had created a great deal of hurt and anger for his family.

He thanked God he'd had parents who set a good example and expected the best from their two sons. They showed respect and love for each other in spite of occasional differences and passed that valuable lesson to their boys.

Alex wanted Marco to learn about the respect and unselfishness that made relationships thrive. Maybe, just maybe, he could help Scott learn those lessons, too. He would try his best to include Scott in some of the things he and Marco did, with Trish's blessing, of course.

He smiled at the thought of the fiery redhead. Some men might try to tame her, but it was her spitfire approach to life he liked. She had surprised him when she spoke fluent Spanish to the workers in the orchards. He could speak a little Spanish and understood quite a bit, but he wasn't fluent like she demonstrated. Trish exhibited independence and determination. He appreciated her toughness and knowledge, and looked forward to knowing her better.

Right. The last thing I need is a relationship. I lost the love of my life. I don't need to complicate it. Trish is intriguing, but Marco comes first.

Marco had no role models at all in his early years. A loving mother figure would be good for him, but Alex didn't want to add that complication anytime soon. The priority, for now, was to adjust to the two of them living together as father and son. Trish was a distraction Alex didn't need. He would have to be careful not to shut his son out because he couldn't keep his mind off of the woman next door.

~

One week after arriving in North Fork, Alex left Jess Atkins' office as the new owner of McBride Orchards, and an agreement to work part-time for Jess beginning in October. When Alex talked about buying a fruit ranch, Marco began reading books about country living and growing fruit. Alex had arranged to call Marco once the papers were signed. Marco sounded excited about the prospect of moving to North Fork and living in the country. The city was all he had known. "August is forever," he told Alex. "It's hard to wait."

"I agree, but the wait will be worth it. I've taken a lot of pictures. I'll show them to you when I get back."

"When?"

"Monday or Tuesday. Not sure yet. I have some arrangements to make with local contractors so we can get started on the house." Alex smiled. "You'll need to be thinking about what color you want your bedroom."

He heard Marco chuckle. "You can bet it won't be white or gray. Some shade of blue sounds nice. Like the sky."

Alex laughed. "I'll bring some paint swatches and you can pick one out. By August it should be painted and ready for you to move in."

"Sweet." A moment of silence stretched between them. "Thanks, man."

"You're welcome. See you next week."

~

Trish had invited Alex to supper the afternoon after they'd signed the final papers. She promised him that Scott would be on his best behavior. Alex accepted and realized he'd have to be careful not to say something that might trigger the pent-up anger Scott seemed to harbor.

The wooden steps creaked as Alex climbed them to the porch of Trish's home. He braced himself and rang the doorbell. Scott opened the door. They stared at each other a moment.

Alex offered Scott his hand, which Scott accepted.

"Good to see you again, Scott."

"I'm sorry about how I acted the other day."

Alex stepped inside. "Apology accepted. I'm sure it isn't easy to see your way of life change. I hope we can get better acquainted. And I'm anxious for you to meet my son, Marco. He's your age."

Scott led Alex into the living room. "So when's he

125

coming?"

"Not until August." The aroma of beef permeated the air.

Before Alex could say more, Trish entered the room, wiping her hands on a kitchen towel.

"Welcome." She smiled.

Alex's heart beat a little faster. "Something smells good."

"I hope you like pot roast. Otherwise, we have a problem."

"Love it."

"This way, then. It's ready to eat." She ushered him through the dining room into the kitchen. "Hope you don't mind eating in the kitchen. It's where we take most of our meals."

"Not at all." Alex sat in the chair Trish indicated. When everyone was seated, he waited for Trish to offer a blessing. When she didn't, Alex took charge.

"Do you mind if I say a blessing?"

Trish eyed him a moment. "That would be fine. Kids." She bowed her head. Scott cast her a "What's that about?" look, then shrugged his shoulders and bowed his head.

"Lord, we thank you for this opportunity to share your bounty. We thank you for the next chapter of our lives. I pray we can live in harmony with each other and You. Amen."

"Pass the potatoes," Scott said.

Alex smiled, thankful Trish agreed to the prayer. It was important to him to thank God for all things. He hoped Trish felt the same and wasn't just being polite.

Alex accepted the meat platter from Meghan. "Your mom tells me you like soccer."

"Uh huh. It's fun."

"Good exercise, too, I'll bet."

"I guess."

That conversation was going nowhere. He turned his attention to Scott. "I understand you're an athlete like your dad. What's your favorite sport?"

His mouth full, Scott said, "Football, I guess."

"Don't talk with your mouth full," Trish admonished.

Scott frowned at her and swallowed. "I play basketball and baseball, too. Right now our baseball team is undefeated."

"That's great. What position do you play?"

"Which sport?"

Alex smiled. "All of them."

"I'm shortstop on the baseball team. I pitched in Little League, but I like playing infield better. Quarterback in football, and point guard in basketball."

"Good for you. Sports can be very satisfying and productive when you do your best. Playing sports kept me out of trouble and garnered me a scholarship to college."

Scott frowned at him, and Alex wondered if he'd said too much.

"Does your son play sports?" Trish asked.

"He's interested in basketball and baseball but hasn't had the opportunity to play much. Maybe Scott can help him out."

Trish eyed Alex and frowned. Scott shrugged and

127

continued eating.

Trish and Alex discussed the orchards and what needed to be done next. When Trish placed a banana cake on the table, Scott asked to be excused. "Can I take mine to my room? I have homework. I'll clean up later."

"You may. And you're excused from kitchen duty tonight."

Scott smiled. "Sweet."

"Can I watch TV?" Meghan asked.

"Is your homework done?" Megan nodded. "Go ahead."

Meghan grabbed her cake and followed Scott from the kitchen.

Trish settled in her chair and sighed. "Well, that went well."

"You have great kids," Alex said. "You've done a good job with them."

"Thanks, but I threatened them within an inch of their lives to be on their best behavior tonight."

"It worked."

"This time. Too often I wonder if I'm doing anything right. But I love them both and wouldn't trade them. Farm them out sometimes, but not trade them." The dimples at the side of her mouth deepened.

"You sound like every other parent I know." He took a bite of cake. "This is delicious, just like the rest of the meal. You're a good cook."

Trish smiled. "Thanks. I had two good teachers—my grandmother and my mother."

"Do your parents live around here?"

The smile faded. "They were killed in a car accident on the way to their winter home in Arizona, about ten years ago. I miss them very much."

"My condolences. We seem to have that in common." When she looked puzzled, he added, "Loss of family to vehicle accidents. That's how I lost my wife and son and our unborn daughter."

Trish blinked. "I am so sorry. I didn't know."

"It happened five years ago."

"My husband died when his gas truck wrecked on slick roads. That was a little over five years ago."

"I, too, am sorry." He met her eyes. "It seems we've both experienced tragedy in our lives."

"Sometimes I wonder what might have happened if . . ."

"I've learned that living with what might have been doesn't do any good. Moving on is imperative. Life goes on, and God expects us to make the most of it."

"That's good advice. Unfortunately, I've had trouble moving on. Maybe selling the orchards is a start." She stood and began gathering up plates and utensils.

"Let me help you." Alex rose and took his dishes to the sink.

"You don't have to. The dishes will wait."

"You don't want to have to face them later." He looked at her dishwasher. "You load, I'll carry." He returned to the table and gathered up more dishes. As they talked about the next steps for the orchards, they put the food away, loaded the dishwasher, and washed and dried the pans.

Trish turned from the sink, dishrag in hand and smiled

at Alex. "Thanks for your help."

She stood inches from him. Her dimples appeared again, and Alex had a compelling urge to kiss her. They stared into each other's eyes for an eternity; in reality, a few seconds.

She cleared her throat. "Let me wipe the table off and then we're done."

Alex folded the dish towel and laid it on the counter.

"Would you like more coffee?" she asked.

"That and another piece of cake, if you don't mind."

"I don't mind at all."

She filled their mugs and dished out two more squares of cake. "I really shouldn't have another piece. I'll be apologizing to my scales in the morning."

Alex chuckled. "The way I've been eating since I arrived in North Fork is shameful. Between Wanda's meals and the one I just had, I'll need to go on a starvation diet for the next two weeks."

They visited until late in the evening. By the time Alex returned to his hotel, he was ready for a good night's sleep. As he pulled the covers over his tired body, the day's events replayed in his mind. But the memory that lingered was the urge to take Trish in his arms and smother her with kisses. He hadn't been that aroused by a woman since Amy.

He resigned himself to the fact his desire probably wasn't going away any time soon. He was bewitched by a red-haired imp. Yes, that's how he saw her. If she ever let her true personality come out, instead of the guarded one she displayed, he would have his hands full. He always did like a good challenge.

"First things first," he whispered. "Get settled with Marco. Then see what else life brings. Right, Lord?"

Right.

K.L. McKee

CHAPTER 11

As he approached Floyd Hill on I-70, Alex was reminded why he'd left Denver behind and sought the solitude of the Western Slope. The encroaching smog irritated his eyes as he negotiated the teeming freeway traffic. Although air quality in Denver had improved over the last few years, the air still felt thick and oppressive.

Or had Alex gotten used to the crisp, clean air of North Fork? And less traffic. He hadn't planned on moving to North Fork specifically, but God always had something good in mind when Alex sought His guidance.

Dumping his bags in his condo's bedroom, Alex punched in the phone number for his realtor. He could trust Ed, who had sold the house he shared with Amy and Alex, Jr. Moving out had been hard, yet it was even harder to stay.

Too many memories—loving, laughter, backyard barbecues, teaching Alex Jr. to catch a ball. He'd saved a few mementos. Amy's favorite painting that hung over the fireplace, Alex Jr.'s teddy bear and favorite Matchbox car, and lots of pictures. The condo had served him well, but it wasn't home. No longer having a need for a home in Denver, it was time to sell.

"Ed. Alex Lambert here. I need to put my condo up for sale."

"Alex. What gives? I thought you liked it there."

"Did. I'm moving to the Western Slope."

"You're kidding. When?"

"Couple of weeks, or as soon as I get packed. When can you get it listed?"

"Yesterday."

Alex grinned at Ed's answer. It's why he liked him. He moved quickly and got things done. "Works for me."

"I'll be by tomorrow at nine to take pictures and discuss price. Will that work?"

"See you at nine."

After his meeting the following morning with Ed, Alex visited the Denver Department of Youth Services office. He wanted to get the change of address out of the way before he saw Marco.

Once Alex informed the caseworker about the change in residence, a huge burden lifted from his shoulders. He anticipated some resistance when he asked for a transfer of the adoption case to Delta County, but the caseworker took the change in stride, promising to initiate the paperwork immediately and send it to the Delta County Child Welfare Department. A caseworker there would be responsible for overseeing the final year-long adoption process. She assured Alex that he would be contacted.

The next day, Alex visited Marco. He paced the visitor's area, anxious to show Marco pictures of his new home. After an initial hug, they settled at one of the tables, Alex sitting beside Marco.

"So, would you like to see your new home?"

Marco smiled. "Yeah, man. I'm tired of just hearing about this paradise you keep talking about. No way it's as great as you've described it. You like to exaggerate, you know."

"Me? Exaggerate? I beg to differ. Have a look, then tell me if I'm exaggerating."

Alex let Marco scroll through the pictures on his digital camera, explaining each one and the proximity to the orchards he'd bought. Marco studied each picture. When the last picture—one of the orchards and the bare spot that would soon be their home—appeared on the screen, Alex held his breath, waiting for a reaction.

Marco looked at Alex, a slight wetness in his eyes. "These are real? You aren't making this up?"

Alex frowned. "Of course they're real. Why would I make it up?"

Marco shrugged. "I guess I didn't believe places like this really existed. It's amazing. I love the mountains and the trees, and the town. I especially like where the house will be. It's great."

"I'll make copies for you."

"Sweet." He scrolled back to the picture Alex had taken of Trish, Scott, and Meghan. "They're our neighbors?"

"Yep. They live a short distance down a graveled road from us. Nice family. Scott's your age, so you'll be in school with him. He's quite the athlete—football, basketball and baseball. You won't be able to participate in football this next fall, but basketball and baseball are both possibilities, if you're interested."

Marco handed the camera to Alex. "I doubt I can compete with kids that have been in sports all their lives."

"Whoa, don't sell yourself short. I've watched you play basketball and baseball here. You're pretty good. It might take a little practice to get you up to speed with the public school kids, but you can do it. I'll help, and I think we can talk Scott into giving you some pointers. The rest is up to you and what you want to accomplish."

"You have lots of confidence in me." He sighed. "Guess trying won't hurt."

"The only hurt you'll have is sore muscles." Alex grinned. "I brought along a copy of the blueprints for the house. Thought you'd like to see them, too."

They pored over the design for a 3500 square foot house, Alex explaining it in detail to Marco. When they were through, Alex rolled up the plans and secured them in a cardboard tube.

Marco sat silent for a while. "Sometimes I think I'm dreaming, and all this won't happen." He stared at his hands resting on the table. "I didn't do anything to deserve this."

"About five months and it will be a reality, Marco. You can count on it." Alex clamped a hand on Marco's shoulder. "As for deserving this, you made the effort to turn your life around in spite of the odds against you. You definitely deserve this . . . and so do I."

"Thanks, man."

"That's Dad to you." Alex slipped his arm around Marco's shoulders and hugged him. "Get used to it." He saw a tear slip from Marco's eye.

~

With his new Ford F250 pickup, Alex backed the small camper he'd purchased into a spot next to the foundation of the new house. That morning, Trish had gone with him to the dealership in Delta, so she could drive his Expedition home.

Alex had spent the previous two weeks packing up what he wanted from his condo. He left most of the furniture. A new house needed new furniture, and the old stuff held too many memories. His new life started with the move to North Fork. The past was where it belonged.

The builder had made great progress in spite of a few stormy days. Most of the house was framed and the contractor had started the roof. The workers had gone for the day, so Alex wandered through the rooms of plywood floors, inspecting the work, satisfied it was going as planned. He took a moment to write Jeremiah 29:11—*"For I know the plans I have for you," declares the Lord, "plans to prosper you and not to harm you, plans to give you hope and a*

137

future."—on the bare wall between two studs in the dining room. He'd memorized the verse once he'd moved forward with his life after the accident. A small blessing for his new house and his new life.

Trish's recommendation of a contractor, along with Jess Atkins' approval, had been right on. He liked the quality of work he saw. Alex had no complaints.

Although the complete wiring would take time, limited electricity had been provided to the house, and at his request, an outside receptacle had been provided for power to the camper. He'd have to buy groceries in the morning. Until then, Wanda's North Fork Burger beckoned.

~

"There's a freeze warning out tonight," Trish said as she and Alex walked through one of the peach orchards a few days after Alex's return. April weather remained unpredictable, with chances for sudden temperature drops and hard freezes that could ruin an entire crop. The freeze danger began in March when the tender buds formed, or sometimes February, depending on the year, and could last until May 1st. Growing up, he'd seen a few years that freeze warnings lasted until the middle of May.

Red Havens, Cresthavens, and Red Globes were some of the peach varieties in the orchards Alex bought from Trish. They walked through an orchard of Early Red Havens, an early peach already in bloom. The cherries and apricots had hit full bloom the day after Alex arrived back in North Fork. The other varieties of peaches and the apples weren't far behind.

"Guess we better be sure the wind machines are working properly. I heard twenty-eight degrees for the low tonight." Alex glanced at Trish. "Is the spray machine filled with water and ready to go?"

"It is. Guess you get baptism by fire on your first few days back. Mother Nature isn't very accommodating."

Alex grinned. "She certainly has her own time schedule, that's for sure. Where does the alarm sound when the temperature drops?"

"In my bedroom and in the kitchen. When it goes off, I'll call you."

"Sounds good." Alex stopped walking. "I'm sorry to inconvenience you this way. I'll have alarms installed in the house, but that's a bit down the road."

"No problem. Consider it part of the consulting fee you're paying me."

Alex watched her eyes as she smiled. A bit of orneriness sparked from them. "You going to drive the tractor while I spray the cherry and apricot blossoms?" he challenged.

Her expression turned serious. "If you'd like. It takes two people. Manuel, my foreman, and a couple of hired hands will be handling the wind machines in the peach orchards."

"Does Manuel live close by?"

"About a mile down the road. He has alarms set up in his house, too, so he'll know when to head this way."

"Good," Alex said.

~

A loud banging on his camper door startled Alex awake.

"Alex! Get up! Temperature's at thirty-one degrees. Time to get going." Trish's voice, loud and clear, spurred him to move. He groped for his pants, pulled them on and opened the door. "What time is it?"

"2:30. Let's go."

"Why didn't you call?"

"I did. You didn't answer. Meet you in the shed." Before Alex could utter a response, Trish turned and left.

He finished dressing, grabbed his coat and gloves, and hurried to the equipment shed. On the way he checked his phone. Missed call. He'd forgotten to turn the volume up. He met Trish inside the shed.

"You driving or spraying?" she clipped.

"Spraying." She didn't sound in the mood for an explanation of his failure to answer his phone. He didn't have a good one, anyway.

Trish jumped on the tractor and coaxed it to life. Alex climbed onto the spray machine, like the one his parents owned, and adjusted the controls. As the tractor rumbled out of the shed and toward the first orchard, a smile tugged at the corners of his mouth. He shook his head. He shouldn't be enjoying this—it was drudge work—yet he felt a sense of gratification that he was engaging in physical labor. When he was a kid, he'd hated middle-of-the-night alarms during early spring. He dragged his feet more often than not when it came to climbing out of bed in the dark and cold. Funny how his outlook had changed as he grew older. Tonight he was doing something he wanted to do, and it felt great.

Alex heard the rumble and whine of the propane-powered wind-machine motors engaging. Manuel, or whoever was monitoring them, would have a hand-held temperature gauge to monitor the giant fans' effectiveness. The motors powered the blades at about three to five miles per hour, and that could buy them three to eight degrees for ten acres of fruit, the difference between having a bountiful harvest or none at all.

Once in the first cherry orchard, Trish drove slow and steady, and Alex began spraying blossoms with water, hoping the temperature didn't drop too much or their effort wouldn't be worthwhile. With any luck, the water would freeze around the blossoms, protecting them from a harder freeze as the temperature dropped. It was a gamble worth taking. They'd be spraying the blooms with water until the temperature warmed enough to melt the ice around the blossoms.

Before the night was over, Alex and Trish filled the spray tank several times with water. By nine a.m., the temperature had risen enough to call it quits. They were both tired, and Trish steered the tractor toward the shed. Inside, Alex jumped down and helped Trish from the tractor seat. As he set her feet on the cement floor, he studied her face. Her eyes drooped, but her mouth looked inviting.

"Alex?" Her soft voice brought him up short. "Are you okay?" She touched his face with her gloved hand.

No, he thought. I want to kiss you. *Now, however, is not*

the time. He didn't want to be attracted to her. He didn't need the complication. He had another person in his life who required his full attention for a while.

"Alex?" she said again.

"Tired." He cleared his throat. "I'm exhausted, and I imagine you are, too."

"Done in is a better description." She stepped toward the door. "I'm going to get a hot shower and go to bed."

"Not going to the library today?"

"Think I'll call in and beg off, at least until the evening shift. Sarah's very understanding considering the time of year."

"Your plan has merit. Think I'll do the same." He stepped back and moved to the door. "Thanks for your help."

She fell in step beside him. "Like I said before, that's what you're paying me for." As she exited the shed, she stopped and turned toward him. "It's in the blood, you know. I couldn't have stayed away tonight no matter what. Good night . . . morning, Alex."

He watched as she straddled the four-wheeler she'd driven from her house and headed down the road toward her home. She was right. It was in the blood, and he liked having someone around who understood that.

~

Warmed from a hot shower, Trish climbed into bed and closed her eyes. The kids had gotten themselves up and off to school without her help. She left a message on Sarah's work phone that she wouldn't be in for her afternoon shift, but would make the evening shift. With nothing to disturb her for several hours, she welcomed sleep, but the time spent with Alex played over in her mind, keeping her awake.

Alex understood getting up in the middle of the night to protect the blossoms from freezing, although when he didn't answer his phone, she feared she had another Clay on her hands. Clay had grumbled every time he had to do it, and half the time he dragged his feet. Several times she'd reawaken him to get him going. After a while, she quit trying and let him sleep. *Thank goodness Alex proved my fears wrong.*

She couldn't forget the look in Alex's eyes when he helped her down from the tractor. For a moment she thought he was going to kiss her. When he didn't, she felt a stab of disappointment. "And what would you have done if he had?" she whispered. Trish wasn't sure she wanted that kind of attention from Alex. They had established a working relationship—a friendship—she enjoyed. That would do for now. Anything beyond that became complicated and more than she wanted to handle.

She did something she hadn't done for too long. She prayed. "Lord, please let Alex and I have nothing more than a friendship. I can't deal with anything more serious. Friendship is good enough." On that thought, she drifted off to sleep.

~

Over the next few weeks, the temperature cooperated. Warmer days and nights encouraged the fruit trees to flaunt their beautiful pink and white blossoms. The effort that Alex and Trish had put into spraying water on the cherries and apricots paid off. They'd lost a few blossoms, but not enough to hurt the overall crop.

The next step would be spraying insecticide, then thinning the apricots and peaches. Apples would come later. Alex was grateful that Trish had a good crew already in place. Manuel Lopez had worked for Trish's family for nearly twenty years. He knew exactly when to do what and how to do it. That kind of loyalty and knowledge was invaluable. Alex made it clear to Manuel that he wanted him to continue in his role as foreman. Replacing him didn't make sense.

Trish's expertise with the fruit and the time spent working with her in the orchards brightened Alex's days. He enjoyed her company and her knowledge of fruit growing. They worked together irrigating and fertilizing the orchards, Alex learning how the water from the canal was distributed. He found their time in the orchards refreshing and peaceful.

They spent hours together checking to be sure everything was progressing the way nature meant. Sometimes, Trish invited Alex to supper at the end of the day. Happy to oblige, he preferred her cooking and company to being alone and digesting his feeble attempt at cooking. He enjoyed getting to know Scott and Meghan, too. He detected a bit of defiance in Scott, not unusual for a teenage boy.

Near the end of April, Alex was enjoying supper with Trish and her kids when an idea hit him. "Scott," he said, "how would you like to help me work on the house when you have some spare time? I know you're busy with baseball, but that will be over soon, and I could use some help." He watched Scott for a reaction. "I'll pay you— minimum wage."

Scott swallowed his bite of food. "Seriously? I don't know very much about building houses. And I'll have summer baseball starting in June."

"We can work around that. The wiring and plumbing are done, and the contractor is working on the drywall. I've been helping with that, so I can show you what to do, and then I'll need help painting, laying tile, other stuff. I'll be glad to teach you what I know."

"I might be interested for $10 an hour. That's what Mom pays the H-2A workers from Mexico."

"Scott!" Trish's face turned red with anger.

"Geez, Mom, what's wrong with that?"

Alex intervened. "Sorry, Scott. Minimum wage is my best offer. You're not experienced enough for more than that. And you'll have to earn your pay or you're gone."

Scott looked at Alex and shrugged. "Whatever. Had to try." He looked at Trish. "Is it okay, Mom?"

"I think that would be fine, as long as you don't ignore your responsibilities here."

"I promise." He looked at Alex. "So when do I start?"

"Come by the house tomorrow after baseball practice, and we'll work out a schedule."

"Sweet." Scott picked up his plate and carried it to the sink. "I have homework." As he exited the kitchen he said,

145

"See you tomorrow, Alex."

Trish watched him leave, then turned to Alex. "I am so sorry. He had no right to demand more than minimum wage. He should be thankful for a job."

Alex shrugged. "He's a teenager. They always think they're worth more than they are."

"Still, I'm sorry for his behavior."

"Don't apologize for him, Trish. He's old enough to do that for himself."

~

Marco stared at the pictures on the wall by his bed. Alex had sent him pictures of the trees when they bloomed and the green leaves and flowers spring brought. He couldn't wrap his mind around the beauty of the area where he and Alex would live. If it actually happened. He wanted to believe, but. . .

North Fork. Mountains. Trees that bloomed. Green everywhere. Flowers. He closed his eyes and pinched himself. He knew it was silly, but he needed to remind himself he wasn't dreaming. Alex promised. The sheer beauty in the pictures definitely beat the dirty, depressing neighborhood where he'd grown up. Crowded tenements, filth and garbage everywhere, drugs, and gangs. His mother was one of several prostitutes in his building.

He shook his head to rid himself of past, and best forgotten, memories. After the adoption became official, Marco had practiced writing Lambert, his new name, for hours. The name Rodriguez was history. No regrets.

He scanned the pictures again, hoping there would be a place to plant a garden. He liked growing things.

He still struggled to believe that he would have a home and a father once he was released from youth services. Only God could make such a miracle happen. Reverend Moss had saved him and introduced him to a loving God and Savior. Without that, Marco wondered how his life would have turned out.

Alex played a big part in Marco's redemption. At first he doubted Alex's sincerity, but when he got to know him, he realized Alex was genuine—the real deal. For a man to forgive him for killing his family, and then to love him enough to adopt him, seemed impossible. Yet God had made it happen. Of that Marco had no doubt.

Four months. Only four months and he'd be away from his prison and free to live his life. It felt like an eternity, but then, the last five years seemed to have flown by, mostly with the help of Reverend Moss and Alex. He clenched his fists and took a deep breath. All he had to do was endure the heckling from Tonio, another inmate, without planting his fist in the other boy's face.

Tonio, new to the facility, had been trouble to Marco from the first day he'd arrived. He continually called Marco a suck-up and a coward, said Marco didn't have the guts to stand up to authority and be a man. Tonio had a knack for getting some of the other boys to back him up.

Marco had endured all the heckling by ignoring it, but a day earlier, he'd nearly screwed up his chance to leave when Tonio had teased and beat one of the dogs Marco had been working with. Marco could have killed Tonio right then and there. For a moment he wanted to make Tonio hurt as much as the dog. Focused will-power and a talk with God had calmed him down.

"Mess with my dog again and you'll be sorry," he quietly but firmly told Tonio. "*Nobody* messes with my dog." His look told Tonio he meant business.

Tonio backed off. "Hey, man, it's just a dog."

Marco knelt by the dog, petting and talking quietly to it. "He was being trained to be a service dog to a needy person. If you messed that up, you're dead meat. Comprendè?"

"Whatever." Tonio shrugged his shoulders. "Be a wuss if you want. I don't care. It's just a dumb animal."

Not as dumb as you. Marco had refrained from speaking the words out loud. He wasn't about to say something stupid, start a fight, and ruin his chance at freedom.

He vowed to make the most of the chance he'd been given. He owed that much to Alex and the family he'd lost. And, Marco decided, he owed it to himself. No more screwing up. Life was too important to mess up.

Back at his bunk, Marco had settled on the bed. "Father," Marco prayed, "thank you for the chance to have a better life. Help me to be a good person so that You and Alex—Dad—can be proud of me. I don't *ever* want to live like this again. *Ever.*"

A tear slid down his cheek as he lay back on his pillow and closed his eyes.

CHAPTER 12

Living in his cramped camper was getting old. When Alex had finished his bedroom, he moved his king-size bed in and some of his clothes. He was ready to abandon his cramped quarters and live in the house, but he wanted to wait until Marco arrived. They would occupy their new home together. He'd put a coffee maker and a few cups in the kitchen along with some snacks to have while he worked, but that was it. Everything else remained in storage.

Alex placed another tile on the floor of the master bath. Making sure it was aligned properly and the spacers in place, he set the next one. The house was nearly done. He'd been working until late every evening, the best time for working in the house. The August heat made working inside during the day almost impossible without air conditioning. He had central air installed but didn't have it hooked up yet.

His days were spent overseeing the fruit harvest—cherries and apricots picked, packed, and shipped in late June and early July. Peach varieties Early Red Havens and Suncraft were nearly done. Cresthavens and Red Globes would be ready the latter part of August. The packing shed teemed with non-stop activity since the harvest began. A few local women helped with packing the fruit, along with the H-2A workers.

Gala apples, the first of the apples, would be close behind the late peaches. The harvest would end in late October with the Rome Beauties. Although the Romes belonged to Trish, he'd help her with her harvest. It was only fair.

Tomorrow he'd work inside during the day, as the forecast called for cloudy with an eighty percent chance of rain, which would make picking impossible. He smiled, remembering the book, *Cloudy with a Chance of Meatballs,* he used to read to Alex Jr. He doubted he'd ever have a chance to read the book to a son or daughter again, but he could always hope for a grandchild or two. The thought warmed his heart.

He cleared the memories from his mind and concentrated on his work. When he finished the master bath, he'd be done except for Marco's bedroom. All the rooms had been painted, but Marco would have a say in decorating his own room and the other rooms upstairs, including the two baths.

He'd sold his condo a few weeks after Ed listed it and for the price he wanted. What money was left over from building the new house would go toward furnishing it; the rest he'd put in savings for a rainy day or other needs. Amy's life insurance and the insurance settlement from the accident that took his family had given him a new start, paying for the orchards. But when you owned fruit orchards, there were always unexpected expenses, or a bad year—sometimes two or more in a row. *It's good I'll have a part-time job with Jess Atkins.*

Only two weeks until he and Marco began a new life together. Marco's criminal record would be expunged as long as he stayed out of trouble. He would serve six months' parole under the direction of Colorado Health and Human Services. The woman overseeing Marco's case was pleased to learn Alex had adopted Marco. Having a father and a stable home gave him a better chance at succeeding in the real world. The adoption paperwork had been delivered to Delta County's Child Welfare Department, and Alex had already introduced himself to the caseworker. She had visited the house in progress and deemed it suitable. In less than a year, the scrutiny of their lives would be over and done with, and Alex looked forward to that day.

Alex recalled Marco's fascination with the photos he'd shown him of their new home. The young man, who had known only the worst part of Denver and the worst life could offer, treasured the pictures. Alex kept him apprised on the progress of the house. Marco's wonder and excitement tugged at Alex's heart. He had taken so much for granted about his own youth and all its advantages. The Marcos of this world considered what Alex had as fantasy. Alex had the chance to show at least one boy that love, family, and a safe place to live were real.

He wished Marco could have participated in the majority of the fruit harvest, although he would be able to help with the apples. Marco could definitely help Manuel interpret the migrant workers' Spanish for Alex. Trish's expertise with the language helped, but she wasn't always available. Alex hadn't spoken much Spanish since he'd been in high school.

Getting migrant workers from Mexico proved more a problem than it had been in his youth. Trish had the process well in place, cooperating with other fruit growers and filling out all the H-2A paperwork with the Department of Labor and form I-129. In spite of the frustrating and endless government paperwork, the workers arrived on time to help with the harvest.

Growers no longer used contract labor—local pickers who picked by the box—as they did when Alex was a kid. The H-2A workers were paid transportation from and to their homes in Mexico and lived in government approved housing—a bunkhouse at the southern edge of Trish's property. They received an hourly wage, between ten and twelve dollars an hour. Labor was a big expense for fruit farmers under the new system. No more kids picking fruit for a summer job.

If more American citizens stepped up to do the work, life would be simpler. But that wasn't the case. Instead, growers had to rely on the migrant program and all its requirements. The government pulled surprise inspections at the bunkhouse and in the orchards, often at the worst possible times. Alex had to quit overseeing the picking and packing to accommodate the inspector, who always seemed to nitpick and take twice the time needed.

It had been an excellent year for fruit. "Next year." Alex remarked aloud. "Marco will get his real initiation next year." He smiled at the image of Marco in the orchards.

Alex's decision to hire Trish as a consultant proved priceless, worth every bit he paid her and then some. She not only kept detailed books of years past, but she worked as hard as he did. Habit, he knew, was partly responsible. He speculated she still thought of the orchards as hers. He didn't mind. He had no problem sharing them.

The other good decision he'd made was hiring Scott to help him with the house. He turned out to be a good worker, willing to learn from Alex. Spending time with Scott only made Alex more anxious to have Marco home.

"Alex?" Trish's call interrupted his thoughts.

He stood and called out the bathroom door. "In the master bath. Come on back." He washed his hands in the sink and gingerly stepped past the tiles he'd finished laying.

Trish stuck her head in the bedroom door. "I

knocked. Guess you didn't hear me." She shrugged. "The door was open."

"You're welcome any time." He gestured around him. "So what do you think?" He spread his hand toward the spacious bedroom with more than enough room for his king-size bed. Large windows let in an abundance of light. A mahogany desk with a computer sat in an alcove on the north side. Dark teal covered the wall behind the bed, the other walls about three shades lighter. Blinds with varying shades of brown and splashes of teal covered the windows.

"I like. Great colors. Thought you were living in the camper."

"I am. Didn't think it would hurt to move the bed in. In two weeks, Marco and I will occupy the house at the same time. The less to move in that doesn't affect Marco, the better."

"Sounds fair."

"Thanks for the decorator recommendation. Ann did a great job and was easy to work with. She listened and came up with great ideas."

"I've known Ann for a long time. We graduated together. I always thought she had good taste." Trish grinned and her dimples stood out. "Much better than mine. I do my best work outside."

"I like what you've done with your house."

"Can't take the blame for that. My mother and grandmother were the decorators. I haven't changed anything."

Alex smiled. "Must be in the genes somewhere."

Trish shrugged. "I think Meghan got all the decorating genes."

He nodded toward the unfinished bath. "'Bout done with the master bath. Just finishing the floor."

Trish peered through the door. "Nice. Awfully big for one person, isn't it?"

"I like my space. Besides, a generous master bath has its resale merits."

She frowned. "You planning on selling anytime soon?"

"Nope. Plan on being here a long time." He gestured for her to follow. "You should appreciate this." He opened the door to a walk-in closet the size of a small bedroom. "My wife, Amy, would have loved this."

"Oh, my." Trish stared at the empty rods on one wall. Another wall had one rod with some shirts, slacks, and a few suits. Built-in drawers and shelves covered the remaining wall space. "You're right. A woman would kill for a closet like this."

Alex chuckled. "I figured as much."

"So, you're planning to remarry then?"

He shrugged. "Who knows?" He stepped back and closed the door. "I had it great once, though. Maybe that's all that was meant to be."

"I envy you. I didn't make a very good choice the first time." A shadow of regret passed over her face. "Maybe that's all *I* was meant to have." A tear slid down her cheek.

They stood only inches apart. Unable to resist, Alex reached up and wiped the tear away with his thumb. Her skin was soft and the sadness in her eyes pierced his heart. He leaned down and gently brushed his lips over hers. His hand slipped behind her head and he pulled her to him. As their bodies met, he deepened the kiss. Her hands pressed against his chest, ending the moment.

He stepped back. "I apologize." Bad move, he thought. "That was uncalled for."

She touched her lips with her fingers and looked at the floor. "Yes, it was. I've had enough of that kind of complication." She bit her lip.

"I understand," Alex said. *Awkward. Change the subject.* He cleared his throat. "My adopted son is my priority right now. I have to think about him."

"Tell me about him . . . your son. When will he be here?"

He looked around. *Maybe the bedroom isn't the best place to be talking. At least she didn't slap me.* "Let's go to the kitchen. I'll give you the short version over a cup of coffee."

The kitchen was spacious, surrounded by oak cupboards and two large pantries. Black appliances and granite countertops in marbled gray added a modern touch with a work island dividing the kitchen. A breakfast nook with an oval oak table and a curved wooden bench under a bay window occupied the east wall. Red plaid curtains covered the bottom half of the window with a matching valance. They settled on wooden stools at the breakfast counter, with two mugs of steaming coffee and a plate of Oreos. The tension from earlier had disappeared. Alex relaxed.

"As you can see," Alex said, "I don't bake."

"I love Oreos. They're my favorite." She twisted the chocolate cookie and skimmed the creamy center into her mouth. "Ann did a great job in here, too. It's very homey."

She dipped the chocolate cookie into her coffee. "So, about your son . . ."

"Marco comes from a troubled background. His mother was a prostitute hooked on drugs. He got in a little bit of trouble and has spent some time in youth services in Denver. I met him through the court system. I've never seen such a change in one kid. He connected with a minister at the facility and became a Christian. He's completely turned his life around." Trish didn't need to know the reason Marco was in youth services. That was up to Marco to tell, not Alex. Small-town gossip could be brutal. Marco needed to make his own impression on the residents without his past influencing his acceptance into the community.

"His mother was found dead a few years ago, and he has no idea who his father is. Over the last four years, I've come to know and love Marco. In March I officially adopted him. He'll be here around the fourteenth or fifteenth."

"Just before school starts." She sipped her coffee. "You're doing a good thing."

"I'd appreciate you keeping his background to yourself. I'd rather even Scott didn't know. I want people to accept him for the young man he's become, not judge him for the troubled boy he was."

"It's between us, I promise."

Alex smiled. "Thanks."

"I see now why you want to help other boys who've made wrong choices. I'm guessing you'll succeed more than you fail."

"That doesn't upset you anymore?"

Trish looked into her half-empty cup. "I'm sorry for that. I was out of line. Wanting to help troubled kids is good. You've helped Scott a lot."

"With God's help I think I can make a difference, at least for a few boys."

"That's the other thing I envy about you."

Alex frowned.

"Your faith." She sighed. "I've struggled with mine for many years. Quit going to church for a while. I've been better at attending lately, but I still struggle. I don't feel God has helped me much. He's taken away my parents, my heritage, even my husband, although that wasn't a great loss, considering. I know that sounds cold, but Clay wasn't much of a husband, or father to Meghan. I'd planned on filing for divorce before he died. Scott misses him. Meghan doesn't remember him that much."

"Blame Clay if you have to blame someone, but not God." Alex sighed. "I was really good at blaming God for all my troubles. I've made my share of wrong choices.

The tragedy is not learning from them. Truth is, I should have gone with Amy to visit her parents. I wanted to stay home, play some golf, and watch sports on TV. If I had gone with her, maybe the accident wouldn't have happened. Then again, who knows? We can't second-guess what happens in our lives. The point is to move on and trust that the next time our choices will be better. We can't make our lives or our kids' lives perfect. Some lessons we learn the hard way. Right?"

"I suppose so."

"When bad things happen, we learn from them and strive to do better in the future. When we do, God celebrates."

Trish closed her eyes. "I think He's probably scratching his head over me."

"He's done the same with me more than I like to admit. I think I may finally be learning a little, anyway." Alex fiddled with his cup. "Trusting God was hardest for me after I lost my family. But I'm getting a lot better. He brought me here. Can't complain about that."

"Well, He didn't exactly answer my prayer about saving the orchards, but at least He brought me the right buyer."

"I'm glad you think so. Sometimes we have to let go of something to appreciate what we already have and what's in store for us next."

"I'll try to remember that." She glanced at her watch. "I'd better get home. I actually came over to invite you to dinner on Sunday—after church. Thought we'd barbecue hamburgers and celebrate nearing the end of the peach harvest and the beginning of the apple harvest. And the end of your house construction. Scott said you were close to finishing."

"A celebration sounds good. We'll have another one after Marco and I get settled."

Alex leaned against the front door jamb and watched Trish walk toward her home, the yard light on the shed illuminating the highlights of her red hair. Moths flitted around the light, casting tiny shadows. Although the sun had set, the air was still warm. A perfect summer evening.

"Tell you what," he called, "let's forget the hamburgers." She turned to look at him. "Let's make it steak. I'll furnish the steak, you fix everything else. Deal?"

Trish raised her thumb in the air. "Deal," she answered.

~

Long after Trish left, Alex was still thinking about her and the softness of her lips. The kiss surprised him as much as it seemed to unsettle her. He hadn't planned to kiss her. Unfortunately, or perhaps fortunately, the opportunity presented itself, and he couldn't resist. She'd been tempting him for months. Not consciously, of course, but working with her in the orchards made him appreciate her more each day. Her knowledge, however, wasn't the only thing he admired. She was beginning to let her real personality shine. She had a bit of an ornery streak, a passion for farming, liked the outdoors, hated to cook and clean or anything else that kept her inside. But she had a vulnerable side she tried to camouflage with toughness.

She pushed me away, but didn't slap me. I hope she liked the kiss a little, anyway. I did.

He frowned. He was treading on shaky ground. He had to agree with Trish. Neither of them needed a relationship right now. He had Marco to think about—getting him settled in school and helping him adjust to a new home with freedoms he hadn't experienced in years, not to mention the two of them sharing the same living space. That, too, would be an adjustment. Those were his priorities.

Still . . . .

~

Trish lay in bed thinking about her evening with Alex. He had shown her around the house as it was being built, but she hadn't seen any of it since Ann had added her designer touches. The enormous master bedroom left her own lacking, and she loved the spacious kitchen. The house was beautiful. If she didn't treasure her drafty old two-story farmhouse with all its memories so much, she'd love to live in a house like the one Alex had built. Spacious, all the modern conveniences, like central vacuuming, and windows that let in the brilliant sunlight, especially the ones on the east that framed the mountains. She sighed. The walk-in closet was jaw-dropping. She'd

161

love to have that much room for clothes, not that she had that many. Hers were crammed into a small closet with little wiggle room.

She touched her lips. She hadn't been kissed like that in a long time. No, she hadn't been kissed like that *ever*. The warm sensation traveled all the way to her toes and back to her heart. *I wish I'd met Alex a long time ago.*

She had put an end to the kiss for fear of where it would lead. Once her life was settled and on solid ground, she might—*might* being the operative word—think about getting involved with someone. Dating Dale occasionally had been convenient. Something to do instead of sit at home. She had seen herself possibly getting serious down the road, but he'd screwed that up.

Like Clay, Dale had been a poor choice. *Could Alex be right about God letting us make our own mistakes, so we can learn from them?* She knew what kind of man she didn't want. Spending the rest of her life alone was better than making a wrong choice. Years of trying to make a bad marriage work made the thought of any relationship frightening. She had to be sure about Alex before even considering getting serious. Was Alex the right man for her?

Take it slow this time.

She harbored a little resentment toward Alex. He owned *her* orchards. Acting as his consultant made her feel they were still partly hers, but the reality was they belonged to him. Being almost debt-free helped, but it had cost her a lot. And she wouldn't foster involvement with him just to get her heritage back. It wasn't worth the grief of a contentious relationship.

Alex said we have to let some things go to appreciate what we already have. Trish had to admit that her life had improved since she'd sold the orchards. Her connection with Scott and Meghan had been less strained, and the difference in Scott was amazing. Instead of obsessing about keeping the orchards and paying a never-ending debt, she should have been concentrating on the two most important things in her life—her kids.

Trust.

There was another issue she'd have to work on. She found herself trusting Alex in any number of ways. And he had trusted her with Marco's story. That was definitely a point in his favor. She would return that trust by keeping the story to herself.

She was anxious to meet Marco. He sounded like a nice young man. Maybe he and Scott would become friends. If Alex thought enough of Marco to adopt him, she could trust he'd make a good friend for her son.

Scott had changed over the last few months. He talked incessantly at the supper table about all Alex had taught him—carpentry, laying tile, and wiring. He liked painting, taping, and mudding the least but didn't complain about having to do it. He even asked Trish if he could repaint his room.

What would it have been like if Clay hadn't died? Would he have taught Scott anything but sports? Probably not. Alex had attended Scott's summer baseball games except when he travelled to Denver. Scott hadn't even complained about helping with the fruit. And the biggest miracle of all was that he treated Meghan like a little sister instead of a troll.

She'd lost the orchards, but she still had a say in how they were managed, at least for now. Alex had a great background in fruit, and it didn't take him long to adjust to a later growing season. He'd even taught her new methods of fertilizing that his family used. Trish let her heart believe life might finally have a bright side.

"Thank you, Lord, that Alex loves the orchards as much as I do. They're in good hands." She couldn't remember the last time she had said a prayer of thanks. Her prayers were always pleas for help, or angry diatribes about how life wasn't fair. She hated it when her kids pleaded for something they didn't need, or whined and complained about life not being fair. Did she sound like a whining child to God?

The memory of Alex standing in his doorway this evening caused her heart to race. His paint- and dirt-stained jeans hugged his long legs, his holey white T-shirt accented his muscular chest. What wasn't to like? Tall with dark blond hair that needed combing more often than not, and a smile that lit up his blue eyes. The best part, he was honest and unassuming. Although tempted to explore her feelings for Alex, she knew better.

Still . . . .

~

Trish watched Alex flip a rib-eye steak on the grill. Through the open kitchen window, the mouth-watering aroma of charcoal and grilled meat mingled with fresh mountain air and newly cut grass. Country-fried potatoes with onions sizzled on the stove and baked beans warmed in the oven. The egg-lettuce salad was ready. All she had to do was stir in the dressing.

"Meghan, take the plates and utensils out to the picnic table."

"Okay. How come Scott isn't helping?"

"He is. Alex is showing him how to cook the meat just right." She winked at Meghan. "At least that's what he said. We'll see if he's the expert he claims to be when we eat."

Meghan gathered up plates, knives, forks, and napkins. At the door, she stopped and turned back toward Trish. "I like Alex. He makes me miss Dad less."

"I like him, too." And he's nothing at all like your dad, she thought. He's twice the man—far more honest, a hard worker, and doesn't complain. *Okay, you're making him sound like Adonis or Apollo. He's got to have a fault or two.* She suspected, however, that his faults were minimal, compared to Clay's.

She watched her daughter set the table. Alex said something to Meghan, making her laugh. Tears pricked at the back of Trish's eyes. This was how a family should be. She remembered her childhood. It hadn't been perfect, but she always felt loved, with a ton more laughter than anger. "Stop the regrets," she admonished out loud.

"Time to look forward."

"Steaks are ready," Alex called.

"Coming," Trish answered. She emptied the potatoes into a bowl and set them on a tray along with the baked beans and salad and headed for the door, a satisfied smile across her face.

CHAPTER 13

Alex fidgeted in the chair across from the director's desk. Anxious to finally take Marco home, the trip from North Fork to Denver had seemed twice as long as usual. When he'd arrived at Mount Evans Youth Services to pick up Marco, he was told the director wanted to see him. Alex hated waiting. Waiting conjured up worries. Had something gone wrong? He'd had no indication of any problems. Surely they would have let him know.

Where was the director? He glanced at his watch for the umpteenth time. Ten minutes. It seemed like ten hours. Alex startled when the door opened, his heartrate accelerating. The director approached him and offered his hand.

"Good morning, Mr. Lambert. Sorry to keep you waiting."

Alex shook his hand. "There's no problem is there?" He held his breath.

The director smiled. "I just wanted to visit with you for a minute before we release Marco to your custody."

Alex heaved a sigh and settled back in his chair, ready for the traditional lecture the director was sure to deliver about troubled kids in the real world.

"I wanted to tell you what an outstanding young man Marco is. He has shown all of us that it's possible to change for the better and have a real chance at making a successful life on the outside. That said, I believe you and Reverend Moss have had a great deal to do with his transformation."

Alex smiled. "Thank you. You've given him a decent chance here. I appreciate that."

"He was a frightened, troubled boy when he came here. He's leaving a more confident and hopeful young man." He cleared his throat. "There is something you need to be aware of, however."

Alex frowned.

"In the last few months, a new arrival has been harassing Marco, trying to get him riled up. Recently, he beat one of Marco's dogs. Since Marco was due for release, we watched to see how he would handle it. Until the dog incident, he basically ignored the harassment, so we let it play out. But when his dog was hurt, we could see the anger build in him. Had he fought Tonio, touched him in any way, he would have had to be disciplined and his release delayed. But Marco managed to keep his anger to a verbal threat and walked away. We don't know what he said, but it seemed to put Tonio in his place."

Alex gritted his teeth. *Why would they let this Tonio get away with egging someone on, let alone beat a helpless animal?* "And have you disciplined Tonio? Seems to me he's the troublemaker."

"After the dog incident Tonio was transferred to another facility and will be disciplined. We had hoped that Marco's stance of non-violence might influence Tonio in a positive way. Unfortunately, Tonio's a hard case and needs a different structure than we can give him here. We definitely didn't see the dog incident coming, or we would have intervened sooner.

"I'm telling you this so that you'll understand what Marco has endured the last few months and how much his new life means to him. You should be proud of him, but you also need to be aware that he may face some of the same harassment on the outside. You'll need to help him be strong enough to deal with it. As much as we like him, we don't want him back."

"We'll work on it together. And I won't mention this to Marco unless he brings it up."

"I think that would be wise." The director stood. "I wish you and Marco the very best. He deserves a good home and a better life." He shook hands with Alex again. "He's waiting for you right outside. Take him home."

Alex couldn't get to the door fast enough. Marco sat in a corner chair in the outer office, two small duffle bags at his feet. Alex met him with a bear hug.

"Are you ready to blow this joint?" Alex asked.

Marco smiled, moisture in his eyes. "I've been ready for a long time."

"Then let's go see what the outside looks like."

They ate lunch at a Taco Bell—Marco's choice—then Alex took him to their hotel room. For a long time Marco stared out the twelfth-floor window at downtown Denver. Alex gave him a few minutes to absorb his freedom before joining him.

Clamping a hand on Marco's shoulder, Alex asked, "So, what do you think?"

Marco took a moment to answer. "It's a city. I'll be happy to shake it from my shoes."

It was an answer Alex hadn't expected. "Sounds like you're anxious to see North Fork and the house."

"The sooner the better."

"Then we'll head for Grand Junction first thing in the morning."

Marco frowned at Alex. "Why Grand Junction?"

Alex grinned. "Because you have some bedroom furniture to pick out, along with our living room furniture and furniture for the extra bedrooms. Can't live in a house without furniture."

"Really? You'll let me pick out my own stuff?"

"You're the one who has to live with it. That okay with you?"

"*Awesome.*"

"By the way," Alex handed him a box. "Time you had this."

Marco opened the box to find the watch Alex had given

him at Christmas. Once secured on his wrist, he smiled and hugged Alex. "Thanks."

Marco was up before the sun, urging Alex to get going. Alex chuckled at his eagerness. He couldn't blame him. Being cooped up in the same compound and small room for five years, then suddenly experiencing freedom, would make anyone anxious. Not long after the sun peeked above the eastern plains of Colorado, they were on I-70 headed west.

~

"I like this one." Marco pointed to a bedroom set made of mahogany with a matching desk. He was willing to settle for a twin bed, but Alex talked him into a queen-size bed.

They found a living room set they both liked with the needed accessories and a dining room table and chairs. For the extra bedrooms, they chose bunkbeds and dressers to match. Alex made arrangements to have their selections delivered to North Fork the following afternoon. Because they had gotten an early start, they still had most of the day left. After purchasing bedding and bath accessories at a local department store, Alex surprised Marco with a visit to the local animal shelter.

"What're we doing here?" Marco asked.

"Thought maybe you'd like to pick out a dog to take home with you."

"Seriously?"

"Seriously."

Marco hugged Alex. "Thanks, Dad."

Alex fought back tears. It was the first time Marco had

called him Dad without any prompting.

Marco took his time, checking out both older dogs and puppies. He finally settled on a six-month-old black and white Australian cattle dog and border collie mix. "This is the one," he said. "She's smart, and she likes me." He grinned at Alex as the puppy licked his face.

"She's yours. You understand she will be an outside dog."

"We'll have to build her a dog house."

"That can be done."

Alex made arrangements to pick the dog up first thing in the morning. With plenty of time left in the day, Alex had one more surprise left for Marco—a visit to Alex's family and their fruit farm in Palisade, about fifteen miles east of Grand Junction. Marco's new grandparents and uncle and aunt greeted him with hugs and made him feel a part of the family. His two younger cousins also made him feel welcome. They stayed the night with Alex's parents. As he settled Marco in the guest bedroom, Alex asked him what he thought of his new family.

"They're amazing." He frowned. "Do they know it was me?"

"I keep no secrets from my family. They thought I was crazy at first for even wanting to see you, but they've come to understand the need for forgiveness. As you can see, they have accepted you as I have."

"Grandpa and Grandma—I can call them that, right?"

"You can."

"They called me their newest grandson. I've never had

grandparents."

Alex hugged him. "You do now."

~

"I think I'll name her Lucky," Marco told Alex when they picked the dog up the next morning on their way to North Fork.

"Why Lucky?" Alex asked

"Don't you think it fits? We're both lucky to have a new home and a new family."

Alex chuckled. "I guess it does fit."

When they left the desert and farm lands surrounding Delta and reached the valley leading to North Fork, Alex watched Marco for a reaction. Marco stared out the window, his eyes wide. Lucky had fallen asleep on his lap.

"Well, what do you think?"

"I-I don't know. It's like the pictures, except it's real. Man, it's *awesome*."

Alex pointed to the two tall mountains closest to them. "That's Mt. Lamborn and Land's End to its south—right." He wasn't sure Marco knew the directions yet.

Grand Mesa had shadowed them on the east and north as they made their way from Grand Junction to North Fork. Marco had asked numerous questions about the largest flattop mountain in the world. Alex assured him there were nearly 400 lakes and ponds that they could explore when time allowed.

"What's that rocky-looking mountain way back there?" he asked as they drove the final miles to North Fork.

"That's the Raggeds, the highest point is Ragged Mountain. I think it's the most beautiful and majestic of all the mountains."

"It sure is."

"The one that's just a little closer is Marcellina. We'll go by it when I show you Kebler Pass."

"Tomorrow?"

Alex chuckled at Marco's enthusiasm. "Maybe in a few days. We need to get settled in the new house first." Alex turned off the highway toward home, while Marco continued to stare out the window. When the car stopped in front of the house, Lucky stirred, but Marco sat riveted to his seat, the seatbelt still buckled.

"This is home, Marco. Don't you want to get out and see where you'll be living?"

"I-it's so big."

"It's comfortable. Come on. This is home."

Once out of the vehicle, Marco let Lucky relieve herself, then picked her up and followed Alex into the house. Alex didn't object to Lucky being inside this one time.

Marco wandered through the downstairs, his eyes wide, an expression of disbelief on his face. When Alex showed him his new bedroom, he sank to the floor and cried. Alex knelt beside him, an arm around Marco's shoulders.

"This is *stupid*," Marco said after a few moments. He wiped his eyes and nose with the back of his hand. Lucky licked his face. "I'm acting like a baby."

Alex squeezed his shoulders. "It's all yours. Enjoy it. I'll check on the ETA of the furniture."

The furniture was due to arrive around three that afternoon, so Alex called Trish at the library.

"Marco and I are here. He's taking in his room right now."

"Does he like it?"

"I think he's a little overwhelmed at the moment."

"It's a major change for him."

"It is. I called for two reasons. I want to take Marco to Granny's for lunch. Would you like to join us?"

"Thank you for asking, but I think you two need the time alone."

"Don't hesitate to join us if you change your mind."

"What's the other reason?"

"I got Marco a puppy, so you may hear some whining and barking for a few nights until she gets used to her new home. Just wanted to give you a heads up."

"I appreciate that. I promise not to complain too much."

"Maybe we'll see you tomorrow. Let you and the kids get acquainted with Marco."

"I'm looking forward to it. Catch you later."

Alex closed his phone and contemplated the call. He hadn't planned on asking her to lunch. He'd missed her, and he hadn't been gone that long. Funny, he thought, how a person gets used to having another around without realizing it. He turned as Marco descended the stairs.

"You like it? Did I get the color right for the walls?"

"Man, it's amazing. It's all mine? I don't have to share it when we have other boys here?"

"You don't have to share it. Ever. There are other

175

bedrooms upstairs, or didn't you notice? The ones the bunkbeds go in."

Marco grinned sheepishly. "I didn't notice. Guess I'll have to look again."

"There's plenty of time. Right now I'm going to treat you to the best hamburger this side of heaven."

~

Long after she'd hung up, Trish contemplated Alex's call. Not scheduled on the reference desk until late afternoon, she could have accepted Alex's invitation. She wanted more than anything to see him and meet Marco, but something told her she needed to wait. Even though Alex hadn't been gone long, she missed him. Every time he left for Denver, she missed him. Missed walking through the orchards with him, talking to him about the fruit, the future of the orchards, and life in general. He was so easy to talk to; he made her want more of his time and attention.

"I must be crazy," she whispered. How could she have gotten so close to him in such a short time? He shared her goals and her beliefs. She had to admit his faith was stronger than hers, but she was working on trusting God more and herself less. He'd had a good marriage and lost everything. She'd only lost Clay—half of a failed marriage. She still had Scott and Meghan, but Alex had lost so much more. All Alex had was an adopted son . . . and memories.

Both her kids had become attached to Alex. Meghan adored him. He treated her with the same attention he gave Scott. He'd asked Meghan to pick out the colors for the two extra upstairs bedrooms. Scott couldn't stop talking about how much he'd learned from Alex—not just the construction, Trish mused, but life lessons. Scott didn't come right out and say he'd learned to be a better person, but since he began spending time with Alex, he had become a better person. Even Cam Morgan, Scott's counselor, commented on the change in Scott.

Trish worried things would change once Marco arrived. With his own son to concentrate on, she hoped Alex wouldn't ignore her kids. She couldn't blame him. After all, Marco should get Alex's full attention. But she wondered what effect that might have on Scott.

"You look deep in thought."

Trish glanced up at Sarah standing beside her desk. "Just thinking about the change in Scott and Meghan."

"They do seem like different kids. You must be doing something right." Sarah settled on the chair by Trish's desk.

"I don't think it's me." Trish sighed. "I think it's Alex's influence. The kids look up to him."

"I need to meet this Alex. Sounds like a great guy."

"He's a man of integrity. That's good for Scott."

"But something else is bothering you."

"Alex has an adopted son that has just come to live with him. I'm afraid Scott and Meghan will take a back seat now that he's here. Not that it's wrong, but I still worry they'll feel rejected."

"Valid. But if this Alex is the kind of man you say he is, don't sell him short. I'm guessing he'll find time for all three."

"You're such an optimist, Sarah."

"It's a good thing to be. Try it sometime." Sarah rose. "And don't sell yourself short. I've seen a change in you, too, which is bound to effect Scott and Meghan. Say some prayers for guidance and let God handle it. He's good at such things, you know." She smiled and walked away.

Trish closed her eyes and thought about Sarah's advice. *Okay, God, I'm putting things in your hands. Don't let Scott and Meghan feel left out now that Marco is here. They need Alex. I need Alex.* Her eyes flew open at the last thought. Where had that come from? She glanced at the clock above her desk. No time to worry about it now. She had books to order and reference desk duty in an hour.

~

"She's nice," Marco commented.

"Trish? Yes, she is," Alex agreed as he turned down the drive to their home.

Before returning home, they had stopped at the library to get Marco a library card. Alex could have waited, but they had time to kill before the furniture arrived. And if he were honest with himself, he wanted to see Trish and introduce her to Marco.

After stopping by the lumber yard to pick up materials for a dog house, they headed home, arriving only a few minutes ahead of the furniture. With the furniture placed in the rooms, they went to work building the dog house.

Lucky growled, followed by several barks. Both Alex and Marco looked up from their work.

"So, what's all this?"

"Scott." Alex put his arm around Scott's shoulders. "It's a dog house."

Scott glanced at Marco. "Already in trouble?"

Marco frowned.

Alex dropped his arm. "Scott, this is my son, Marco. Marco, this is Scott, our neighbor."

The two boys eyed each other for a minute, then shook hands.

"It's for Dad," Marco said with a straight face.

Alex relaxed. He had assured Marco that no one knew of his background, and Marco had evidently taken him at his word.

Scott grinned. "Sounds right."

"Hey, wait a minute. What makes you two think I deserve the dog house?"

"Well," Marco said, "it couldn't be us. We're the good guys."

Alex let out a guffaw. "Ha! We'll see who needs it."

They all laughed. Lucky barked and joined in the fun.

"Neat dog. What's his name?" Scott asked.

"*Her* name is Lucky." Marco picked her up and rubbed her neck.

"Sweet. So, can I help?" Scott asked.

"Up to Marco," Alex answered.

Marco looked at Scott, then handed him a hammer. "Nail that board to the cross beam."

"You got it."

Alex stepped back. The two boys went to work on the

dog house as though they'd been working together for months. *This is how it's supposed to be. Thank you, Lord.*

~

Trish picked up a bouquet of carnations, alstroemerias, daisies, and a couple of tiger lilies. A welcome gift for Marco. What little she'd seen of him at the library she had liked. She hoped he and Scott would become friends.

"Where's Scott?" Trish asked Meghan as she walked in the door.

"At Alex's. He saw the furniture truck go by, so he went over as soon as he finished his chores."

"Oh." Trish looked through the refrigerator. Not much there. She could make a tuna salad fairly quickly. She had chips and crackers to go with it. That should do.

Trish and Meghan walked to Alex's with the salad, chips, crackers and bouquet of flowers. As Trish approached the house, she couldn't believe her eyes. Marco and Scott worked on what looked like a small house, Alex supervising. She shook her head. Unbelievable. As they approached, they were met with barks from a black and white puppy.

Alex looked toward them. "Well, boys, look who's here."

Both boys glanced up, and then went back to work.

"I brought supper." Trish indicated the bowl she carried. "And a welcome home gift." She raised the flowers.

"Great. I forgot all about supper. We got busy building Lucky's house. She'll need it tonight."

"She's so cute!" Meghan knelt before Lucky.

"You can pick her up if you want," said Marco. "Her name's Lucky. I'm Marco."

Meghan picked up Lucky and grinned at Marco. "Hi. I'm Meghan." She snuggled against the puppy and was rewarded with a wet kiss.

Alex took the bowl from Trish. "Let's take this stuff in the house and let these kids get acquainted. I think they're about done with the house except for painting it." Alex turned to the boys. "When you've finished putting it together, come in for supper. Paint can wait till tomorrow. Meghan you're welcome to stay out here or come in."

Nearly in unison, both boys and Meghan answered, "Okay."

Inside, Alex handed a vase to Trish, then pulled out plates and utensils. "I think there's enough pop and iced tea in the frig."

Trish arranged the flowers in the vase and set them on the breakfast table. "This okay?

"Perfect." Without thinking, Alex approached Trish and gave her a hug. To his surprise she didn't flinch but returned the hug. "You and the kids have made our evening," he said as he stepped back. "Marco and Scott hit it off immediately."

"I'm glad. They looked like they were enjoying themselves."

"Completely shut me out."

"I'm sorry. Maybe Scott shouldn't have—"

"Trish, it's okay. I'm thrilled."

"Then so am I."

~

From his bed, Marco stared out his window at the starlit sky. He'd never seen so many stars in his whole life. The country-fresh air drifted through the open window. He fought back tears. "I'm so lucky. I don't know why, after what I did, but thank you, God," he whispered.

He liked Scott, and enjoyed his help with the dog house. Meghan was cute and kind of quiet. He'd had fun getting acquainted with both of them.

Before going to bed, he'd put a dog bed and a hot water bottle in Lucky's new house. They'd attached a chain to her collar so she wouldn't wander away. Marco would train her to stay on the property and let them know when strangers approached. He'd teach her both verbal and hand signals and couldn't wait to get started.

His own dog. He'd checked on her several times that night before Alex insisted he go to bed and get some sleep. His clock radio showed well past one o'clock, and he still couldn't sleep. He could see Lucky's doghouse from his window and listened for Lucky to whine or bark, but no sounds came from her. *Guess she's adjusting better than me.* He closed his eyes and prayed. Sleep finally overtook him.

He dreamed he was back in a small room in a locked facility and awoke with a start. Climbing out of bed, he stared out the window at the open spaces and inhaled the fresh air. In spite of the cool evening, he broke out in a sweat. Did his dream mean he'd end up in jail again? If he messed up, would Alex abandon him? A tear slid down his cheek.

CHAPTER 14

Marco stared at the mirror surface of the lake, the rugged East Beckwith Mountain reflecting back at him. He had said little on the trip to Lost Lake Slough, gazing out the window at the quakie trees flanking Kebler Pass. He asked about the mountains as they drove: Gunnison, Marcellina, the Beckwiths, the Rubies, and, of course, the Raggeds that he had seen at a distance when he'd first arrived in North Fork.

"So, what do you think?" Alex asked.

"Man, it's amazing."

"There's another Lost Lake a short hike from here. We'll do that another time. You'll be even closer to that mountain than you are now." Alex nodded toward the peak that towered over the lake.

"Seriously?"

Alex smiled. "Seriously. Today we'll fish here, and if we're lucky, we'll have trout for supper tomorrow night."

Alex patiently taught Marco the fine points of fly fishing. Marco was awkward at first, but he soon managed to avoid snagging a nearby bush or tangling his line and landed the fly in the water. When he snagged his first fish, his excitement exploded. After that there was no stopping him from casting out his line again and again.

The Monday following their arrival in North Fork, Alex had taken Marco to the high school and enrolled him. Marco's transcripts would come from Jefferson County School District, which had overseen his education while he was in youth services. School started on Wednesday, and Marco was assured he would be welcome, even if his transcripts hadn't arrived. He was given a tour of the school before meeting with Cam Morgan, the school counselor.

After questioning Marco about what he'd been studying, Cam set up a schedule for him. Marco and Alex both signed off on it.

Cam shook Marco's hand. "Welcome to North Fork High School, Marco. I hope you'll be happy here."

"Thanks."

"Alex, it's nice to finally meet you. I've heard a lot about you from Scott Ryan."

"All good, I hope."

Cam smiled. "You've made a difference in Scott. He looks up to you."

"He's a great kid. He and Marco have already hit it off."

"Good. Scott can help him get acquainted."

Before going home, Marco and Alex stopped at Jess Atkins' office to check on the progress of the land trust he had asked Jess to work on and pick up any papers he needed for clients assigned to him. At Jess's urging, Alex had started working part time for Jess a little earlier than originally agreed. The extra income helped and kept his legal skills current. Jess handed Alex several files—work he could do at home. If he needed to meet with a client, he could do that at the law office.

On the way home, Alex had suggested the fishing trip. "Let's put some food in a cooler and head to the mountains," Alex said. "I hear a few fish calling."

Marco had jumped at the chance to see the surrounding mountains and lakes. On the way to Lost Lake, they had seen a groundhog, numerous chipmunks, and a couple of deer, leaving Marco wide-eyed with wonder. He still had trouble taking in everything since he'd been released from youth services. He wondered what had he done to deserve all this.

Marco's gaze followed a hawk soaring over the lake. The afternoon went quickly and before Marco knew it, the sun had slipped behind the horizon.

Alex called to Marco. "It's getting late. Probably should head home."

"Come on, Lucky. Time to go home." Marco reeled in his line.

Lucky barked once and followed them to the pickup.

As they stowed their gear in the pickup bed, Marco grinned at Alex. "Man that was great! Thanks, Dad."

"You're welcome. Some fun, huh?'

Marco nodded and took a deep breath. "Dad, I need to tell you something."

Alex shoved the cooler onto the pickup bed and looked at Marco. "Okay."

Marco stared at the ground. "The last few months at the center a kid named Tonio bullied me. Called me a suck-up and some other things."

"Doesn't sound like a nice kid. What did you do?"

"I mostly ignored him, but one day he beat the dog I was working with." He gritted his teeth at the memory. "I nearly decked him."

"Can't say as I blame you."

"If I had, I wouldn't have been able to leave when I did. I didn't want to mess that up. But I threatened him. Told him he'd be dead meat if he did that again."

"Would you have harmed him if he had?"

"I don't know." Marco clenched his fists. "I came real close to clobbering him. Going home with you was the only reason I didn't."

"You didn't act on your threat, and that's good. I'm proud of the way you handled the situation. What happened to Tonio?"

Marco shrugged. "He got transferred, that's all I know."

"Thanks for telling me about it."

"Just want you to know how important all this is to me."

Alex smiled and put his arm around Marco. "That, son, means a bunch to me. I'm glad you told me." Alex closed the tailgate on the pickup. "Load up. Let's go home."

Marco climbed in the passenger seat and Lucky followed, settling on the cab floor at Marco's feet. "Have you and Scott been fishing?"

"Nope. Wanted to do that with you first."

"Can we invite Scott next time?"

"If you want."

"Does he know? About me, I mean."

"No. I told you, it was up to you if you wanted people to know. Otherwise, it's our secret. No one needs to know unless you want them to."

"Okay."

~

Alex looked up from his paperwork and stared out the window of his home office. The first week of school had been an adjustment for Marco, but Scott had helped him settle in and introduced him around. He seemed to like the school and teachers.

He even likes spending time with me in the orchards, Alex thought. He's genuinely interested in learning about the fruit and how to take care of the trees. *Wait till spring, son, you'll get baptism by fire when the freezes hit.*

He and Marco had established a comfortable routine. They worked together fixing meals and cleaning the house. Marco was responsible for cleaning his own room and bathroom and needed little prodding from Alex.

Homework was done as soon as he got home from school. He and Scott sometimes studied together in the evening for tests in classes they shared. Even Lucky had adapted well and was learning all kinds of skills from Marco, who had a natural knack for working with dogs. Alex felt content for the first time in many years.

Alex loved attending the high school football games with Marco. Scott had won the starting quarterback position, unusual for a sophomore. They attended the away games as well, making Marco feel more a part of the school. Alex sat with Trish and Meghan, while Marco joined the kids in the student body section. The homecoming game in mid-October was no different. When the Eagles scored their first touchdown against their biggest rival, Trish hugged Alex. He liked the spontaneous affection from her. The Eagles cruised to an easy win, with Scott scoring one touchdown and passing for two more.

Alex couldn't help grinning over Marco's enthusiasm after the game. He high-fived Alex and Trish, a grin as wide as the Grand Canyon across his face.

"Man, that was awesome. We were the underdog, and we blew them away!"

"It was a good game," Alex said.

"So, there's a homecoming party after the game that Scott and I are invited to. Can I go?" Marco asked.

"Where's the party?"

"Some kid's house. I forgot."

"Not good enough. I need to know where and who."

"Danny Hirsh," Trish interjected. "His mother, Sarah Morgan, is my boss and his stepdad is Cam Morgan. Danny's a great kid. It should be fine. I told Scott he had to be home by midnight. Since it's homecoming, I'll give him a little leeway."

Alex looked at Marco. "It's fine. Curfew midnight. Be careful and enjoy yourself."

"Oh, and can I go to the homecoming dance tomorrow night?"

Alex grinned at Marco's enthusiasm. "I don't see why not."

"Thanks!" Marco yelled as he turned and jogged toward a group of kids celebrating the victory.

"I told Scott he could have the pickup tonight. Hope that's all right. He's been very responsible with his driving. And since he's had his license for a few weeks, he's allowed a passenger."

Alex hesitated a moment. He couldn't shake the uneasiness he felt. "I guess that's all right." At some point, he had to let go and trust. That's probably what was bothering him. He had kept Marco close since they'd gotten home. He needed to show Marco and Scott he trusted them. Now was as good a time as any.

"I'll need a ride home," Trish said.

"Be happy to accommodate you and Meghan. I think I know where you live."

"Meghan's staying the night with a friend, so it's just me. Can you handle that?" she asked, a twinkle in her eye.

"How about I treat you to some hot chocolate and Oreo cookies before I scc you home?"

"Sounds good. You're on."

~

Alex placed the package of Oreo cookies on the breakfast bar across from where Trish sat. "Two hot chocolates coming up."

He heated the milk, poured it over the packages of hot chocolate mix and carried the cups to the bar. As he set them down, he studied Trish. Her hair was in disarray from wearing a stocking cap, her nose and cheeks still a little red from the cold. She'd never looked more beautiful or inviting.

"You look great tonight, Trish."

She forked her fingers through her hair. "I'm a mess, but thank you."

Alex rounded the counter, turned Tish's stool around, and cupped her face with his hands.

"You look scrumptious," he said and kissed her.

She put her hands against his chest, putting a small gap between them. "Please, Alex. I'm not ready—"

Without removing his hands, he studied her face a moment. "When will you be ready? Time to stop being afraid and embrace the possibilities. I have no intention of hurting you. I'm not Clay, and I'm not Dale. I don't use or abuse women, I don't lie, I don't think I'm selfish, and I think I'm falling in love with you."

He kissed her again, and this time she didn't push him away. He stepped back and smiled at her. "That's better."
He could see tears form in her eyes, and he pulled her against him. "It wasn't that bad, was it?"

He heard a muffled giggle. At least he prayed that's what it was. "I hope you're laughing and not crying."

She lifted her head and leaned back to look at him. The

tears were evident, but she was smiling. "A little of both."

"And?"

"It wasn't so bad." She shrugged. "Okay, I liked it, but it scares me. I've had a hard time trusting men, and yet I find myself trusting you." She leaned against the counter and Alex moved back a fraction. "I see how much you love the orchards. I love the way you treat Scott and Meghan, and I've watched you with Marco. We seem to see eye to eye on most things. You're the kind of man my father and grandfather were."

"I consider that a compliment. So?"

"So, I find myself wanting to be with you." She winked at him. "I say let's try that again. I think I could get used to it."

He lifted her off the stool, stood her in front of him and kissed her, deep and long.

~

Scott motioned to Marco over the heads of the students crowded into the Morgan's living room. Marco worked his way to Scott.

"What's up?" Marco asked.

"Let's blow this joint," Scott said.

"Why? I'm having fun."

"Well, I'm not. I know where there's a better party." Scott waved at Danny Hirsh, their host. "Dude, we're headed out. Thanks."

Marco followed Scott out the door. "My Dad thinks I'm here."

"It's okay. We're just party hopping."

They worked their way down the street to Scott's pickup. Marco glanced back at the house and then looked into the pickup cab. He paused for a moment but got in. Scott drove out of town along a narrow road.

"Where are we going?" Marco asked.

"You'll see."

Marco noticed an orange glow in the distance, and as they got closer, he realized it was a large bonfire. Numerous kids—some he knew, some he didn't—were gathered around, laughing and drinking out of bottles.

Scott parked the pickup, and as they walked toward the crowd, Marco realized the party-goers were drinking beer. He suspected some were probably drinking whiskey or something like it.

"Scott, let's leave. We shouldn't be here."

"Come on, Marco. Live a little."

Marco frowned. "No. I don't need this."

"Don't be such a wuss. A little booze won't hurt. It's a party, man."

Marco stopped and shook his head. "I'll wait for you in the pickup. Be careful, dude. You shouldn't be drinking."

Scott waved him off and headed for one of the coolers a short distance away from the fire. Marco gritted his teeth and returned to the pickup. He waited for almost an hour, dozing once, but Scott hadn't returned. It was inching closer to midnight and their curfew. He went in search of Scott and found him weaving and slurring his words.

Grabbing Scott by the arm, he pulled him toward the

pickup. "Come on, Scott, we need to get home. It's almost midnight."

"You going to turn into a pumpkin?" Scott asked and burst out laughing.

"No, but you might."

Marco half dragged, half pushed Scott toward the pickup. "Give me your keys," Marco demanded.

"You can't drive, you don't have a license," Scott slurred.

"Tough. You're in no shape to drive."

"Oooh, you sound threatening." Scott pointed the beer he had in his hand at Marco. "I'm driving. Get in."

Marco tried to get Scott to hand over the keys, but Scott had already slid behind the wheel.

"Get in or I'll leave you here."

"You're too drunk to drive. Come on, give me the keys."

"Get in." Scott slurred.

Marco hesitated. He didn't want to ride with a drunk, but he didn't have any way to get home. Maybe he could at least keep Scott alert. Reluctantly, he climbed in the cab.

As Scott drove back the way they'd come, Marco noted he drove a little too fast and prayed they'd make it home without incident. He shook and his mouth went dry when he thought about what he'd done the one time he'd driven drunk. As they rounded a curve, headlights from another vehicle flashed in Marco's eyes.

"Look out!" Marco yelled. He grabbed the steering wheel and the pickup lurched toward the side of the road.

K.L. McKee

CHAPTER 15

Trish awoke with a start to someone pounding on the front door. Grabbing her robe, she hurried downstairs. She flipped on the porch light and peered out.

"Trish, open up."

The door flew open. "Alex, what are you doing here? What time is it?"

"Almost 1:30. Get dressed. The boys are in trouble."

"What?" She stood back to let Alex in. "Are they all right? What's going on?" She realized she hadn't heard Scott come home.

"I got a call from a Deputy Morgan. The boys are at the sheriff's office."

She'd fallen asleep thinking of Alex and the kisses they'd shared. She had felt warm, cherished, and truly happy for the first time in a very long time. Trish couldn't believe what she was hearing. Fear overtook her and washed away those feelings.

Alex grabbed her arm and pushed her toward the stairs. "Get dressed. *Now.*"

Halfway up the stairs she looked over her shoulder. "Why didn't they call me? Are they hurt?"

"I told Deputy Morgan I'd get you. At least they're not in the hospital. I was told they were being held, and we needed to get down there ASAP. *Now get dressed.*"

Trish raced up the stairs and threw on jeans and an old sweatshirt in record time. Alex was waiting in his pickup, the motor running. She grabbed a coat and joined him.

"I don't understand," she said as she fastened her seatbelt.

"Neither do I," Alex said and gunned the pickup toward town.

~

"I'm Kale Morgan," the deputy said and offered Alex his hand. "You must be Mr. Lambert." He nodded at Trish who followed Alex into the Sheriff's office. "Trish."

"Why didn't you call me first? I want to see Scott. Now!" Trish glared at Kale and then at Alex. "I should have known Marco would get Scott in trouble."

Alex touched her arm. "We don't know what's happened. Let's save judgment until we know the facts."

"Spoken like a true lawyer." She shrugged away from his hand.

"Trish, Mr. Lambert's right," said Kale.

Alex turned his attention to Deputy Morgan. "I prefer Alex. Where are the boys?"

"They're in separate interrogation rooms. I need to talk to both of you before you talk to the boys." He escorted the two of them to his office. Once they were all seated, he related what had happened.

"It seems the boys went to a party up Minnesota Creek with lots of alcohol available. On the way home, they were in an accident. Neither of them was hurt—a few bumps and bruises—but there was another car involved. The occupant of that car was pronounced dead at the scene."

Alex felt his stomach drop. This couldn't be happening again. Marco wouldn't have allowed it. His freedom was too important. Something wasn't right. *Please, God.*

"Scott wouldn't drink," Trish declared. "This has to be Marco's fault."

Kale held up his hand. "Scott *was* the one drinking, Trish, not Marco."

"What?"

Alex closed his eyes. *Thank you, God.*

"Marco tried to make it look like he'd been drinking, but he hadn't. I could tell that right away. Scott, on the other hand, had an alcohol level of .17. He's had some coffee and water. That and the accident have helped him sober up a little."

"I don't believe it," Trish reiterated. "Was Marco driving?"

"Believe it, and Marco wasn't driving, although he said

he was," Kale returned. "We have someone who witnessed the accident. She saw Marco exit the passenger side of the pickup and pull the deceased driver, Wes Johnson, from the car. He started CPR on Mr. Johnson and yelled at the witness to get help. She drove to the nearest house and called us.

"When I arrived, Marco smelled of beer, but it was obvious he hadn't been drinking, and the breathalyzer confirmed that, though I haven't shared the results with the boys. I suspect Marco poured beer over himself to make it look like he was drinking. If he'd been drunk, he wouldn't have reacted so fast to help the other driver. I suspect he's covering for Scott."

Alex wondered what Marco had been thinking. None of this made sense. Why would he make it look like he was at fault? He noticed tears in Trish's eyes.

"You must be wrong. Scott wouldn't . . ." Trish covered her mouth, unable to finish the sentence.

"A man died in the accident. That will affect the charges, won't it?" Alex already knew the answer, but he wanted Trish to hear it.

"Depends on the outcome of the autopsy. I've asked the coroner to put a rush on it for several reasons. The witness said she saw Mr. Johnson's car swerve into the boys' lane, not the other way around. Trish, you and I both know Wes Johnson was an alcoholic. The fact that his driver's license is suspended and that he had at least two heart attacks in the last year could put the accident in a different light." He looked at Alex and shrugged. "It's a small town.

"At any rate, I can't get the boys to change their stories.

They insist Marco was driving drunk. I think they're lying."

"What do you intend to do?" Alex asked.

"They both insisted they wanted to talk to you—their lawyer. I'm hoping you can get the truth out of them. I haven't mentioned the witness or our suspicion about Wes. A man died tonight. They need to think about that for a while. It's my belief that a big dose of fear and uncertainty is good to make adolescent boys think twice before doing something stupid again."

"I want to see Scott," Trish insisted.

"He says he's not ready to see you, which is why I didn't call you first. I'm going to honor that request for the moment. I promise, however, that you'll get to talk to him soon. You can wait in here or in the lobby."

"I have a right to see my son, Kale."

"In due time." Kale stood. "Alex, if you'll follow me, I'll let you talk to the boys. Which one first?"

"Marco."

"Alex, if you do anything to hurt Scott—"

"You *know* better than that, Trish." Alex glared at her. "We'll get to the bottom of this, but you need to take a deep breath. Praying wouldn't hurt."

Alex followed Kale to an interrogation room. Before entering the room, Kale stopped him.

"I know about Marco's record. It came up when we did a check. It's still active. I didn't want to say something in front of Trish."

Alex nodded and entered the room. Marco sat in a chair, his arms on the table and his head down. When Alex entered,

Marco looked up.

"Alex."

Alex sat beside him. "What happened to Dad?"

Marco shrugged. "I don't deserve to be your son." His voice caught. "Guess you'll cancel the adoption."

Alex felt a stab in his heart. How could Marco think that? "I don't know where that came from, but you are my son, and nothing will ever change that."

"But I messed up." Tears streamed down Marco's cheeks.

"Yes, you did. But that doesn't change how I feel about you. We'll see this through together and handle whatever comes."

Uncontrollable sobs racked Marco's body, and Alex held him, fighting back tears of his own. When Marco settled down, Alex asked the one question that burned inside him.

"Why did you lie about drinking and driving?"

Marco took several shuddering breaths. "I didn't. I drank too much, but I wasn't as drunk as Scott, so he let me drive."

Alex took a deep breath and sat in a chair next to Marco. "Marco, I know you better than that. You would never jeopardize your freedom. I've seen the resolve in you. Why are you protecting Scott?"

Marco shrugged.

"I can't help either one of you if you don't tell me the truth. For what it's worth, Deputy Morgan is sure you're lying." Alex squeezed Marco's shoulder. "The one thing I expect from you is the truth. How about it?"

Time clicked by. Alex waited.

Marco stood and paced, then turned to Alex. "I lied because I've been locked up. I know what it's like and I can handle it. Scott has a chance to get a football or baseball scholarship for college, but he won't if they find out he was drunk and driving." He fought back a sob. "That man died. They're not going to ignore that."

"And that's why you lied. Marco—"

"Scott's the only friend I've ever had. He's scared. I can deal with the consequences. He can't."

Alex stood and gathered Marco into his arms again. "It's great to be loyal to a friend, but you're not doing Scott any favors by lying for him. He needs to take responsibility for his actions just like you did five years ago. Otherwise, he'll believe he can get away with anything." Alex released Marco. "Think about that while I go talk to Scott."

"Please don't tell Scott about my past," Marco pleaded.

"Either you tell him or I will. I won't let you ruin your life. It's time he knew what you're giving up by lying for him. And if he's a real friend, he won't let you ruin your life." Alex turned the doorknob. "I love you, Marco. Nothing changes that."

When Alex entered Scott's interrogation room, Scott looked up and attempted a smile. His right eye was puffy and beginning to swell. "Bet you're not too happy with us, huh?"

"Wipe the smile off your face," Alex ordered. "This is nothing to take lightly. You've disappointed not only me, but your mom."

"So, I got a little high. It's nothing serious."

"You left the party you were supposed to be at, you got drunk and drove a vehicle while intoxicated, and were involved in an accident where someone died. And to top it off, you let a friend lie for you. I call that *very* serious."

"Marco was driving. I swear."

"A witness says different. Want to change your story?"

"What witness?"

"The one Marco sent for help while he tried to revive the other driver." Alex took a deep breath. The silence in the room was deafening. "I'm waiting."

Scott slumped in his chair and hung his head. "Hey, I didn't ask Marco to lie. He offered to say he was driving."

"No, but you *let* him lie for you."

Scott shrugged. "What difference does it make? He doesn't have a license to lose or a position on the football team to lose."

"Is that all that matters to you?" Alex rubbed his hand through his hair in frustration. "You're a better person than that. A man died in that accident, and Marco's being blamed."

Scott grimaced but said nothing.

"Why don't you ask Marco why he lied? You might be surprised. And don't let him convince you it's because you're his friend. Make him tell you the *real* story and the consequences of his taking the blame."

Alex turned to leave. "You're a good kid, Scott. What happened tonight doesn't reflect who you are or define you unless you let it. Think about that, and demand the truth—from yourself and Marco."

~

Trish paced Kale's office. Alex told her to pray. She'd tried. What was taking so long? She almost convinced herself that Marco was the cause of all the trouble. After all, he had a record. He'd been incarcerated for five years. Scott wouldn't jeopardize his starting position on the football team. Yet a feeling of uneasiness kept creeping back into her thoughts. Maybe Scott had a little too much of Clay in him.

She chastised herself for the thought. She had to stop blaming Clay for everything. Why wouldn't Scott talk to her? She resented Alex for getting to see her son before she did.

The office door opened and Kale walked in.

"*Now* do I get to see Scott?" Her tone was more sarcastic than she intended.

"At Alex's request, we're going to put the boys together and see what happens. Thought you'd like to listen in."

"I've known you a long time, Kale, and I'm not very happy with you right now. Why does Alex get his way, and I'm stuck wondering what's going on?"

"Because I think you'll be surprised at what you hear, and you need to hear it before you talk to Scott."

Trish followed Kale to a one-way window, allowing them to see into the room where both boys sat. Alex was already observing.

"So, what do you think?" She heard Scott ask Marco.

"We're in big trouble."

"Alex said there was a witness to the accident. Did you

203

know that?"

"Yeah."

Minutes passed before Scott spoke. "Why'd you lie for me?"

"Because you have a chance at a great future in sports. I didn't want that ruined for you."

Scott shrugged. "I might have been suspended for a couple of games for getting drunk."

"Dude, a man died. Do you know what that means?"

"He swerved into our lane. I remember that."

"Doesn't matter. He died. Do you *really* know what that means?"

Scott shrugged again.

"It means criminal action. It means getting locked up for vehicular homicide." Marco stood and paced the room.

Scott's face paled. "What do you mean, 'vehicular homicide'? How would you know?"

Marco turned and glared at Scott, his face red. "I just know, that's all!"

Scott stared at Marco, who tried to get control of his emotions.

"So tell me why you lied."

"Because you're my friend."

"Alex says there's more, and I should make you tell me the truth. Something about consequences."

Marco sat, leaned his arms on his legs, and stared at his shoes.

"Look, Marco, I have a right to know." He sighed. "Alex is right, a friend doesn't let a friend lie. So, I'm going to tell the truth—that I was driving."

"You can't."

"Why? *Tell* me."

Marco shook his head. "Because I know what it's like to be locked up for the same thing. It's horrible and you couldn't handle it!"

Scott's eyes got big. He rested his arms on the table. "Dude. You were in jail?"

"Youth services for five years. I was ten when it happened. They couldn't charge me as an adult, so I ended up in a youth facility in Denver."

"So who was killed?" Scott asked.

"Alex's family," Marco said quietly, a hitch in his voice.

Scott was silent for a few moments. "No way. If that's true, how come Alex adopted you?"

Marco half smiled and tears trickled down his face. "That's the million dollar question, isn't it? There's no way he should ever want anything to do with me, and yet I know he loves me. I don't deserve it, but he does."

"Man, I can't get my head around this."

"It's true. It happened."

"Tell me."

Marco related the story of how he had celebrated his birthday by driving drunk and killing Alex's family. As his story unfolded, Trish couldn't believe what she was hearing. She looked at Alex and noticed tears in his eyes. When Marco finished his story, including how Alex had forgiven him and then adopted him, Trish couldn't stand it any longer.

"Alex, is this true?"

He nodded.

"I'm so sorry. I didn't know."

He looked at her. "I'd just as soon no one did. Marco and I have both made a new start. That's why I wanted you to understand the significance of him lying for Scott. His freedom and a new start mean everything to him."

"But why did he lie for Scott if he knew he'd be put away again?"

"Because Marco values Scott's friendship more than his freedom."

"Oh." Trish had nothing more to say. She was overwhelmed with what she'd learned about Marco, and disappointed in what she'd discovered about Scott.

"I think we've heard enough," Kale said. "Let's get this straightened out."

The three adults joined the boys in the interrogation room. Kale took the lead. "So, boys, anything you want to add to what you've already told me?"

Scott looked at Alex. Alex nodded.

"I was driving," Scott said. "Marco didn't have anything to drink. He poured beer on himself to cover for me." Scott looked at Trish. "I'm sorry, Mom."

Trish's temper surfaced. For a moment she saw Clay, the resemblance between father and son uncanny. "How *could* you, Scott? You're just like—" She caught herself. "You *know* better than to drink. Or let someone lie for you."

"You were going to say I'm just like Dad."

Trish blinked. There was no denying . . . nothing she could say.

"You were. I hate Dad! I don't want to be anything like him. I want to be like Alex!" Scott burst into tears and Trish put her arm around him, letting him sob into her shoulder.

"You're not at all like your dad. You're a much better man than he was. And you're grounded." As she held Scott, she noticed Alex and Marco in an embrace and heard Alex tell Marco he knew his confession to Scott had been difficult and that he was proud of him.

Kale left the room for a few minutes. When he returned, he asked Alex to join him outside. Trish looked at Marco. He slumped in a chair with his chin resting on his chest.

"Marco," she said. He lifted his head. "I know it was difficult to share your story, but you've done Scott and me a great favor. You've shown us what love and forgiveness and loyalty are about. I'm glad to know you. You're a fine young man."

Marco smiled a little for the first time that evening. "Thanks. That means a lot."

"And so are you, Scott. Remember that," she said.

Kale and Alex returned and each settled in a chair.

Kale spoke. "Well, boys, Mr. Lambert and I have talked. As your lawyer, he has agreed to certain terms. Here's the scoop. We're waiting word from the coroner about the cause of Mr. Johnson's death. We suspect he was drunk and may have died of a heart attack. Our witness said he swerved into your lane. If our suspicions are correct, there will be no vehicular homicide charge."

A collective sigh could be heard throughout the room.

"However, there are consequences for driving drunk."

He looked at Scott. "I'll consider reducing the charge from a DUI to a DWI under two circumstances. Give me the name of the person or persons supplying the alcohol to underage kids, and first thing Monday morning, tell Coach Campbell what happened."

Scott's face reddened. "I'm not a snitch."

"It's in your best interest, Scott," Alex said. "A DWI isn't as serious as DUI."

"Everybody'll know it was me."

"We'll handle it so that it looks like the information came from another source" Kale said. "I promise you won't be implicated. The only people who will know are sitting in this room."

Scott looked at Alex, then at Trish. She nodded. "Tell him. Do *something* right tonight."

Scott stared at his hands. "Eddie Franklin. He's been doing it a long time."

"That corroborates what we already suspected. You did the right thing. And your coach? If you don't tell him, I will."

Scott nodded. "I'll tell him."

"Good. Since you've agreed to plead guilty to the charges, Scott, you won't need to see a judge. I'll need your license before you leave. It's been suspended for three months and four points will be taken away. Just remember, if the autopsy report comes back different from what we suspect, we have the right to change the charges and the consequences." Kale stood. "Marco, I'm impressed with the way you tried to save Mr. Johnson's life. That was admirable."

"I'm sorry he died."

"He was working on borrowed time as it was. I doubt he could have been saved. You boys can go home now. I don't *ever* want to see you back here unless you decide to go into law enforcement. That said, I think we're done here."

Once Kale was gone, Trish caught Scott's eye. "You're suspended from driving anything but the tractor and the four-wheeler for six months. *My* rules."

"Aw, Mom," Scott said as they left. But Trish could tell it was a half-hearted complaint. Scott knew he'd gotten off easy. What was it Kale said? Small town. Trish was never more grateful she lived in a small town.

Chapter 16

Alex dropped the pickup keys on the breakfast bar. He clamped his hand on Marco's shoulder. "Shower and go to bed. We'll talk in the morning."

Marco nodded. "I'm really sorry, Dad."

"I know. Get some sleep."

Alex settled in bed, closed his eyes, and contemplated the night's events. He'd made headway with Trish, until the call from Deputy Morgan. By the time the events played out at the sheriff's office, he was the bad guy again. His wife, Amy, had been so easy going. Trish was a challenge. Her Irish temper should have put him off, but he couldn't help being attracted to her. Give her time to settle down and think things out, he told himself. She'll come around . . . or she won't.

He felt for Marco. Freedom was a new concept to him, and he hadn't exercised it in the best way. Yet he'd had the good sense not to drink. He tried to save a man's life. That made Alex proud. Would another kid have done that? Alex fell asleep with a prayer of thanks on his lips.

~

"Are you up for all day?" Alex asked as Marco shuffled into the kitchen just after ten the next morning.

"Huh?"

"My dad always asked me that question when I slept in."

"Oh." Marco grabbed a glass and poured himself some milk.

"I made blueberry pancakes for breakfast. Yours are warming in the oven."

Marco smiled. "Thanks."

While Marco wolfed down the pancakes, Alex broached the events of the previous night.

"You know you were lucky last night that something worse didn't happen." Alex couldn't keep the sternness out of his voice.

Marco nodded. "I know. I'm really sor—"

"No more 'sorry.' I hope you've learned a good lesson from this." Alex frowned.

Marco grimaced. "Big time."

"So, from now on you'll think twice before getting yourself into a similar situation. Monday, I'll get you a cell phone. Next time something comes up—you break a shoestring, need a ride home, anything—you call. Anytime, anywhere. I'll come get you."

"Okay." He swallowed the last bite of pancake and shrugged. "Scott was my ride home. I was supposed to be with him, and I felt stranded. I didn't know he was going to a kegger."

"I understand. However, you should have stayed at Danny's and called me. At least you made the right decision about drinking. Drinking would have clouded your judgment, and you wouldn't have been much use to the other driver or Scott. No more lying. Period. It only causes problems. Understood?"

Marco's face paled. He set his fork down and nodded his head.

"You're grounded for two weeks. No video games, no football games or extra school activities. No Homecoming dance."

Marco half smiled. "That's a relief. I don't know how to dance, anyway."

"You will also write Deputy Morgan an apology for lying and thank him for keeping you out of trouble."

"Seriously?"

"Seriously."

"Okay." He finished the glass of milk. "Can I go work with Lucky?"

"You may."

Marco headed for the back door and glanced over his shoulder. "Thanks, Dad."

Alex smiled for the first time that morning.

Half an hour later, the doorbell rang. Alex opened the

door to Trish and Scott. "Come in. Coffee?"

Trish and Scott followed Alex to the kitchen. He placed a cup on the breakfast bar for Trish. "Scott?"

Trish looked pointedly at Scott. Scott shook his head and focused on the countertop for a moment before looking at Alex. "I'm really sorry for what happened. I shouldn't have let Marco lie for me."

"Apology accepted. Don't do it again. And no more drinking."

"I won't. I promise." Scott fidgeted. "And thanks for bailing me out."

The corner of Alex's mouth twitched. "That's what your lawyer is supposed to do." With a nod of his head, Alex indicated the back door. "Marco's out working with Lucky. Go on out."

Scott wasted no time hitting the back door.

"I came to apologize, too," Trish said. "I wasn't very nice to you, and I prejudged Marco. I should have had enough patience to wait and find out what happened."

"Again, apology accepted. In all fairness, you reacted the way any parent would."

"But you didn't react that way."

Alex grimaced. "You have no idea. I was fuming. I had to work not to show it."

"You have better resolve than I do."

He winked. "I guess the lawyer side of me kicked in."

She took a deep breath. "I'm still trying to get my head around what Marco told Scott." Tears glistened in her eyes. "I can't fathom that kind of forgiveness. How did you do it?"

"Let's sit." Alex indicated the breakfast nook. "I'll tell you how and why."

~

Scott slumped onto a patio chair and watched as Marco worked with Lucky. Marco gave no verbal commands, only hand signals, and Lucky responded to each one. After a few minutes, Marco verbally commanded Lucky to stay and joined Scott on the patio.

"Hey," Marco said.

"Hey."

A slight breeze ruffled the dry leaves on the lawn. A robin swooped to the ground a few yards away and hopped several paces before flying off.

"So, where'd you learn to do that?"

Marco shrugged. "Read some books, then started working with a volunteer at the youth facility. He showed me how to train dogs. I trained service dogs for people."

He held his palm out at his side. Lucky trotted over to him. Marco then moved his hand up as if to touch his shoulder. Lucky sat. From his shoulder, Marco moved his hand toward the ground, palm-down. Lucky lay down.

"Cool, but why the hand signals?"

"Some people can't speak, but they can use hand signals. It's nice to train the dogs to respond to both."

Scott nodded. "Does she only respond to you?"

"Unless I tell her to mind someone else." He looked at Lucky, moved his hand from his side and toward the back. Lucky stood. "Lucky, go to Scott." Marco pointed to Scott.

215

Lucky trotted over to Scott and stood in front of him.

"She'll respond to you until I tell her otherwise."

"Does she respond to words?"

"Yep."

Scott smiled and looked at Lucky. "Sit."

Lucky sat, and Scott patted her. "Good girl."

Marco grinned. "Verbal rewards are always good. Lucky." Marco patted his chest and Lucky moved to where Marco sat. He moved his arm with palm-down to the ground. Lucky settled at Marco's feet. Marco pulled a treat out of his pocket and gave it to her. "Good girl."

"So," Scott ventured, "I'm really sorry about last night. I just wanted to have some fun."

"Guess we'd better figure out something else to do for fun, huh?"

Silence filled the space between them.

"Look, I shouldn't have let you lie for me. I was scared."

"Yeah, I know."

Scott looked at Marco. "So why did you?"

"You're my friend. I didn't want you to mess up your life."

"But you—"

"Been there, done that."

"Thanks, man."

Marco smiled and gave Scott a light punch on the arm. "Last time, dude. Won't do it again."

Scott grinned. "Won't ask you to. Man, I have one nasty headache."

"I'm grounded," Marco said, "so can't go to the dance

tonight."

"Me, too. Two weeks for sure."

"Two weeks for me, too."

"Mom won't let me get my license for six months. That sucks."

"Better than not getting it at all."

Scott smiled. "Guess so."

~

Trish listened as Alex told her all that had transpired after the accident that killed his family. He explained that hate and bitterness had nearly destroyed him.

"I needed to talk to Marco and find out why he did what he did. I also needed to forgive him. What I didn't expect was to have a relationship with him. I just wanted answers. I nearly lost my job by visiting him. But it was worth the risk. Now look at us." Alex smiled. "Never in a million years did I expect to love Marco, let alone accept him as my son. God is amazing in the miracles He brings about."

Trish fiddled with her coffee cup. She felt a tear wet her cheek. "You never cease to amaze me, Alex. You have such a big heart."

He put his arm around her shoulders and pulled her against him. "It's God who has the big heart. He's forgiven worse." He kissed the top of her head. "Just let go, Trish. Don't fight it. I got tired of fighting God. Something finally cracked open in me. I began to see things in a new light. He made me a new man. Gave me a new life."

A sob escaped Trish. "I struggled for so long trying to

make a hopeless marriage work. It hurts to admit failure. It's not in my nature. I would be lying if I said otherwise." She looked up at Alex. "Will you stick with me? Help me get it right?"

Alex rubbed her arm. "With God's help, I think we can make that happen."

Trish nodded and relaxed against Alex. She was falling in love with this strong and gentle man. And for the first time in many years, she wasn't afraid to let go, as Alex suggested. She'd have to trust God to do the leading and the healing. Not easy for her.

~

Scott's backpack thudded to the floor. He tugged open the refrigerator.

Trish stopped peeling a potato and turned from the sink. "Deputy Morgan called this afternoon." Scott turned to look at her, a bottle of milk in his hand. "Mr. Johnson's blood alcohol level was .2, and he had a massive heart attack. The coroner figures that he either swerved into your lane because he was drunk, or the heart attack caused him to swerve. Either way, Mr. Johnson is responsible for the accident and consequently his death. You'll only be charged with the DWI."

Scott set the milk on the counter. "I'm sorry about Mr. Johnson."

"Your driving suspension still stands."

Scott nodded.

Trish knew Scott hated riding the bus, but that was the

consequence of losing his license. He was fortunate that was all he lost. "So what did Coach Campbell have to say?"

Scott poured a glass of milk, grabbed a handful of cookies, and settled at the kitchen table. "I'm suspended from playing for two weeks. I can still practice, but no games."

"I think you got off easy."

"Guess so, but it still sucks."

Meghan dropped her school books on the table. "So how long before Scott can drive me places again?"

"Six months."

"That *really* sucks." She slumped onto a kitchen chair.

"Maybe so, but that's the way it is."

"Thanks a lot, Scott. You had to go and get drunk. You messed up my life."

Scott frowned at her. "I'm the one who can't drive, so quit bellyaching."

Meghan grabbed her books and a couple of cookies. "Who's going to take me to soccer practice?" She took a bite of cookie. "My friends were jealous of me having my big brother take me places. Their mom's take them."

"Well, you're stuck with this mom taking you places for a while, so get used to it," Trish said.

"It still sucks. And I *hate* riding the bus." Meghan moved toward the stairs. "I have studying to do."

Scott stood and grabbed his books. "Sometimes little sisters can be a real drag."

Trish turned her back and smiled. "And sometimes big brothers can be, too. You're lucky to have each other. I wasn't so lucky."

"Whatever," Scott said as he headed for his room.

~

West Texas, October 2008

Clyde Johnson settled in the worn brown recliner that occupied one corner of his small apartment. He scanned the sports page of the *North Fork Weekly*, looking for news about Scott Ryan. Clyde, as he was known, left the name Clay Ryan behind after the accident. Clay Ryan didn't exist anymore, but he couldn't help wondering how Scott was doing. After he'd gotten a roustabout job in the oil fields of West Texas, he'd ordered his hometown newspaper so he could at least see if Scott was pursuing sports. It made him proud to discover that Scott was starting quarterback as a sophomore. He regretted he couldn't be at the games to cheer him on.

"That's the price I paid for getting out of my debts," he muttered, "and out of my marriage. Not so sure it was worth it, though, if I can't be there to see Scott play."

He'd felt such euphoria when he first walked away from the wreck. He'd taken the time to exchange clothes and IDs with his unconscious passenger before he sent the gas truck over the edge of the highway. They had visited enough for Clay to discover that Clyde Johnson was an orphan. He'd run away from foster homes numerous times until he was sixteen, and then he wandered from state to state, finding odd jobs, never staying in one place for long. He was four years older than Clay, but they looked somewhat alike. Once Clay grew a full beard, he resembled Johnson's worn photo enough that he could pass for him. Johnson carried his Social Security card in his wallet, so Clay easily made the transition to a new identity. Freedom never felt so good. No more nagging, no more driving a lousy gas truck. Johnson was a drain on society, anyway. Good riddance.

He'd lucked into his oil field job and was making over $70,000 a year. He had money to do anything he wanted. No obligations to anyone but himself. He didn't mind the small apartment. Cheap rent with enough money left over to spend on a fancy pickup and anything else he wanted. No more getting permission from Trish for how he spent his money.

Life was great, but he was missing out on his son's activities. Maybe, just maybe, he thought, there was a way to get it all back—his family, everything. He didn't hate Trish. He hated the orchards. He hated North Fork where everyone knew his history. In West Texas, all people cared about was whether you did your job or not.

He'd seen in the paper where Trish had sold most of the orchards. Maybe she was tired of them, too. A plan began to form in his mind. He could claim amnesia. Something could happen to trigger his memory. He'd reconcile with Trish and move his family to Texas. Texas was known for its outstanding football teams. Scott could really go places with a great program behind him. Pro football wasn't unattainable for someone like Scott if he had the right experience in a place bigger and better than North Fork.

Clay put the paper down, picked up the television

remote and smiled to himself. Clyde Johnson was a person of the past. He would reclaim his name and his family. Tomorrow he would go to the library—okay, he hated libraries. Maybe he could Google amnesia and read up on it. He'd have to be convincing or it wouldn't work. Patience. He'd need to exercise patience to pull it off, but it could be done. He was sure of it.

He opened his laptop and began to implement his plan. Boy would Scott be surprised. Trish would take some convincing. He'd have to turn on the charm, but that was easy for him. He'd charmed her into the backseat of his car when he was in high school. Of course, that had led to a forced marriage, which he hadn't planned on. He almost walked out when Trish lost the baby, but then she got pregnant again and Scott was the result. Meghan had come along, too, but she wouldn't be playing sports or have a shot at going pro. He supposed a daughter was okay. Maybe she could marry a pro player. Whatever. Scott was his main focus. He needed his son.

"North Fork, look out. I'm comin' home and claiming my family. And nobody's going to stop me."

CHAPTER 17

February 2009

Trish looked up from the Reference desk as Alex walked toward her. How did she always sense when he was near?

He smiled as he approached. "I hear there's a damsel in distress needing a ride home. Know where I might find her?"

"You're a tad early. We don't close for another fifteen minutes."

"Don't want you going out in the dark alone. No telling what kind of dragons await."

Trish laughed. "Okay, Sir Knight, I'll be ready shortly."

As Trish settled in Alex's pickup, she apologized. "I'm sorry you had to come out so late to get me. I barely made it to town this afternoon before my pickup quit right in the middle of the street. Vince at the gas station was kind enough to give me a tow. He said the fuel pump died. It'll be a day or two before it's fixed."

Alex reached for her hand and held it. "I don't mind at all giving you a ride. Anytime. You know that."

"Thanks, anyway. Now all I have to do is figure out how to get to work the next couple of days."

"As I see it, you have two choices. Either I can take you and pick you up, or you can borrow the Expedition for a couple of days. Personally, I like the idea of chauffeuring you." He squeezed her hand. "But I trust you with the Ford if you'd rather."

"How can I resist being chauffeured? Are you sure it won't inconvenience you?"

"Nope. Have to stop by the law offices anyway."

He parked the pickup in front of her house. Instead of letting go of her hand, he pulled her close to him and kissed her.

Trish melted into the kiss, relishing every moment. She treasured this man who had restored her heart, her faith in men, and possibly her faith in marriage. She pulled away, her heart racing. Her kids had mentioned marriage a few months ago, and she'd felt that same flutter of panic at the thought. Marriage and intimacy frightened her. Alex had never mentioned getting married, so where had that thought come from? Was she really ready for such a big step? Was he? Their relationship was going somewhere, but marriage?

"Are you okay?"

"Fine." She gave him a quick kiss. "Just tired. I think I'd better go in. I have to be at work at eight in the morning. Makes for a short night."

"I'll see you about 7:45 then. Sleep tight."

Trish waved at Alex from the door before going inside. After shedding her coat, she settled on the bay window seat and stared at the star-studded night sky. She loved living away from the city lights. The night sky, carpeted with millions of twinkling lights, gave her solace. She'd come a long way since she'd sold the orchards to Alex. Although something she thought she'd never have to do, the sale had actually given her new life, new hope, and a new outlook. She was beginning to believe that God *did* work for the good of all and happy endings were possible.

Alex was part of her new-found attitude. Love had blossomed between them. Many a Saturday night or Sunday noon the two families shared a meal either at Alex's or in her home. Laughter filled the room as they ate, and when they pulled out a board game, lots of good-natured teasing ensued. The three kids tried hard to beat Alex and Trish at Trivia or Apples to Apples. They fared better at a fast-paced card game called Imp.

Just before Thanksgiving, Meghan had confronted Trish during supper about her relationship with Alex. "So, Mom, are you and Alex an item?"

Scott cleared his throat. "Yeah, Mom, what gives? Everybody's talking about you two."

Trish reddened. "Who's talking?"

"All the kids." Meghan giggled. "They want to know if

you're 'doing it'."

"Absolutely not! You can put that rumor to rest immediately."

"So, what does give between you two?" Scott asked.

Trish smiled. She and Alex had tried to be careful around the kids, but agreed to be honest with them if they suspected anything. "I guess you could say we're an item. We care a great deal about each other." She picked up her empty plate and carried it to the sink. Turning toward the table she asked, "What do you two think? Is it all right?"

Scott shrugged. "Fine with me. I like Alex. If you're happy, then go for it."

"Meghan?"

"I think it's romantic. Are you going to get married?"

Trish fought down the rush of panic she felt. "We haven't talked about that. We're taking things slow for now. Getting to know each other."

"If you get married, where will we live?" Meghan had asked. "Here or at Alex's? I really like his house."

"I think you're getting ahead of yourself, Meghan. Let's just enjoy things the way they are right now."

The conversation ended and the kids headed to their rooms to do homework. Trish had pondered their reaction for the rest of the night. At least they had seemed okay with Alex. Since that conversation, she hadn't thought about marriage until tonight. Why did she always panic at the thought of marriage?

Trish and Alex worked in harmony in the orchards, Alex easily demonstrating his know-how from growing up in the business—like riding a bike, he told her. They had gotten a good start on pruning for the year. The winter had been more open—slightly warmer and drier—than usual, and less snow made it easier to access the orchards. Manuel, along with a small crew, helped with the work. Seldom speaking, she and Alex communicated by gestures and looks as they pruned the trees. Marco and Scott kicked brush, putting the trimmings in the open space between rows to be picked up later and burned. Trish took comfort in knowing Alex loved the fruit as much as she did.

Scott and Marco helped as their time away from school and sports allowed. On the days they all put in long hours, Meghan fixed supper. She was actually becoming a pretty good cook and loved doing it. Marco asked endless questions about the fruit and took to orchard work like he'd done it all his life. Scott still grumbled a little about getting out in the cold, but held his own. Life was good.

Trish smiled at the change in Scott since the accident. His grades were up, and he had taken on more responsibility at home and at school. Both boys were involved in basketball, which kept them busy throughout the week and most Friday and Saturday nights. Scott and Meghan were getting along better, and Marco fit right in. He teased Meghan like he was her brother, but she didn't seem to mind. She gave as good as she got.

Trish rose from the window seat and climbed the stairs to her room. Lights were still on in the kids' rooms. She knocked on both doors as she passed. "I'm home. Sleep tight."

"Night, Mom," came from both rooms.

Trish showered and settled into bed, but her mind refused to shut down. The holidays had been split. Alex declined Trish's invitation for Thanksgiving dinner. He and Marco spent the holiday in Palisade with Alex's family. For Christmas, however, Alex invited Trish and the kids to his house to meet his family. The love Alex's family shared was contagious; they laughed, played games, sang Christmas songs, and stuffed themselves with ham, sweet potatoes, green bean casserole, homemade rolls and delicious desserts that Alex's mother and sister-in-law had made. The day reminded her of the way things were when she was young, and Trish relished every moment.

The latter part of October, Trish, Alex, and Jess Atkins had begun working on plans to form a land trust in Delta County. True to his promise, Alex wanted to put some of his orchard land into the trust to preserve it for agricultural use, not housing developments. The three of them had worked evenings and weekends to put it all together, using the resources of the Mesa Land Trust in neighboring Mesa County as a model.

In a few days they would present their plan to a meeting of farmers and ranchers in the North Fork area. Trish closed her eyes and said a prayer for success. And then she asked for guidance where Alex was concerned. She still wasn't sure she was ready for a more committed relationship with him. She hadn't been successful in her first marriage. Was she cut out to be a wife, or would she be better off staying single?

~

Jess Atkins called the meeting to order. Jess, Trish, and Alex sat at a table at the front of the meeting hall. The room was packed with local cattle ranchers, fruit growers and farmers. Trish noticed Dale Thorndyke sitting in the middle of the room. Biting her lip, she hoped he wouldn't cause trouble. He'd be at least one voice of strong dissention. Realizing she was clenching her hands, she took a deep breath and tried to relax.

"Thank you for coming tonight," Jess said. "We've asked you here to present a unique idea for preserving the agricultural land in this valley. I'm going to turn the meeting over to Alex Lambert and let him explain what we're proposing."

Alex stood, placed an apple on a cutting board and picked up a knife. "This apple represents the earth." He sliced the apple into quarters and set aside three of the pieces. "These three quarters represent the oceans of the world.

"The fourth quarter roughly represents the total land area left." He sliced the quarter in half. Setting aside one eighth, he explained, "This piece represents the land inhospitable to people—the polar areas, deserts, swamps, and very high or rocky mountainous areas. The other eighth is land area where people live but do not necessarily grow the foods needed for life."

He picked up the knife again and sliced that eighth into four pieces, each representing one thirty- second of the earth. Setting aside three of those pieces, he said, "These pieces are

229

areas that are too cold, too steep, or with soil too poor to actually produce food. They also include areas of land that could produce food, but are buried under cities, highways, shopping centers, suburban developments, and other structures built by people.

"This leaves us with a one thirty-second slice of earth. Carefully peel this slice," he demonstrated, then held up the skin, "and you have the surface, the very thin skin, of the earth's crust upon which humankind depends. Less than five feet deep, it is a fixed amount of food-producing land."

Alex waited for a few moments to let the demonstration sink in. A small buzz of conversation filled the room.

"As food producers," he continued, "we must find a way to preserve this precious land for agriculture, or our world will face an even bigger challenge than it's already facing—worldwide hunger, not just in third world countries, but right here." He cleared his throat. "Jess, Trish, and I have been working on a way for landowners to put their acreage into a land trust, still maintain ownership, parent-to-child inheritance, and retain the right to sell it. The stipulation is that the land will always remain in the trust, and when it is sold, it must be used for agricultural purposes.

Mesa County has done this successfully with the Mesa Land Trust. We propose to do the same thing here. We've already filed papers with the IRS and are ready to move forward. I will put sixty acres of my fruit orchards into the trust. Trish has also put her five acres of apples into the trust. Jess has added 100 acres of his ranch. As you can see with Jess's contribution, the acres in the trust don't have to be contiguous. We hope others will follow suit."

Alex returned to his seat.

"How does this work?"

"What's in it for us?"

Questions came from around the room.

Jess stood. "We've filed for a 501 (c) 3 organization. Money for the trust to function will need to be donated. I've put in $20,000 to get us started. For every conservation easement in the trust, with the stipulation of non-public access, a qualified appraiser for the IRS must do the property valuations. We know your land is worth more if you sell it for housing developments, so you'd be foregoing the option of ever subdividing your property, but you will pay less in taxes because of the valuation as agriculture. With the money given to the trust, we will also have the ability to put claims on property in arrears. Because of the hard work that Mesa Land Trust has already done, we will have an easier time getting our trust set up."

"So the land would still be ours," said an older man wearing a well-worn cowboy hat, scuffed boots and Levis, "to do as we please, and it will not be open to the public, as long as we grow or produce food."

"That's right, Tom" Jess answered. "The land is still yours, it's still private property, and you can sell it whenever you want, but it will always remain agricultural."

Dale Thorndyke stood. "Everyone here should think very carefully about giving up your rights to your land. You can make a lot more money if you let someone like me develop it. People still need places to live."

Tom turned in his chair and squinted in Dale's direction. "Well, they aren't going to live very long if they run out of food." Laughter rippled through the crowd. Tom stood and addressed Jess. "I like what you're doing. My family's been ranching here for over a 100 years. We don't know, or want to know, any other kind of life. I'll consider putting three-fourths of my land into the trust."

Jess smiled. "Thanks, Tom. That means a lot."

A younger man stood. "I'd like to consider putting some of Karlson Dairy and our irrigated lands into the trust. Is that possible?"

"Absolutely, Jake." Jess answered. "Dairies are food producers by definition."

From the back of the room, JD MacCord stood. "I'll put all but 10 acres of my land into the trust, and I'll donate $500,000 to the trust to secure land for the future."

Jess smiled. "Thank you, JD. That's very generous."

Murmurs ran through the crowd, and then applause resounded throughout the room.

"You people are crazy." Dale Thorndyke stood and surveyed the room. "Just because some rich and famous movie star is willing to throw his money and land away, doesn't mean you need to follow suit."

A few boos and comments of "Shut up, Thorndyke" echoed throughout the room. Dale turned red and stormed from the meeting. Trish grinned at his receding back.

"Unless there are further questions," Jess continued, "I'll adjourn this meeting. We'll meet again in a few weeks to elect a board of directors. For those of you ready to be part of the trust, you can call my office and make an appointment. In the meantime, if you have questions, feel free to call me or Alex. Thank you for coming."

"We did it!" Trish high-fived Alex and Jess. *Thank you, Lord, for a successful meeting.*

Alex hugged her and shook hands with Jess. "Nice to have JD MacCord's support."

"It is," Jess answered. "He's my brother-in-law, but I didn't twist his arm. Just invited him to the meeting. Come on. I'll introduce you."

~

Trish placed a mug of coffee on her kitchen table for Alex. Cradling her own cup, she sat next to him. "I'm so relieved the meeting went well. I hope more landowners will join us."

"It doesn't hurt that Tom Watson and JD MacCord were on board. I'm still reeling from JD's monetary contribution. That will help insure the trust will be successful."

Trish laid her hand on Alex's arm. "Thank you for following through on the promise you made me when you bought the orchards. I was skeptical and shouldn't have been."

"Agricultural land is too precious to leave it to land developers." He winked at her. "I don't think Thorndyke was too happy with what transpired."

"That's his problem."

Alex leaned toward her. "And you're mine." He kissed her lightly on the lips.

"You think I'm a problem?"

"Let's just say you have me wrapped around your little finger, but I'm not complaining."

They kissed again, deeper and longer. Trish's heart sang.

"Enough already." Meghan stood in the doorway.

A flush warmed her cheeks, and Trish smiled sheepishly. "Never. Do you need something?"

"Came to get a snack."

"Where are the boys?"

"In Scott's room playing video games."

Alex rose and took his mug to the sink. "Tell Marco it's time to go home. Tomorrow's a school day." When Meghan was gone, Alex pulled Trish to her feet. "So, what are you doing Valentine's Day?"

"No plans that I know of."

"Good. I'll take you out to dinner. I think the boys are going to the school dance that night. Can Meghan stay by herself for a while?"

"She can, but she may decide to stay with a friend. We'll figure it out." Heavy footsteps pounded on the stairs. "Sounds like the boys."

Alex kissed her again. "Good night." He met Marco at the foot of the stairs. Trish locked the door behind them and waited until the taillights disappeared before heading to bed. As she snuggled under the covers, she thanked God for Alex. She couldn't imagine life getting any better. She was content for the first time in many years.

~

At home, Alex hung his coat in the hall closet. The taste of Trish's lips still lingered.

"Night, Dad."

"Wait a minute, Marco. I want to talk to you."

"Something wrong?" Marco looked a bit apprehensive.

Alex smiled. "I hope not."

They settled in the living room. Alex leaned his arms on his legs and cleared his throat. "I want to ask Trish to marry me. But I need your permission first."

Marco smiled. "You don't need my permission."

"Yes, I do. You and I are a family. A pretty new family at that. Asking Trish to marry me changes the dynamic by three, and that effects both of us, but especially you."

"Well . . ." Marco hesitated and Alex held his breath. "I think you should. I like Trish. She'd make a great mom. I'd also gain a brother and sister. That's cool. Never had that before."

Alex sighed in relief. "Asking her is only the first step. She could say 'no.'"

"I don't think so." Marco stood. "She'll say yes. When are you going to ask her?"

"Valentine's Day." Alex rose and looked at Marco. "Is that too corny?"

"Nah." Marco hugged Alex. "'Night, Dad."

"Good night, son." Alex watched Marco take the stairs two at a time. Life had a way of inserting the unexpected. Five years ago, if someone had told Alex he'd have a nearly

235

grown son, let alone be contemplating marriage at this point in his life, he would have called them crazy. The twists and turns of the last six years had led him to a stronger faith, a forgiving heart, and endless possibilities. God was truly great.

CHAPTER 18

"Mom," Meghan yelled, "you got flowers!"

Trish looked up as Meghan entered the kitchen with a large vase of light-orange roses and baby's breath.

"Are you going to throw these away like you did the last ones?"

Trish chuckled. "Depends on who they're from."

"I bet they're from Alex." Meghan wiggled her eyebrows.

"Let's find out." Trish pulled the card from the holder.

Looking forward to tonight.

Alex

"You're right. They're from Alex. I'm definitely keeping them."

"Crap." Meghan turned and rushed to the stairs. "I gotta

finish packing. Janna's mom is picking me up in ten minutes!"

Trish breathed in the sweet scent of the roses. These were more beautiful and more meaningful than the ones Dale had sent. How had Alex known she liked orange shades of roses, not red?

~

Alex dropped Marco off at Trish's when he picked her up for their Valentine's date. Scott and Marco had their own plans for the evening, going stag to the school's Valentine dance.

"I thought you didn't know how to dance?" Alex asked Marco when he had learned of Marco's plans to attend the dance.

Marco had shrugged and smiled. "Scott and Meghan have been showing me some moves." He moved his hips and arms like he'd been dancing all his life. They both laughed.

Before leaving with Alex, Trish planted herself between the boys and the television. "No alcohol. No leaving the dance early to go anywhere else. Come straight home after the dance. Curfew is midnight."

"I *know*, Mom." Scott rolled his eyes. "You don't have to tell me a million times."

Marco clamped his hand on Scott's shoulder. "Hey, man, don't feel singled out. I got the same lecture at home. They have to tell us those things." He glanced at Alex and Trish. "Maybe you should just say 'rules three, six, and nine. We'd know what you mean." He grinned.

Alex laughed. "Okay. Three, six, and nine, and don't forget ten." He winked.

~

Alex chose a restaurant thirty miles away in Delta, far from the prying eyes of North Fork residents. He wanted the night to be special for the two of them. He hadn't decided how he was going to pop the question, which made him nervous, but the ring was secure in his jacket pocket. While waiting for Trish to finish getting ready, Alex had taken Scott aside.

"I'd like permission to ask your mom to marry me."

Scott stared at him for what seemed like an eternity. "Seriously?"

"Seriously."

"So why ask me?"

"Because you're the man of the house, and it's important to me that you approve."

Scott hung his head for a moment. When he looked at Alex, moisture had gathered in his eyes. "Thanks for thinking of me that way." He stared at the floor. "I know my dad was a jerk to my mom and did some things he shouldn't have, but sometimes I still expect him to walk through the door and tell me we're going fishing. Is that crazy?" He looked at Alex.

Alex put his hand on Scott's shoulder. "No, Scott, it's not. You loved your dad, and you did a lot of special things together. It's natural to miss him."

"Thanks."

Alex smiled. "That said, I still want your permission to marry your mom."

"Mom's really been happy lately. She even sings sometimes when she thinks she's alone." He took a deep breath. "Big decision . . . but I say go for it. If she's says 'no' I'll have a talk with her." He grinned, and Alex had relaxed.

~

Alex and Trish lingered over chocolate sundaes. She wore a peach long-sleeved dress accented with a matching orange and green floral scarf.

"You look beautiful tonight," Alex remarked. The vibrant colors of the scarf brought out the green of her eyes and complimented her dark red hair. She glowed with the radiance of a precious jewel.

Trish blushed. "Thank you."

"That color suits you well."

"One of my favorites, besides shades of green."

"Both bring out the color of your eyes. I like that."

She dipped her head and smiled, before taking her last bite of sundae. Watching her across their small table, Alex decided the restaurant wasn't the place to ask her to marry him. He wanted to be alone with her.

"Let's go," he said as soon as they finished eating. He paid the check and ushered her to the pickup. They drove toward North Fork, but instead of going home, Alex detoured and turned onto the road that wound out of town toward Overland Reservoir. Finding a turnout that overlooked the valley, Alex parked and killed the engine.

Trish turned toward him, impishness reflecting in her eyes. "My dad always warned me about 'parking' with a guy."

"You want me to take you home?"

She shook her head and laughed. "No. Dad wouldn't have worried knowing I found a guy like you." With a more serious tone, she said, "I trust you Alex, and that hasn't been easy for me." She lowered her head for a moment, and then stared out the windshield. A three-quarter moon shone brightly over the valley and surrounding mountains. Lights flickered and shone throughout North Fork. "It's a beautiful evening."

"And I'm spending it with a beautiful woman." Alex lifted the console that divided them, opening the seat between. He wanted no barriers keeping them apart. He reached in his pocket and handed a small velvet box to Trish. "I got you a little something," he said.

She took the box, a slight frown forming on her brow. "The roses were enough. I love them. By the way, how did you know I like the orange hues?"

He shrugged. "I didn't. You just don't seem the red-rose type." He nodded toward the box. "I hope you'll like this even better."

She opened the box. A round solitaire diamond set in a rose-gold band sparkled in the dim light. Tears filled her eyes and streamed down her cheeks.

"Marry me, Trish. I love you. I didn't think I'd ever love again, but you've changed that. We make a great team, and I can't imagine my life without you, or the kids."

"Oh, Alex." A sob caught in her throat.

Fearing that she'd turn him down, he forged ahead. "I've already asked Scott for permission. He said it was okay. Marco is on board with it, too. I'm sure we can get Meghan's approval—"

Trish put her hand on Alex's mouth. "Shush. You're rambling." She took a deep breath. "The answer is maybe."

His stomach dropped, and he stared at her. "Maybe?" He glanced away. "That's not what I expected." Taking her face in his hands, he smoothed away her tears with his thumbs. "I've upset you. Not my intention. Explain 'maybe'."

Trish looked down at the ring box and closed it. "It's about dreams. Making a difference. Wanting to make the world a better place."

Alex sat back and slowly shook his head. "You're not making sense. What dreams?"

"Yours." Trish sniffed. "I know what it's like being married to someone who doesn't share your dreams. Someone who fights you all the way." She found a tissue in her purse and blew her nose.

"I'm confused. I don't see you fighting me. We both love the orchards."

"Clay hated the orchards. He even hated my dream of becoming a librarian. When I told him I'd support his getting a degree, he said that was my dream, not his.

"We also have to consider that if we got married, the kids and I would most likely move into your house. It's more spacious and would work better for all of us. You have enough bedrooms for each of the kids to have their own. I don't."

"If you want to stay in your house, we can make it work." Alex searched her face. "Is that what this is about?"

"It's not about my house." She placed her hand along his cheek. "You built your house so that you could help boys like Marco. That won't be possible with all of us living there." She bit her lip. "I don't want to take that dream away from you. But I think the five of us adjusting to living together and being a family will be challenging enough."

Alex let out a breath and grinned. "Is that all? No wonder I love you so much." He kissed her lightly on the lips.

"Alex, this is serious."

"I know." He took her hand. "I came to the same conclusion when I realized how much I love you. You're right, blending two families together is challenge enough. Truth is, I don't need to take on troubled boys right now. Marco and I are still adjusting in some ways. If God wants *us*—you and me—to help troubled boys in the future, He'll show us how. But I'm convinced now is not the time."

Alex took the ring box from her hand, removed the diamond, and held it up. "This means I've put aside one dream for a new dream. One that's much more important to me." He slipped the ring on her finger. "God brought us together and that's what counts. If your answer is no, then just take the ring off and hand it back. If your answer is yes, the ring stays where it is." He looked into her eyes, hoping for the right answer.

243

Trish closed the empty velvet box he held and smiled.

Alex gathered her in his arms, pulled her close, and soundly kissed her. "I know we can make this family work." He kissed her again, long and deep. Holding her tightly, he vowed he'd never let her go. God had given them both a second chance at love. He wasn't going to squander it.

~

Alex stopped the pickup in front of Trish's house. "There's a light on in Scott's room. Do you think everything's okay? It's only 11:00." Trish pushed open the passenger door and hurried up the porch steps. Alex unbuckled his seat belt and followed her.

Inside, Trish called up the stairs. "Scott, are you home?"

After a moment, Scott appeared at the top of the stairs. "Hey, you're home early."

"And so are you," she said. "What gives?"

Marco appeared next to Scott. "The dance was lame, so Danny brought us home early. We've been playing video games. Can I spend the night?"

Alex looked at Trish and she nodded. "Sure. What about church in the morning?" he asked.

"Can't we skip it?" Scott asked.

Trish turned her back to the boys. "Let's do skip church tomorrow. You can come over for breakfast, and we'll break the news to the kids all at once. Janna's mom said she'd drop Meghan off early."

Alex smiled. "Works for me." He looked up at the boys. "Okay. But don't make it a habit. I'll see you here for breakfast in the morning."

Both boys spoke nearly in unison. "Awesome!"

Trish watched as they returned to Scott's room. She couldn't be sure, but she thought she heard Scott say, "You think he did it?"

In the kitchen, Trish set a bottle of Riesling and two wine goblets on the table. Alex poured and handed her a goblet. He lifted his glass to her. "To us," he said, "the kids, and a bright future together."

They clinked glasses and sipped the wine.

Trish studied Alex sitting next to her. A few strands of gray flecked his hair at the sides. His penetrating blue eyes warmed her each time he looked at her. She reached out and traced his strong jawline. "I'll bet the women jurors fell right in line when you argued cases." She grinned.

He moved his head slightly and squinted at her. "Just what are you accusing me of?"

"You're handsome, charming, and *very* convincing."

"I was a great prosecutor." He feigned a hurt expression. "I won my cases fair and square."

"I have no doubt about that." She kissed his cheek. "You've convinced me of something I never thought possible." Setting her wine on the table, she sighed.

"And what's that?"

"That I could love someone other than my children so completely. That men of integrity really do exist. That a loving and happy relationship is possible."

"I'm glad you feel that way. Would hate for you to not like me." He winked.

"Tell me about Amy."

He leaned back and watched her for a moment. "What brought that on?"

"If we're going to be married, I would like to know more about her."

"She's not a threat to you. I don't compare apples and peaches. I love you for who you are. Isn't that enough?"

Trish fidgeted with her wine glass. "You know all about Clay and our struggles. You know what kind of person he was, but I've never heard you talk about Amy. Not *really* talk about her." She felt wetness in her eyes and swallowed. "I don't feel threatened by her. I just want to know *about* her. It's important."

Alex leaned his arms on the table and stared at his hands. "I don't talk about her because of Marco. I don't want him feeling uncomfortable. She's my past; he's my future, as you and the kids are."

"I understand, but she's part of you. You were in love. Knowing something about her will help me know you better."

He was silent for what seemed like an eternity. When he finally spoke, she let out a sigh of relief.

"Fair enough." He cleared his throat. "Amy could make the best lasagna you ever tasted, but she couldn't make cookies." He chuckled. "She always burned them. She had a compassionate and loving heart, always worrying about those who were hurting or needed help. She worked at our church's soup kitchen once a week and volunteered at the homeless shelter."

He scooted his chair away from the table and rested his right foot on his left knee. Trish could see him fighting for composure.

"Go on," she said.

"She was big on practical jokes, trying to catch me off-guard as often as she could. Her laugh was infectious, and if she laughed too hard, she snorted." He smiled at the memory. "I teased her relentlessly about that.

"She had a stubborn streak a mile wide, which used to frustrate me to no end. Once she made up her mind, nothing could change it. I was the disciplinarian. Little Alex had her wrapped around his finger, yet she had a knack for getting him to behave. She chewed her nails while watching television. I couldn't get her to stop." He paused a moment before continuing. "And she loved caramel—sundaes, candy, caramel flavored lattés—if it had caramel flavoring, she was there."

"She sounds like someone I'd be friends with."

Alex looked at Trish. "Yes, I think you two would have been friends. She treasured her friendships and was genuine with others. You knew where you stood with her, much like you."

Alex finished his wine and stood. "I think I'd better get home and get a little sleep, if I can." He pulled Trish to her feet and kissed her, long and tenderly. "I'd better go before I'm tempted to stay the night," he whispered against her lips.

Trish put her arms around his neck. "Thank you for sharing Amy with me. You're welcome to do so any time. If something reminds you of her, then don't be afraid to say so.

We're in this together, you know."

Alex nodded. "We are, and you have a deal. I loved Amy. And now I've fallen in love again. God knew I needed you." He kissed her cheek. "You're welcome to come home with me." He wiggled his eyebrows.

She laughed. "I would like that, but not yet. Soon, though."

He walked to the kitchen door and then turned to look at her. He cocked his head. "You don't know what you're missing out on," he said and strode to the front door.

"Oh, I think I do," she whispered. She fingered the diamond ring on her left hand. Alex's pickup rumbled to life. The light tap of his horn made her smile as the truck tires crunched over gravel.

CHAPTER 19

"Good morning." Trish greeted Alex as he stepped through the sliding-glass doors into the kitchen. He wore a blue sweater and jeans and looked a lot fresher than she felt. She'd had a hard time settling into sleep the night before, second-guessing her decision to marry Alex. Was she ready for such a big change?

He kissed her on the cheek. "Boys up yet?"

His open and natural display of affection washed away all her doubts. She would love him forever.

"I heard some noises from upstairs. I think they're stirring." She poured him a mug of coffee. "Meghan's on her way." She grabbed her own mug, leaned against the counter, and took a sip. "Are we ready for this?" She fingered the diamond on her left hand with her thumb.

Alex leaned in and kissed her. "We are, but are the kids? The boys were all right with it when I asked them. However, when reality hits, I hope they don't have second thoughts."

"Me, too." She set her coffee on the counter and moved to the stove. "Bacon, scrambled eggs and waffles for breakfast."

"What can I do to help?"

The front door opened and Meghan wandered into the kitchen. She stopped when she saw Alex beating eggs. "Alex, how come you're here?"

"Your mom invited me to breakfast."

She smiled. "Where's Marco?"

"He spent the night," Trish answered. "He and Scott will be down shortly."

"I'm going to take my stuff upstairs and get ready for church."

"Don't worry about changing clothes. We're not going to church today."

Meghan stared at Trish. "Seriously?"

Trish nodded. Alex winked at Trish.

"Tell the boys breakfast is about ready," Trish said to Meghan's receding back. She looked at Alex. "Before or after we eat?"

"I think before."

Pounding footsteps on the stairs announced the boys' arrival, with Meghan close behind. All three stormed into the kitchen.

"I'm starved," Scott said. "What's for breakfast?"

Trish took a deep breath. "We'll have breakfast in a minute. Alex and I want to talk to you."

Scott elbowed Marco. "I told you he did it." He looked at Alex. "So, when are you getting married?"

"Married?" Meghan's eyes widened. "You're getting married?"

Alex chuckled. "We are. Your mom said 'yes' last night."

Trish smiled and held up her left hand. Meghan rushed to her mom and hugged her. "Awesome." She carefully examined the ring. "It's beautiful." The boys seemed indifferent.

Alex waited a few moments, then asked, "Any objections from the peanut gallery?"

Marco was the first to speak. "'Bout time you gave me a mom." He grinned.

Alex looked at Scott. "Well?"

Scott frowned. "Do you think you can handle her?" He tried to suppress a grin but failed.

"I can handle her. And you and Meghan." Alex raised his eyebrows. "What about you? Can you handle Marco and me?"

Scott shrugged. "Piece of cake. But if things don't work out, I'll contact my lawyer."

Alex nodded. "As your lawyer, I'll consider taking the case."

Everyone laughed as they settled at the table for breakfast. Trish watched each one as they ate, marveling at how easily they conversed, at ease with each other. This was truly a family. Her heart swelled with pride and happiness.

West Texas—February 2009

Clay Ryan, aka Clyde Johnson, slammed the door to his apartment. How *dare* they fire him. So what if he'd fudged his hours a few times. He worked harder than most of the men on the rigs. He figured the oil company owed him a little extra.

He grabbed a beer from the refrigerator and sorted through his mail. Picking up the *North Fork Weekly*, he looked for any news of Scott in the sports section. The North Fork Eagles had taken the conference in basketball. Scott and Marco Lambert, some kid he didn't know, had been named to the all-conference first team. Clay's heart swelled with pride. He could see all kinds of scholarship offers when Scott was a senior.

"Boy, you're doin' good and makin' your old man proud." He tipped the beer bottle, gulped half of it, and then looked to see what he had to fix for supper. Not finding anything, he picked up the phone and ordered pizza.

After his second beer, and while waiting for the pizza, he read the article about Scott. "Maybe it's a good thing I got fired." Walking to his computer, he pulled up the research he'd recently done. "Maybe it's time to play the amnesia card."

Amnesia meant he could return to work in the oil fields under his real name. There'd be no record of him getting fired. By shaving his beard and mustache, no one would recognize him. He smiled. Life was good. He couldn't have planned things better.

He contemplated how he'd surprise Trish and the kids. He knew they'd be glad to see him, but he wanted to check out "the lay of the land" before he approached any of them. He'd figure out how to handle that first meeting once he got there. In a few weeks, he'd head to Colorado and reconciliation.

North Fork, Colorado—March 2009

Alex, Trish, and Meghan settled on the bleachers and waited for the baseball game to start. Trish was more nervous than Scott, Alex, or Marco. Although Scott preferred football, he liked all sports, excelling in each one, baseball no exception. Trish worried he'd suffer the same fate as Clay—an injury dashing his dreams of playing college ball and maybe even pro ball. She took a deep breath and sipped her Coke. The buttery aroma of fresh popcorn wafted up from a few rows below. Trish's stomach growled. A small dirt devil picked up soil from the infield and deposited it on the grass a few feet away.

"You okay?" asked Alex. "You seem a bit nervous."

"I'm okay. Just hoping Scott and Marco will both play well."

"They'll be fine."

She nodded and shrugged. "Sorry, I just want them to do their best."

She slipped her arm through Alex's. He was the solid rock in her life. She depended so much on him to keep her centered. They had decided to wait until October and the end of the harvest season to get married. They wanted to be able to take some time for a honeymoon, and from now until October, there would be no time to get away.

They had finished pruning by early March. A few warm days the latter part of February had brought on concerns about fruit buds swelling too soon. But Mother Nature had cooperated. Now that it was the middle of March, the weather was cooler. They watched the fruit trees daily and prayed the cold nights would not drop below twenty-eight degrees once the fruit bloomed. With temperature alarms installed in both houses, they were covered if the temperature plunged. The propane tanks that powered the wind machines were full and ready to go at a moment's notice. Mother Nature was fickle. It could be sixty-plus degrees one day, and drop to thirty the next, with nighttime temperatures even lower.

"Penny for your thoughts," Alex said.

She smiled. "Just thinking about how much my life has changed in the last year." She laid her head on his shoulder. "Thanks for making life so great for me and the kids."

Alex slipped his arm around her waist and pulled her closer. "That goes both ways, you know."

A cool breeze ruffled her hair, and she pulled her jacket tighter. She noticed several people glancing their way. "We're the talk of the town. Everyone is looking," she murmured.

He laughed. "Not everyone. Just the nosey ones."

JD and Stacey McCord settled on the bleachers behind them. "Nice day for a game," JD remarked.

"Sure is," replied Alex.

Stacey gave Trish a hug. "I understand congratulations are in order."

"Yes." She showed Stacey her ring. "I couldn't be happier."

The umpire shouted, "Play ball!" They turned their attention to the game. When North Fork came up to bat, Scott was the lead-off man. He hit a double into center field. A shrill whistle came from the crowd.

Trish stiffened. That whistle could have come from anyone, but it sounded exactly the way Clay used to whistle. She glanced around but couldn't tell where the whistle came from. This is crazy, she chided herself, relaxed, and concentrated on the game. In the fifth inning, when Scott hit a home run, she heard the same whistle again along with "Way to go, Scott!" Chills ran down her back. Looking around again, she saw a man standing at the edge of the bleachers clapping. When he turned her direction, her Coke slipped from her hands, hit the plank at her feet, and splattered onto the ground below.

Alex turned and frowned at her. "Are you okay? You look a little pale."

"I-I'm okay." But she wasn't. Although he had a beard and mustache, the man looked a lot like Clay, but that was impossible. He'd died almost five and a half years ago. No way could he be here now. She scanned the crowd again, but the man had disappeared. She wondered if she was going crazy.

"You look white as a sheet," Alex said. "Do you want me to take you home?"

"*No*," she said more forcefully than she intended. "I'm fine," she lied. "I don't think the Coke set well with me."

"You sure?"

"I *don't* want to miss the game." She placed her hand on Alex's knee. "I'll be fine."

North Fork won the game eight to three. As they were leaving the ballpark, Trish scanned the crowd for the man. *This is crazy.* He was nowhere to be seen. *I'm letting my imagination get the better of me. Clay is dead. Get a grip.*

When they arrived at Trish's, Alex joined her in the kitchen and Meghan headed to her room. The boys settled in front of the television. Trish had put a crockpot of ham and potato soup on that morning. She removed the lid and stirred the contents.

Alex took the spoon from her hand, pulled her into his arms, and held her. "Are you sure you're okay? You've been distracted ever since the game. What's wrong?"

"Nothing. I'm fine."

Alex set the spoon on the counter and cradled her face in his hands. "I know you better than that. You were looking for someone after the game."

She looked away from his penetrating eyes.

He persisted. "I love you, Trish, but if we're going to make this work, we need to be honest with each other. If you can't confide in me, then we're in trouble."

She looked at him, tears pricking at her eyes. "It's stupid, really. Not even worth mentioning."

"It is if it's bothering you this much."

She took a deep breath. "I thought I saw Clay today at the game."

"You what?" His head jerked back, and he stared at her. "Trish, he died over five years ago."

"I *know*. I don't know what's wrong with me."

"Sit down and tell me why you thought you saw him."

Once they were settled at the table, she told him about the whistle and then seeing a man yelling for Scott. "I looked for him after the game, but he'd disappeared. I keep telling myself that I imagined the whole thing, but it seemed so real."

Alex smoothed her hair away from her face and smiled. "Maybe you're just a little nervous about getting married again. Lots of people yelled for Scott today. I'm told Abby Karlson has quite a whistle. Maybe you heard her. I'm sure you just saw someone who resembles Clay. At any rate, it's nothing to worry about."

"I guess you're right. Clay never had facial hair like this guy." She sighed. "I'm happy for the first time in many years, and I don't want anything to spoil it." Trish placed her hand along his jaw. "What would I do without you?"

He took her hand and kissed the palm. "I don't plan on letting you find out. *Ever*."

~

Trish pulled into the library staff parking lot a few

minutes early on Monday. As she exited her pickup, she caught movement out of the corner of her eye. When she turned, the man she saw at the ballgame approached her. She gasped.

"Mornin', Babe. It's good to see you." Clay smiled, took her by the arm, and tried to pull her close.

She resisted and fought the cold chill slithering down her back. Despite the beard and mustache, there was no mistaking Clay. He *was* alive. She felt her legs starting to buckle and gritted her teeth.

"Sorry to surprise you like this, but I didn't want to come to the house and upset the kids. Thought it would be best to see you first."

She tried to pull away from him, but he held tight. She glared at him. "Y-you're supposed to be dead!"

"I'm not dead. I've come home."

Without thinking, she slapped him.

He flinched. "What was that for?"

"H-how . . . w-why . . . ." She tried to free herself again. "Let me go!"

"Is there a problem here?" a male voice asked.

"Yes, there is." Her fury was tempered only by the welcome site of Gary, head of library security. "This man has accosted me and won't let me go." She tried to pull away from Clay again.

Gary strode up to them, placing himself close, his steely gaze settling on Clay. "I strongly suggest you let Ms. Ryan go. This is your first and only warning."

"You back off!" Clay spat. "I'm her husband."

"I happen to know Ms. Ryan is a widow. Let her go *now*."

Clay studied Gary's tall and imposing demeanor a moment, then dropped Trish's arm. "We're not through yet," Clay said to Trish. "I'll see you later."

Clay strode to his pickup and peeled out of the parking lot.

Trish shuddered.

"Are you all right?" Gary asked.

"N-no. Tell Sarah I'm not coming to work today. I'll call her later." Trish turned to climb into her pickup.

Gary pulled out his phone. "I'll call the sheriff."

"*No*. He's gone. I don't want any trouble." She climbed into the truck cab and started the engine. As Trish pulled away from the library, she left Gary with a look of confusion on his face, his cell phone to his ear.

Tears flowed down Trish's cheeks, which made her angrier than she'd been a few minutes ago. Clay was alive. How could he be? Where had he been? She hated him.

"Please be home Alex." She clenched the steering wheel. "*Please*." She caught a glimpse of a pickup following her. Clay?

At Alex's she flew from the pickup and stabbed the doorbell. When he didn't answer, she continued pushing it, glancing behind her as she did. No one had followed that she could see. The other pickup must have been a coincidence.

Alex opened the door and frowned. "Trish, what's wrong?"

She fell into his arms and sobbed. "H-he's alive," she

choked.

"Who?"

"Clay." She looked at Alex. "H-he showed up at the library. Oh, Alex, he's alive."

CHAPTER 20

Alex lifted Trish in his arms and carried her to the living room. He settled them both on the couch and held her tight. Smoothing her hair away from her face and wiping away the tears, he spoke softly. "It's okay. Just breathe and tell me what happened. You're not making sense."

She hiccupped as she took a deep breath. Her words came pouring out. "I-I know it sounds crazy. He accosted me in the library parking lot. If Gary hadn't shown up, I don't know what would have happened." She sniffed. "Clay called me 'Babe,' his nickname for me. The same man I saw at the game."

"You're sure it's him?"

She nodded her head and began sobbing again. Alex held her tightly. He could hear Lucky making a fuss in the yard. Someone unfamiliar had driven up.

"Let me go quiet Lucky. I'll be right back." He kissed Trish on the forehead.

When he opened the door, a bearded man, stocky and muscular, stood on his lawn, Lucky circling him, alternately barking and growling.

"Call your damn dog off!" the man yelled.

"Lucky, come."

Lucky trotted to Alex's side. "Sit," he commanded.

Lucky complied but continued with guttural growls toward the man. Alex had never seen her act this way with any stranger. She'd bark, but she was never menacing.

"State your business," Alex directed the man.

"I came to see my wife. She's here, isn't she?"

"Depends who your wife is."

"Trish Ryan. I'm Clay. I followed her here. That's our pickup."

Alex gritted his teeth. "Thought you were dead."

"Well, l ain't, and I want to see her."

Alex clenched his fists. He didn't like Clay's demeanor or demand. "I don't think she wants to see you right now. She's had a bit of a shock. I'm sure you can understand that."

"Well maybe if I talk to her she'll feel better."

"Why don't you tell me where you're staying, and I'll let her know. She can get in touch with you when she's ready."

"Mister, you got no right to keep me from seeing her." Clay started toward Alex. Lucky stood, bared her teeth, and let out a warning growl. Clay stopped.

"Lucky, sit," Alex said. She obeyed. "Name's Lambert," he said, "and I have every right. I'm her lawyer, and she doesn't want to see you right now. I suggest you leave and wait for her to call."

Clay glared at him. "You'll be sorry, Lambert," he threatened. "I saw you with her at the game." He glared at Alex for a moment. "I'm staying at the North Fork Motel. She can call me there."

"I'll tell her." Alex watched as Clay retreated to his pickup, scattering gravel as he drove away.

Inside the house, Alex sat next to Trish, put his arm around her, and drew her close. She had stopped crying, but she still sniffed with short breaths. She couldn't control her shaking.

"Was that Clay?" she asked between sniffs.

"It was. I told him you'd call him when you were ready."

"Bet he wasn't happy about that."

"That's his problem," Alex said.

"Oh, Alex." Her anger surfaced. "How could this happen? He's supposed to be *dead*."

"I think you'll have to ask him that." He rubbed her arm. "I'm guessing there was someone else in the truck when it burned. The remains they found obviously weren't his."

She took a deep breath and wiped away the wetness on her cheeks. "Then whose were they?"

"Trish, I don't have any answers. But I'm guessing Clay does."

Her tears flowed again. "Why?" She buried her head in

Alex's shoulder. "Why couldn't he just stay dead?" She wiped her nose with a spent tissue. "This is going to have a terrible impact on Scott and Meghan. Especially Scott. Meghan barely remembers him. But Scott." She sat forward. "What am I going to do?"

"You're going to have to break the news to them sooner or later. Do you want to tell them before or after you talk to Clay?"

"I don't know. I'm so confused." She fished a fresh tissue out of her pocket and blew her nose. "I guess I'd better talk to Clay first, so I'll know what to tell the kids."

"I think that's wise." Alex rose and pulled Trish to her feet. "Come on. Let's talk about this over a cup of coffee."

Trish settled on a bar stool and took the mug of coffee from Alex. He sat beside her and waited for her to voice her thoughts. He was in no hurry. She needed time to process what had happened.

"Scott idolized Clay," she finally said. "He took Clay's death really hard. He was ten at the time. He has no idea what kind of person Clay was…is." She inhaled and let out a large sigh. "He remembers Clay as the dad who taught him to fish, throw a football and hit a baseball."

"Does Scott know Clay's the reason you sold the orchards?" Alex asked.

"I told him Clay had gambling debts that needed to be paid off. Scott's never asked for details."

"Scott is older and somewhat wiser," Alex said. "He'll eventually figure out a few things for himself." He paused a moment. "You're going to have to be prepared for Scott to be happy about his dad's return from the dead. He's going to want to spend time with him." He cleared his throat. "He might even expect the two of you to get back together."

Trish frowned at Alex. "How could he?"

"Because you're family, and Clay is his dad." Alex let the thought sink in.

"I was planning to file for divorce before the accident."

"Does Scott know that?"

Trish shook her head. "No."

"It probably won't matter to Scott that you and I are planning to get married. Now that Clay is back, Scott will want things to be the way he remembered them. He didn't know the extent of the problems between you and Clay."

Trish stared at her coffee mug for several minutes. Alex refilled his cup and returned to sit beside her. The rich aroma of the coffee did little to settle his churning thoughts. He'd give anything if Clay had stayed dead, but, he reminded himself, he wasn't in control. God was, and Alex would have to trust that He would work things out for the good of all.

"I'm still going to file for divorce. I don't care if Clay has changed, which I doubt. I've moved on. Scott and Meghan will have to understand that."

Alex breathed a little easier. He didn't believe in divorce, but in Trish's case, he felt that was best for her. "Don't expect Scott to accept it right away. You'll need to be straight with both kids and tell them before you file, not after."

"I know." She took a sip of coffee. "*Why?*" Tears filled her eyes. "Why did God let this happen?"

Alex shook his head. "I'm no expert, but I guess God knew that things needed to be settled with Clay before we got married." He tried to smile. "I'm pretty sure God knew he was alive."

Trish eyed Alex for a moment and almost smiled. "Guess it would have been a lot more awkward if he'd shown up after we got married." She fingered the diamond on her left hand. "I was so happy." She placed her hand along Alex's jaw and managed a small smile. "I found the perfect guy." She let her hand drop and looked away. "Everything was going right. And now this."

"*This* can be handled."

"I'm sorry you've been dragged into this mess. I didn't know what else to do. All I could think of was coming here." Her hand flew to her mouth. "Oh my gosh. I *slapped* him."

Alex suppressed a smile. "Probably didn't make him too happy."

They sat quietly for a little while. Finally, Trish slipped the ring off her finger and handed it to Alex. "Under the circumstances, I don't think I should wear it right now. I'm still married."

Alex turned her stool so she was facing him. "You keep it."

"I don't want Clay finding it and causing you problems. Besides, it would be my luck he'd find it and pawn it." She looked up at Alex and smiled. "I'm going to want it back, so don't lose it."

Alex kissed her lightly on the lips. "You can have it back any time."

"I guess I'd better call Clay and get this over with." She heaved a big sigh. "I'll tell the kids tonight. Then we'll see what happens."

"You need to decide what you're going to ask Clay when you see him."

"I guess I'll ask what happened, and where has he been for five and a half years? He'll have some excuse, I'm sure. He was always good at excuses."

"Do you want me to go with you?"

She turned to face him. "Under the circumstances, I don't think it would be wise." She gave him a peck on the cheek. "I love you so much. Thank you for being here."

"No need to thank me." He pulled her close and kissed her. "We're in this together. Thick and thin. I love you and intend to marry you, no matter what. Hang on to that while you're talking to him and call me when you're done."

"I will." She said. "Say a prayer. I'm going to need it." Trish took a few more minutes to settle down, and then freshened up in Alex's bathroom. She told Alex she didn't want Clay to see she'd been crying. Calmer, her eyes less puffy, she pulled her cell phone out of her purse and called the motel.

Alex watched her from the doorway as she backed out of his yard. *Lord, watch over and protect her. Help her to stay calm while talking to Clay. And bring her back to me. I love her and need her.*

Realizing Trish had never gone to work, Alex called Sarah to let her know what happened. He promised to have Trish call her later. As soon as he ended the call, his cell rang. The Sheriff's office number appeared on the screen.

"Alex, Kale Morgan. Is Trish all right? I tried her house but she didn't answer. I understand there was an altercation in the library's parking lot. Their head of security called me."

Alex smiled at Gary's efficiency, thankful he'd called in the incident. "Clay Ryan just showed up in town, alive and well," he explained.

"Clay Ryan?" Deputy Morgan let out a low whistle. "I'll be damned. Gary said the guy claimed to be her husband, but I thought he was just a nutcase."

"Nutcase is probably accurate, but Trish said there's no doubt he's Clay."

"That's one I didn't expect."

"I'd appreciate it if you or another deputy dropped by the North Fork Motel and kept an eye out for Trish. She's meeting Clay there. You don't have to go in, just be available."

"I'm on it. Won't interfere unless we need to. Looks like there are some unanswered questions we need to resolve."

"Thanks, Kale. I'd rather Trish didn't know I asked."

"Between us. Catch you later."

~

Trish parked at the edge of the motel parking lot. Her stomach churned, and she swallowed the bile rising in her throat. *Stay calm. He's not going to hurt you anymore. You have the upper hand. Don't let him rattle you.* In spite of her self-talk, she shook as she exited the pickup.

When Clay opened the door to his room, he was all

smiles and clean-shaven. As Trish entered the room, Clay grabbed her and pulled her close. He tried to kiss her, but she turned her head and pushed him away.

"Stop it!"

"What's wrong with you, Babe? I thought you'd be glad to see me."

She glared at him. "You're the *last* person I ever expected to see, or *wanted* to see for that matter."

"Ouch! That hurt." Clay feigned disappointment. "I know this is all a shock to you, but I can explain."

"Then let's hear it. I haven't got a lot of time or patience."

"I've had amnesia. I didn't remember who I was or what had happened until a few weeks ago." He shrugged. "I was working the oil fields in West Texas, and a co-worker was reading his hometown paper. It was the *North Fork Weekly*. I saw a picture of Scott in the sports section, and it all came back."

Trish frowned. "A few weeks ago? And you're just now contacting me?" She barely controlled her anger. Clay was always creative with his excuses, but this was a doozy. "Go on."

"Please, Trish, sit down." He gestured toward the only chair in the room.

Trish perched on the edge and waited.

Clay sat on the foot of the bed. "I didn't remember everything right away. It all came back kind of slowly. I was going by the name Clyde Johnson. When I finally remembered what happened, I realized I wasn't Clyde, but

Clay.

"You see, I picked up a hitchhiker in Rangely. I know I wasn't supposed to do that—company policy—but I felt sorry for the guy because of the weather. When I lost control of the gas truck, I was thrown clear. Before I could help him out, the truck exploded and knocked me to the ground. When I came to, I couldn't remember who I was. I found a wallet on the ground with an I.D. for Clyde Johnson. I figured that's who I was. Since it was an I.D. and not a driver's license, I figured the driver was killed in the accident."

He rested his arms on his legs and clasped his hands in front of him. "I wandered down the road and a while later a man picked me up. He dropped me off in Grand Junction, and I found a place to sleep for the night. The next day I set off for Utah, because I remembered someone saying something about Utah."

Trish stared at Clay. His story didn't make sense, but she was too upset to figure out what was wrong with it. It was too incredible to believe, yet here he was insisting he'd had amnesia for over five years.

"Did you try to find out about Clyde Johnson?"

"I figured if that's who I was, there had to be some records somewhere. I didn't find out anything. I eventually ended up in West Texas, working in the oil fields until a few weeks ago."

Trish shook her head. "How can I believe you, Clay? You lied to me over and over while we were married."

"I want to come home, Trish. I'll turn over a new leaf." He looked at her with pleading in his dark brown eyes. "I want my family back."

He almost had her believing his story, but he'd used that look on her too many times, and then did something to make her distrust him again and again.

"You hated living in North Fork. You hated the orchards, and you gambled them away." She stood and glared at him.

He moved toward her. "What do you mean, gambled away the orchards?" He tried to look confused, but he didn't fool her. He knew exactly what she meant.

"I'm sure it will come back to you."

"Come on, Trish. I've changed. I'm not the same guy."

"I've forgiven you over and over and taken you back too many times. Not this time. I've moved on, Clay. You should do the same. There's nothing between us anymore."

"Is it Lambert? Is he the one you moved on to?" he sneered.

"I don't love you anymore, haven't for a long time. It's that simple."

She watched him clench his fists and narrow his eyes. She held her breath.

He pasted an ingenuous smile on his face. "I'll change your mind. You'll see."

"Don't count on it." She walked to the door. "Once I've broken the news to Scott and Meghan, you'll be welcome to see them but on my terms. You'll need to call each time and clear your visit with me. If it's not convenient, I'll say so."

"I was hoping to move back into the house. I can't afford to stay here too long."

"That's your problem. You're not welcome to move back."

"Trish—"

She opened the door. "I'll let you know when you can come by the house to see the kids. Don't try to see them before that."

She slammed the door behind her and ran to the pickup. Inside the cab, she locked the doors and grabbed the steering wheel with shaking hands, trying to calm her anger. "Amnesia my foot!" she said under her breath. She drove past a patrol car sitting on the street near the motel. Pulling out her cell phone, she dialed Alex. "You won't believe what Clay just told me."

CHAPTER 21

At Trish's hasty retreat, Clay exploded. He picked up a lamp but caught himself before smashing it onto the floor. He didn't need to end up in jail for destroying motel property. At the moment, however, he needed to hit something or someone.

"Hell, I should have ignored the dog, clobbered that smug lawyer and gone in and gotten Trish." Lambert was on his list. He wasn't going to put up with Trish hiding behind another man. Lambert was going to pay, somehow. He'd just have to figure out a way to do it.

"Nobody messes with me and my family." He took a deep breath. Trish was angry, but he didn't know why. She had a job at the library. Wasn't that what she went to school for? And she'd sold the orchards, so she must not have been as attached to them as Clay believed. True, he'd shocked her by showing up alive after all these years, but she shouldn't be angry. She should be happy to see him.

He'd give her a few days to get used to the idea he was back, and then he'd move home and take up where they'd left off. All she needed was a little more time to get used to him as a husband again, then he'd broach the subject of moving to West Texas. She didn't have anything to keep her here. That would be an argument in his favor.

He'd figure out a way to convince her that their future didn't involve North Fork. For her to see things his way, he would kowtow to her every demand, do everything she asked. She would have no choice but to take him back, and then they could leave this God-forsaken excuse for a town. He smiled and glanced at the time. A cold beer or two was calling. He grabbed his jacket and scooped up his keys. It was time the *good* people of North Fork knew he was back in town.

~

Even though Trish had called Alex to let him know she was all right, he still paced the floor until he saw her pickup. He flung open the door and met her halfway.

Alex lifted her off the ground and kissed her. When he set her down, he noticed the tears in her eyes. He ushered her into the house, and they sat together on the couch.

"Well?"

She laid her head on his shoulder and the tears flowed. He let her cry until she could pull herself together. She spoke in a soft voice, tinged with a hint of confusion and anger. "Amnesia. That's what he said." She spat the words out. "He's had amnesia for five-and-a-half years."

"Do you believe him?"

"He sounded believable and sorry for having put us through the agony of thinking he was dead." Trish sighed. "I definitely don't believe him. I can't explain it, but I know he's lying. His story just doesn't make sense."

"It does sound incredible. Tell me everything he said."

Trish related to Alex what Clay had told her. "I don't trust him. Something isn't right. It seems awfully convenient that the other man's billfold just happened to survive the wreck and Clay's didn't. Clay *always* carried his billfold with his driver's license in his back pocket. It should have been there."

Alex closed his eyes. He'd heard a lot of incredible excuses during the time he worked as an assistant D.A., but Clay's story was a winner in the hard-to-believe category. "Did he tell you what name he'd been using?"

Trish was silent a few moments. "Jones." She hesitated. "Charles, no that's not right."

She shook her head. "I can't remember."

"That's okay. You've been through a lot today. You're not going to remember everything."

"Oh, Alex." She sniffed and looked up at him. "What are we going to do?"

He smiled at her. "We're going to be patient and play Clay's game for a while. It's my experience that sooner or later he's going to mess things up. Guys like him usually do."

A wan smile formed on Trish's face. "You're probably right. Clay usually blew it one way or another." She leaned forward and turned to look at Alex. "I'm going to tell the kids tonight, but I want you and Marco to be there when I do."

He frowned at her. "I don't mind being there, but shouldn't this be between you and the kids?"

She shook her head. "This affects all of us. We were going to be a family, and families stick together. Clay's return changes things for you and Marco, too. Meghan will be shocked, but Scott—I'm not sure what to expect from him. I need you there as a buffer if nothing else. That much I do know."

Alex kissed her on the cheek. "Then we'll be there. Is it all right if I let Marco know what's going on before we come over?"

"Probably a good idea." She rose. "I think I'll go home and find something to fix for supper. That will give me a little time before the kids get home from school."

"Forget worrying about supper. I'll order pizza for all of us. It'll make things easier. You need some time to yourself right now." Her grateful smile told Alex everything.

Distress returned to her face. "How in the world am I going to break this to them?"

Alex hugged her. "Tell them exactly what happened. Don't beat around the bush. Just come out with it." He nudged her to arms' length. "I'll say a prayer for you, and I suggest you take some time for prayer, too. When you break the news to them, God will be with you."

She nodded. "You're right. I'll do that."

"You might give Sarah a quick call. Let her know you're okay."

She nodded and moved to the door. "Could life get any more complicated?" She stepped outside. "See you at six," she said and closed the door.

~

Marco stared at Alex. "Seriously?"

Alex nodded. "Seriously." He put his hand on Marco's shoulder. "Scott is going to need a friend to talk to, so be prepared."

"What do I say?"

"Sometimes a friend doesn't have to say anything. Listen, and let him talk. You'll know what to say when the time comes."

"Man, this is heavy stuff. And I thought I had problems."

"Scott's probably going to want to reconnect with his dad, which means he'll spend less time with you."

Marco nodded. "That's okay. I never had a dad when I was young, so I can only guess what it must have been like for him." He grinned at Alex. "But I have a great dad now."

"I have a terrific son, and no matter what happens, that will not change." Alex hugged Marco. "Go get cleaned up. We're supposed to be at Trish's at six."

He watched Marco take the stairs two at a time and swallowed the lump in his throat. Like God had done with

Job in the Bible, He had given Alex a new family, and Alex was going to fight tooth and nail for all of them.

Alex's cell phone rang. He recognized Deputy Morgan's number. "Alex."

"Kale Morgan here. Sorry to be so long getting back to you. Trish left with no problems that I could tell. Had another call just after that. When I got back to my office, I pulled up Clay's accident report from November of 2003. His showing up puts a whole new light on things. Did he tell Trish what happened?"

"He did. Said he's had amnesia for the last five and a half years. Frankly, from what I know about amnesia, his story doesn't hold water. I dealt with a case where a woman claimed amnesia for ten years, but the testimony of doctors discredited her claim. You might want to talk to Trish. She's pretty skeptical."

"I plan to do that," Kale replied. "I want to exhume what few remains there were and do a DNA test on them. I'll give Trish a few days to adjust to Clay's return, and then ask for her permission. We need to know who the guy was that died in the fire. By the way, Clay registered at the motel as Clyde Johnson. Don't know if that's significant or not."

Trish was close with the name. Alex was pleased Kale intended to look into the accident. "For now, consider me Trish's attorney in this matter; unless she says otherwise. I know she uses Jess for most things and may want to continue with him, but just to be on the safe side, I'll represent her for now. Something about this whole thing stinks."

"You're right, Alex. Something's rotten in Denmark,

and I intend to get to the bottom of it. I was a year behind Clay in school. Never did cotton to him." Kale paused. "He was good at weaseling his way out of things and adept at manipulating people to get his way. Hated it when Trish married him. Figured she deserved better."

"Well, what little I saw today," Alex said, "definitely swayed me toward distrust."

"I'll keep you informed as to what I dig up." Kale chuckled. "Pun intended."

Alex smiled. "Thanks, Kale." He ended the call. The more he interacted with Deputy Kale Morgan, the better he liked him.

~

After a short nap and time spent in prayer, Trish showered. She wanted the smell of Clay's aftershave off her skin and clothes. How *dare* he try to kiss her. He wasn't even gentle about it, just grabbed her. *Forgive me, God, but I despise him. He always thinks I'm going to melt in his arms as though nothing has happened. He's so smug.* She slammed her brush onto the bathroom counter and gripped the edge with both hands. She didn't regret slapping him. He deserved it.

"How am I going to tell the kids?" she whispered. They were both in their rooms doing homework. She closed her eyes and pictured Scott. "Lord, Scott's come such a long way since Clay died. Now what? Will that change? I want him to be the young man he's become, not someone Clay wants him to be." Tears stung her eyes. *Please, God, don't let Scott fall*

279

back into an angry and resentful person like he was for so long. Let him look to Alex, not Clay, as a role model.

Clay wasn't going to be happy when Trish served him with divorce papers. But like it or not, Clay was going to be her ex-husband. She wasn't going to let Clay spoil her future with Alex, who was, she knew without a doubt, perfect for her. She'd finally found a man of integrity, honesty, and genuine love for her and her children. Someone who loved the orchards as much as she did. Someone who's faith had brought her back to God.

Putting the final touches on her hair, she stared at her reflection in the mirror. Red, puffy eyes stared back and weariness strained her features. Tonight wasn't going to be easy. She didn't know what to expect, but with Alex by her side, she could handle anything. That in itself gave her comfort. She headed for the kitchen. Alex and Marco would be arriving in a few minutes.

As she went by Meghan's and Scott's bedroom doors, she knocked and called. "Supper in fifteen minutes."

~

"Pass me another slice of meat lovers," Scott said.

"Please," Trish prompted.

"*Please.*" Scott rolled his eyes. "Geez, Mom, we're family. It's not like we have to behave in front of company."

A knot formed in Trish's stomach. Revealing Clay's sudden appearance wasn't going to be easy. "Nevertheless, you still use your best manners."

Scott shrugged. Alex stifled a grin, and Meghan and

Marco gave each other a funny look. Meghan couldn't hold back a giggle, and soon they were all laughing. Except Trish. She rose and began clearing the table.

"So, Mom, are you feeling okay? You look tired or something," Scott said.

"It's been a rough day," she answered and glanced at Alex. He nodded slightly. She couldn't delay telling the kids about Clay any longer. She returned to the table and folded her hands in front of her.

"I have something I need to tell you, and it's going to change some things for a while."

"I *knew* it." Scott scooted his chair back. "You're sick, aren't you?" he said quietly.

"*No*. I'm not physically sick, Scott. But I appreciate your concern. What I have to tell you concerns your father." She paused, waiting for a reaction.

Meghan spoke for the first time. "Mom, you're not wearing the ring Alex gave you. Why?"

"Because. . ." Trish took a deep breath. "Your father is still alive, which means we're still married, so I can't be engaged to Alex." *There, I said it.* She waited for a reaction.

"Seriously?" Meghan stared wide-eyed.

"Dad's still alive? How do you know that?" Scott asked.

"Because he came to the library this morning, and I talked to him this afternoon. According to him, he survived the wreck but had amnesia. He said his memory came back a few weeks ago."

Scott stared at the table. "Dad's alive. I can't believe it." He looked at Trish. "So why isn't he here?"

281

"Because I—we thought it best to tell you before he saw you."

Scott stood, knocking his chair over. "I want to see my dad *now*. You can't keep him from me."

"Scott, please, I'm not—"

"Scott, settle down a minute," Alex interrupted. "You'll see your dad as soon as it can be arranged. He understands this is a shock for everyone. No one is trying to keep you apart."

"This isn't your call," Scott spat at Alex, "so stay out of it." He turned to Trish. "When do I get to see him? It better be soon."

"We can have him come by tomorrow evening. You have baseball practice after school. Clay understands that."

Scott picked up his chair and sat down. "Okay. I guess I can wait." A smile crossed his face. "He's alive. Dad's alive."

"Does that mean you and Alex won't be getting married?" Tears filled Meghan's eyes.

"'Course it does," Scott said. "You heard Mom. Man, this means we can be a family again." He shrugged and looked at Alex and Marco. "Sorry, guys. I like you, but I love my dad, and he's back."

Marco smiled. "That's okay. I never knew my birth dad. I think I understand a little how you feel."

"Thanks, man."

"Scott you're being mean!" Meghan declared and glared at him. "I don't want Alex and Marco to go. We were going to be a family. " A tear slithered down her cheek.

"Geez, Meghan. Our dad is alive. You should be happy about that."

"I don't remember him like you do. I want Alex to be my dad." She crossed her arms in front of her.

"Well he can't be, because our dad's still alive, so shut up about it."

Tears flowed down Meghan's cheeks. "That's not nice."

"Scott!" Trish admonished. "Apologize to your sister."

"Why should I? I'm just saying the truth. We have Dad back. She'd better get used to it."

"I don't *want* to," Meghan wailed. Trish stood and put her arms around Meghan, attempting to comfort her. "Everything will be fine, Meghan. Please don't cry." Trish glared at Scott. "Meghan wasn't close to your dad like you were. She will have a major adjustment to his being back. You need to help her with that."

Alex cleared his throat. "Scott, you do understand that things between you and your dad will be a bit different. Five-and-a-half years is a long time. You'll both need to take things slow."

Scott frowned. "I think things will be just like they were, only better."

"Mom, you *have* to marry Alex." Meghan sniffed.

"Honey, I can't. I'm still married to your dad."

"Look, Meghan, you'll see how great it will be to have Dad back," Scott said.

"We didn't do things together like you did," she said.

"Well, now you'll be able to. You'll see, it'll be great."

"This sucks!" she said.

"Meghan, it will be all right." Trish tried to use her calm voice. "And Scott, don't expect too much. Alex is right, you'll need to take things slow. Your dad is going to be different. He was living as someone else until a few weeks ago. You'll need time to get reacquainted. He'll need time to remember things."

"Well, it shouldn't take too long. When's he going to move back in?"

Trish paused. "I'm not sure he's going to."

"Great. Just great." Scott stood. "As far as I'm concerned, he should have been here tonight!" Scott stood. "You guys are trying to spoil everything for me. My Dad's alive and I'm happy about it! To *hell* with you guys." He stormed from the room. Marco followed.

Trish closed her eyes and sighed.

Meghan stood. "I *hate* this. Things were perfect until now." Tears streamed down her cheeks. "Dad's ruined everything!" She fled to her room.

Trish looked at Alex. "If this wasn't so serious, it would be funny. I feel like I'm in the middle of a soap opera and at the mercy of the writers." A small giggle escaped. "I shouldn't be laughing. Scott's thrilled his dad is back and expects us to be a family again. Meghan's furious he's back." She shook her head. "What next?"

Alex rose and pulled Trish to her feet. He cradled her face in his hands. "It's going to be okay. You and I and God are the writers, and that's the best possible scenario. Let it play out for a little while. I can be patient." He kissed her lightly on the lips. "I suppose I shouldn't be doing that, since you're a married woman."

She smiled, tears in her eyes. "I love you, Alex Lambert." She put her arms around him and nestled into his embrace. "You give me hope."

"That works two ways," he said and waited a moment, enjoying holding Trish. "Marco and I should go home. You need to talk to Meghan. She seems the most upset right now." He kissed her again and started for the door. "We're going to have to be careful about seeing each other for a while. I don't want to put you in any awkward situations."

"I know. It's not going to be easy, but you're right. Thanks for being here tonight." She sighed. "I apologize for Scott."

"No need. He's understandably glad to have his father back. I only hope Clay doesn't disappoint him."

"So do I."

Alex yelled up the stairs. "Marco, time to go home."

Marco appeared at the head of the stairs. "Can I stay a while?"

Alex looked at Trish.

"He can take the four-wheeler home," she said.

Alex nodded. "Be home by ten."

Trish closed the door after a final goodnight kiss and moved to the stairs. *Lord help me comfort and encourage Meghan without revealing my plans for a divorce. She needs to accept and get to know her dad.* "Okay, Lord, here we go," she whispered as she climbed the stairs. She thought she heard Lucky barking.

285

~

Clay melted into the bushes near Trish's house. Just as he thought, Lambert was more than Trish's lawyer. Rage burned inside. Lambert wasn't going to get away with stealing his wife.

CHAPTER 22

It took only a glance at Meghan's slumped shoulders, tears streaming down her cheeks, and in a flash, Trish was on the bed beside her. She gathered Meghan into her arms and stroked her hair.

"Everything will be fine, Meghan. You'll see."

"No it won't," Meghan sobbed. "He's ruined everything!"

"Meghan, honey, it's good your dad is back. You'll need a little time to get to know him again, but that's okay. He is your dad."

"I don't want him here."

"Oh sweetheart, I hope you change your mind. Give him a chance."

It took a while for Meghan to settle down. Trish had

difficulty convincing her that having her dad back in her life was a good thing. Trish had her doubts about Clay's intentions. He had basically ignored Meghan early in her life because she was a girl. He spent most of his time with Scott. She wondered what Clay would think of Meghan's skill at soccer. She was goalie for the middle school team and good at keeping the opponents from scoring. She'd also taken an interest in volleyball and had excelled at that sport, too.

Trish smoothed Meghan's red hair behind her ear and held her a little tighter. "Are we good?" she asked.

Meghan shrugged her shoulders and sniffed. "I guess."

"Your dad will be very proud of you. I'm sure he'll come to your soccer matches."

Meghan brightened a little. "Do you think so?"

Trish nodded. "I do. He loves sports of all kinds and will be proud of his daughter's abilities."

"I still want you to marry Alex," she said. "He cares about everything I do, not just sports."

Trish closed her eyes, hoping to come up with a good response. She wasn't ready for the kids to know about her divorce plans. That would come later. "There are a lot of things to consider right now. I don't want you to worry."

"Do you still love Dad?"

Trish wiped the wetness off Meghan's cheeks. "When we got news your dad died, it was hard to accept, even though things hadn't been good between us for a while. Now that he's back, there will be a lot of adjustments for all of us to make. I'm not sure everything will be easily fixed." That was a good enough answer for the moment. "I think you need to get to sleep. Tomorrow's a school day."

As Trish exited Meghan's room, she met Marco in the hall. "How's he doing?" she asked.

Marco shrugged. "His dad's alive. Man, that's a real trip."

"Thank you for being a friend, Marco." Trish hugged him. "Take the four-wheeler home. The key is hanging by the back door."

"I'll be sure it's back in the morning."

"Don't worry about it." She waited until she heard Marco close the back door, and then she rapped on Scott's door and entered. Scott was sitting on his bed, holding a picture of Clay that usually sat on his dresser. Trish sat on his desk chair.

"I can't believe he's alive," Scott said. "It's so . . . I can't even . . . oh man. I can't wait to see him. Will you really invite him over tomorrow?"

"I told you I would."

"You're not inviting Alex, are you?"

Trish struggled with keeping her tone neutral. "It will just be the four of us."

"Okay, cuz that's the way it should be." He set the picture aside. "It's so hard to remember what he looked like, even with the picture."

"He really hasn't changed that much." She almost laughed out loud. No truer words were ever spoken. He was still self-centered and belligerent. Scott, however, had never seen that side of him. She hoped he never did.

"You need to get some sleep. It's after ten and you have

school tomorrow."

"Can't I skip?'

"No. Your dad won't be here before supper, and you'll need to get your homework done before he arrives."

"Geez, Mom."

"Just because he's back doesn't mean you can ignore your responsibilities. Got it?" She rose to go.

"Man, I can't believe it," Scott whispered and shook his head.

~

Trish paced the kitchen, waiting for the roast, carrots, and potatoes to finish cooking. The last twenty-four hours had been agony for her. If she could have figured a way to avoid the evening, she would have done it. She sighed. Postponing the inevitable would only make the waiting more intolerable.

The rich aroma of meat cooking did little to settle her nerves. Clay would be arriving in a few minutes. No matter how hard she tried, she wasn't ready for an evening with him.

Would he still expect to move in with them? She wasn't going to allow that, which she was sure would upset Clay. The timer beeped and Trish took the roast out of the oven, carved it into chunks on a platter, separated the carrots and potatoes into glass bowls, and returned everything to the oven, setting the temperature on warm. She added water to the meat drippings for gravy and concentrated on stirring the water and cornstarch mixture into the drippings. The simple task, done automatically, was lost in her muddled thoughts.

The doorbell and the pounding of Scott's footsteps in the upstairs hall jolted her to action. She switched the heat under the gravy to low and headed for the front door. Scott reached the door ahead of Trish and flung it open.

"Dad!" He flew into Clay's embrace, nearly knocking the bouquet of red roses out of Clay's hand.

"Stand back and let me look at you," Clay said after a moment. Scott complied, grinning from ear to ear. "You've sure grown up in the last five years."

Moisture gathered in Clay's eyes, and Trish melted a tiny bit. There was no denying that Clay loved his son.

"Why don't you come in," Trish said.

Clay handed her the roses and placed a light kiss on her cheek. "You look beautiful tonight."

Trish took the roses, noticing that Clay had not yet asked about Meghan.

Clay grabbed Scott's arms near his shoulders. "Can't believe how tall you've gotten. You're going to be taller than me before long."

Scott grinned. "Guess I'm eating right."

"Meghan, your dad's here," Trish called up the stairs. She watched Clay for a reaction, but he was still watching Scott. She gritted her teeth.

"Come on back to the kitchen. Supper will be ready shortly." As she turned toward the kitchen, Meghan sauntered down the stairs.

Clay looked up and smiled. "Is this little Meghan?" he asked. "You're pretty like your mom."

Meghan blushed as she stopped at the bottom of the stairs. "Thanks."

"Come here," Clay said, "and give your old dad a hug."

Meghan reluctantly gave him a short hug.

"You don't remember me, do you?"

Meghan shrugged. "A little bit."

"Well, good. Let's go see what your mom has cooking."

Scott and Clay settled at the table, while Meghan put the roses in a vase and Trish put supper on the table.

Clay leaned into Scott. "I was at your game the other day. You did a great job. If it wasn't for you, the other team would have won."

A smile worked at the corners of Scott's mouth. "It was a team effort, Dad. I wasn't the only one who had hits, and there was lots of good defense. It wasn't just me."

"I beg to differ. You had the most RBIs."

"That's because the other guys got hits before I did."

"Well, you had a great game. I was proud of you."

Trish set the bowl of gravy on the table with a thud. "Meghan is goalie for her soccer team. She's only allowed two goals all season. Coach counts on her."

Clay looked at Meghan. "That's nice."

Clay had already helped himself to meat and potatoes. Trish took her seat and bowed her head.

"Dad," Scott said, "we need to say grace."

"Since when?" he asked.

"Since we realized that being thankful for what we have is important," Trish answered. "Actually, for quite a while now."

Clay shrugged. "Go ahead."

Scott frowned at him and then looked at Trish. "Could I say grace?"

Trish smiled and nodded.

"Father, thank you for the meal and for the hands that prepared it. And thank you that Dad is back in our lives. Amen."

Throughout the meal, Clay pumped Scott about the sports he participated in, never once asking about Meghan's interests. Trish rarely got in a comment. The conversation centered mostly on Clay bragging about his athletic prowess when he was in high school, and about Scott and his chances for a full-ride scholarship to college.

"Good meal," Clay finally said to Trish. "Don't suppose you'd be willing to fix your blueberry pancakes for breakfast, would you? Always did like that for breakfast."

Trish stared at him. "What makes you think you'll be here for breakfast?" How did he remember the blueberry pancakes, which they had only on special occasions?

Clay blinked. "I have my suitcase in the pickup. Figured I'd move back in tonight. Can't afford to stay at the motel much longer." He winked at Trish. "After all, we are still married."

Trish glared at him and picked up the empty potato bowl. "I'm not ready for you to move back in, so you'll have to make other arrangements."

"Already checked out of the motel." Clay stood. "I'll sleep on the couch for a couple of nights."

Trish turned from the sink. "If you need a place to stay,

you can bunk with the migrant workers. You can take your meals there, too."

"I'm not sleeping with a bunch of Spics!"

"Geez, Dad, they're Hispanic." Scott frowned at Clay, then turned back to Trish. "Why shouldn't Dad stay here? It's his house, too. He has a right."

Trish fought the anger rising in her. "He has no right. The house is mine. Lock, stock, and mortgage."

"But Mom—"

"Scott, this is not your concern."

"He can stay in my room," Scott offered.

"No." Trish glared at Clay. "The choice is yours, Clay— motel or bunkhouse. The bunkhouse is free, except for sharing the cost of food."

"Geez, Mom."

"It's okay, Scott," Clay said. He glared at Trish. "Your Mom's not ready to accept that I'm back yet. I'll stay in the bunkhouse. That way I'll be close."

Meghan, unusually quiet through the entire exchange, said, "I think that would work, Scott. You'll be able to see Dad whenever you want."

Trish took note that Meghan had said you not we. She hated to admit it, but the evening had pretty much gone as she had expected. Clay doted on Scott and ignored Meghan, and then expected to move in and take up where he'd left off. She also took note of the underlying anger that Clay tried to hide.

"Well, if I'm going to get settled in the bunkhouse, guess I'd better do it before it gets too late." He looked at

Trish. "May I see you outside for a moment?"

Trish followed him out the door. "I'll go with you to the bunkhouse and let the boys know you'll be staying there."

Clay turned on her, red-faced and furious. "You've got some nerve denying me the right to sleep in my own house!"

Trish smiled. "*This* house is no longer yours. Actually, it never really was yours. Only my name is on the deed and the mortgage. And thanks to your gambling, you owe me 400,000 dollars, which is what it cost me to pay off *your* gambling debts."

Clay stared at her. "What gambling debts?"

He tried to look confused, but his eyes betrayed him. He never could lie to her and get away with it. And if he remembered the blueberry pancakes, why didn't he remember the gambling debts? "You know *exactly* what I'm talking about." She moved toward the bunkhouse, a hundred yards away. "Oh, and I'm sure the insurance company is going to want their $50,000 back, too."

"$50,000?" He tried to look surprised, but failed. "What insurance?"

"Your life insurance, which I used to *bury* you and pay off the pickup." She wasn't being very nice, but she had little patience where Clay was concerned.

Clay grabbed her arm. "Why do you hate me so much?"

"I don't hate you, Clay." She pulled away from his grasp. "I'm just tired of all your lying and manipulating. I'm not going to put up with it anymore. You can reestablish your relationship with the kids—*both* of them, by the way—but you and I are through."

As Clay followed, he pleaded with her. "I don't remember any of that. Honest. Can't we start over?"

"Not interested." Trish knocked on the door to the bunkhouse.

"I'll change your mind. You'll see," he said, and followed her inside the opened door.

Chapter 23

Trish informed the four men in the bunkhouse they had a new roommate and then left without introducing Clay. Clay winced at the pungent odors of green chilies, beans, and sweat permeating the room. He waited until Trish was out of earshot.

Clay looked around. *Time to set the rules.* "Anybody here speak English?" Clay asked.

An older man stepped forward. "I do, señor."

"Good." He pointed to a bed near an open door to his right. "Whoever is sleeping in that first bunk needs to move, and I want clean sheets, blankets, and a pillow. Comprendé?"

"I like that bunk," the man retorted.

"The boss lady and I are married, so what I say goes."

The man grinned. "So why you not staying in the house?"

Clay glared at him. "A minor disagreement that will be resolved soon. Otherwise, it's none of your business. Now, move your stuff."

"This bunkhouse *is* my business. And the 'boss lady' isn't our boss until we work her apples. Right now, Señor Lambert is our boss. Unless he says different, you sleep in whatever bunk is empty. Clean sheets and pillows in the cupboard at the back."

Clay felt his face heat with anger. He narrowed his eyes. Lambert was becoming a thorn in his side along with this peon. And he was anything but happy about being delegated to sleeping in the bunkhouse with a bunch of smelly Mexicans. He slept where he pleased.

With clenched fists, he stepped toward the older man. The other three men watching the exchange stepped forward with challenge in their eyes. One produced a hunting knife, holding it conspicuously at his side. Clay could take the old man, but he didn't want to take on four men, especially when three of them were a lot younger and one was armed. Besides, he reasoned, Trish would be livid if he got in a fight and trashed the bunkhouse. A disingenuous smile crossed his lips. "Okay, *señor*, you win. Can't fault me for trying."

"What you do to make the señora so mad?" the older man asked.

Clay shrugged. "Disappeared for five years. She thought I was dead."

The old man laughed. "Ah, now I understand. Women,

they are tough. They don't forgive so easy."

Clay grimaced. "You got that right, old man."

"Pablo," he said and held out his hand.

Clay hesitated. He didn't want Trish to hear he refused to be civil. He reluctantly offered his hand, then wiped it on his pant leg. "Clay." He picked up his suitcase and stashed it at an empty bunk near the back. He wouldn't be here long. Of that he was sure.

~

When Trish returned to the house, Scott was waiting for her.

"Is that true?" he asked.

Trish blinked. "Is what true?"

"What you told Dad, about the $400,000 dollars."

Trish took a deep breath. "I didn't intend for you to hear that. Yes, it's true."

"When you told me about his gambling, I didn't think it was that much." Scott looked away for a minute. "So how come you had to pay the debt?"

"Because your father tricked me into signing over the house and orchards, and he used them as collateral. Only my name was on the deed." She let that sink in for a minute. "I'm sorry, Scott. You shouldn't have to hear that about your dad."

"He said he didn't remember gambling."

"Maybe he doesn't remember, but it happened. I had to borrow money from the bank against the house and orchards. Borrowed money requires interest, which was six percent.

That's why I had to sell the orchards to Alex. I couldn't afford the debt any longer."

"So it's all paid off? Dad's debt?'

"The house is still mortgaged. I can handle the amount, and it's at a lower interest rate. I still need my library job to make the payments and provide a living for us."

Scott didn't move for a few moments. "I'm sorry."

"You have nothing to apologize for."

"I'm still sorry." Scott hugged Trish, and took the stairs two at a time.

Trish stood motionless, unsure of what Scott had concluded about his dad. She didn't want to disillusion him, but he was old enough to understand all that Clay had done.

~

Since Clay's return, loneliness crowded Alex's days. He missed Trish, Scott, and Meghan. He still attended their soccer matches and baseball games, but he and Trish didn't sit together. They talked by phone after both had gone to bed each night, but it didn't begin to replace the need to talk face to face. He missed the warmth of holding Trish in his arms and the sweet taste of her lips. He thanked God every night for Marco, who helped keep him sane and his days filled with purpose. He couldn't have asked for a better son.

He was pleased that Kale Morgan was actively investigating Clay's accident. Trish had kept Alex informed of the progress. In late March, Clay's "remains" had been exhumed and sent to the state lab for analysis. Kale had requested a rush on the test. In early April, Trish had relayed the findings to Alex.

"The DNA revealed that the ashes and pieces of bone left from the accident belonged to a Clyde Johnson," Trish told Alex over the phone. "Evidently, he was homeless. He didn't have any family. Was raised in an Illinois orphanage. Declared himself emancipated at sixteen with the approval of the courts." She paused and Alex heard her sniff. "No one should ever be without a family."

"How did they find out about the orphanage?"

"I'm not sure. Traced his social security number or something. Anyway, Clay evidently assumed his identity."

"Do you think Clay thought he was this guy?"

Alex heard Trish take a deep breath. "I think Clay figured it was a good way to disappear and get out of his gambling debt."

"You're saying he deliberately killed the guy?"

"Not a pleasant thought, is it? I don't know what I'm saying for sure, but I don't think for a minute that he's had amnesia. I just don't have any way of proving it."

"Did you tell Kale about where Clay kept his billfold?"

"Kale thought that was an interesting point. Don't know what he's going to do about it."

"Or can do." Alex gritted his teeth. Sometimes being a lawyer wasn't an advantage. "You're probably right about Clay, but none of what you've told me so far will hold up in court."

"I was afraid of that. Sometimes you're too much of a lawyer."

"You think that's a bad thing?"

Trish chuckled. "Not for a minute. I love every part of who you are."

Alex smiled. "That goes two ways, you know." He paused. "I miss you."

"It won't be long before we can be together again. I'm going to talk to Jess next week about filing for divorce."

Alex closed his eyes. As far as Alex was concerned, divorce was a "last straw" choice, but in this case. . . "I like the sound of that."

~

Trish closed her cell phone and snuggled into the warmth of her down comforter. She hated being separated from Alex. She needed him like she'd never needed anyone. Their love and future together meant everything to her. Clay couldn't get out of her life soon enough.

Although persistent, Clay had failed at convincing Trish to let him live in the house. He had balked at working in the orchards. Trish made it clear that he needed to earn his room and board and would be paid by Alex for work in the cherries, apricots, peaches, and some of the apples. He would be paid by her when he worked the Romes, the apples Trish still owned.

The migrant workers had spent the last few weeks cleaning up and burning the branches left from pruning. Some days they cleared dead weeds, and others days they cleaned irrigation ditches. Clay refused to weed, but reluctantly agreed to burn the dead limbs and other refuge.

The fruit had come through March without a major

freeze, but April was always unpredictable. In June, if they still had a crop, the workers would begin thinning the apricots and peaches, leaving only enough to get good-sized fruit and a bumper crop.

Trish had allowed Clay to eat with the family one evening a week and on Saturday nights. Clay and Scott talked continually about sports and fishing. Meghan was left out, as usual. Trish had urged Clay to attend Meghan's soccer matches, but he only made one. However, he never failed to attend all of Scott's baseball games, including the ones out of town.

~

A piercing alarm jolted Trish. She sat up, threw her bedcovers off, and hit the off button for the temperature alarm as she dialed Alex's number. He picked up on the first ring.

"I'm on it," he said. "Wake the crew. Temperature is thirty-two and dropping."

"I'll meet you at the shed," Trish said.

She dressed in record time, grabbing her coat on the way out the door. The lights were on in the bunkhouse. Pablo was first out the door.

"Pablo, you start wind machine number one. I'll get Clay on number two. Manuel should be here in a few minutes. You can report to him when he arrives."

"Si, Sēnora. Meester Clay is still asleep. Alarm didn't wake him."

"I'll get him." She entered the bunkhouse and stepped

aside for the other three men to get past her. The lump in the last bunk was Clay.

"Clay wake up." She shook him. "You have work to do."

Clay groaned. "It's dark. It's cold. I'm not budging."

Trish ripped the bedding off him. "Get up and get going. I need number two wind machine started in five minutes!"

"Hell, the peaches aren't even yours, so why are you worried?"

Trish gritted her teeth. "Because I'm being paid as a consultant, and I take my job seriously." She waited a breath. "Just do as you're told."

Clay spewed out a string of nasty words, which Trish chose to ignore. He swung his feet over the edge of the cot. "Why not stay here with me in this nice warm bed? We could get reacquainted." He wiggled his eyebrows at her. "Let the others get cold and hungry." He reached for her but she deftly dodged him.

"Move it!" she spat as she headed for the door.

Late morning, Trish walked through the orchards with Alex. The late-April night had been long and cold, but the wind machines and water had done their magic. The temperature had hovered at twenty-nine degrees for a while until the morning sun began warming the earth and the blossoms. They would lose some fruit to the cold, but nothing substantial.

Trish and Alex were careful to keep a respectable distance between them and kept their conversation neutral. They didn't want to give Clay any reason to think they were anything but business associates. She had talked to Jess a few days earlier, and he would let her know when the divorce papers were ready. She planned to inform Scott and Meghan before Clay was served the papers.

~

The first Sunday in May, Clay invited Scott fishing.

"Isn't it a little early?" Scott asked.

"Not for fishing Anthracite Creek," Clay said. "Just above where it meets West Muddy Creek it's clear and perfect for fishing. I drove up there the other day."

At dawn, they headed east from North Fork toward Kebler Pass. Scott watched his dad as he negotiated the road paralleling the North Fork of the Gunnison River. He enjoyed having his dad back, but there were some things that bothered him. For one, Clay paid little attention to Meghan. All he could talk about was how good Scott was at baseball. Scott knew he was a good player, but to listen to his dad, he was Babe Ruth, Barry Bonds, and Rockies first baseman, BJ MacCord, all rolled into one. He got tired of his dad's bragging about him, and he was sure Meaghan did, too.

Unlike his dad, Alex supported both Scott and Meghan and complimented them when appropriate, but didn't overdo it. Scott knew Alex was proud of him without all the bragging.

"We're going to catch some big fish today, son," Clay said as he drove east past the Paonia Reservoir spillway. "Nobody can fish like we can. I'm going to teach you the fine art of fly fishing."

"Dad, it's not a contest. It's just fishing. We don't have to prove anything. And I already know how to fly fish."

"Really? Who taught you?"

"Alex. Mr. Lambert." Scott knew the minute he mentioned Alex he'd made a mistake. He glanced at his dad.

Clay's face reddened, and he clenched his jaw. "I doubt Lambert knows half what I know about fly fishing."

"Maybe," Scott said, hoping to ease the tension.

Clay forced a smile. "You wait and see. Those fish will beg to get on our hooks."

Another contrast between his dad and Alex, Scott noted silently. For Alex, fishing was about the art, the joy of being outdoors, not how many fish you caught, or how much you knew. He didn't expect Scott to be perfect, just wanted him to enjoy fishing and the time together.

Scott stared out the side window at the quakie and pine covered the hillsides. Cottonwoods grew along the river bank. Flanking the road, meadow grasses were beginning to turn green.

The last few weeks since his dad had returned had been bizarre. *Man, Dad is being investigated over the exhumed body of a Clyde Johnson.* According to his mom, that was the name his dad had been using. He didn't know all the details of the accident, but he couldn't help wondering why his dad didn't show any remorse over someone dying instead of him.

Then there was the gambling and leaving his mom with a huge debt. The whole amnesia thing didn't make sense. He looked amnesia up on the internet. Too many things his dad said didn't fit with what he'd read about memory loss on the medical websites. There were some things about his dad he didn't like. Scott bit his lip. *I'm kinda glad Mom didn't let him move back in. Things are fine the way they are, for now.*

Clay glanced over. "You seem deep in thought."

Scott shrugged. "Just thinking about school and the baseball playoffs."

"You're going to take state. I know that for a fact."

"We're rated number two in the state. If we make it far enough to play the team rated number one, we'll have to work hard to beat them. It's not going to be easy."

"With you on the team, it's a no-brainer."

Scott took a deep breath and gritted his teeth.

They found a spot to pull off the road near the Anthracite. Clay let the tailgate down and proceeded to string his fly rod. Scott followed suit, and soon they were casting their flies on the crystal clear water of the stream. The rushing water soothed Scott's edginess over his dad's attitude, and he found himself enjoying the solitude. By lunch, Clay had two ten-inch trout, and Scott had one eight-inch.

"Look at that beautiful deep-blue sky," Clay commented when they returned to the pickup for lunch. "Ya don't get that kind of sky in Texas. It's the one thing I missed about Colorado."

Scott narrowed his eyes. If he'd had amnesia, how did he remember missing the blue Colorado sky? "Nice and quiet, too," Scott said. Noticing a white and gray bird nearby, Scott grabbed a grape and offered it to the bird. "Look, Dad, a Camp Robber."

"That's a waste of a good grape," Clay snorted.

"Naw, I like feeding them." The bird landed on the ground near Scott and hopped close enough to get the grape, then flew away.

"Better eat your sandwich," Clay said. "We got lots of fishing and drinking to do."

Scott frowned and pulled a Coke from the cooler.

"Put away that Coke. There's plenty of beer for both of us."

Scott glared at Clay. "I'm underage, Dad."

"Nobody's gonna know up here. Go ahead. I won't rat you out."

"Thanks, but no thanks. Coke is fine." Scott twisted the cap off the plastic bottle and took a swig.

Clay grabbed a beer. "Suit yourself."

By late afternoon, Clay had consumed a six pack of beer and started on another. Scott seethed inside. No matter what he said, his dad ignored him and opened another bottle. As the afternoon wore on, Clay got louder, more profane, and stumbled several times. His casting became sloppy, and yet he downed another beer. Scott took note that Clay had left the keys in the pickup ignition, so without Clay noticing, Scott pulled the keys out and stuffed them in his pocket. He wasn't about to ride home with a drunk driver. He'd learned that lesson too well.

As dusk approached, Clay reeled in his line and picked up his creel. "Time to head home."

Scott pulled in his line and followed a weaving Clay to

the pickup. He was glad he had the pickup keys in his pocket.

Clay stowed his fly rod in the pickup and grabbed another beer out of the cooler.

"Put it back, Dad."

"What?"

"The beer. You don't need another one."

"I'm not going to drink and drive. I have time to drink it before we leave."

"We're leaving now." Scott grabbed the beer.

Clay lunged for the bottle. "Hand it over!"

As Scott tried to keep the beer away, Clay knocked the bottle from Scott's hand. It shattered on the ground. A red-faced Clay looked at the glass shards on the ground, then at Scott. Before Scott could move, Clay backhanded him.

Scott stumbled back and rubbed his cheek. Tears stung his eyes, and he fought them back. "Just get in the truck. I'm driving."

Clay swayed as he reached for Scott. "No one drives my truck."

Scott dodged Clay and headed for the driver's side. Climbing in, he locked the door and waited. Clay tried to open the driver's door, cursed, and then climbed in the passenger side.

"You don't mind too well, do you son?"

"Not in this case." Scott started the pickup.

"You know how to drive this thing?" Clay slurred.

Scott put the pickup in gear and pulled onto the road. At the moment, he didn't like his dad.

They didn't speak to each other all the way home. Scott

tuned in his favorite radio station. Clay glared out the front window for a few miles, then fell asleep. When they pulled up to the bunkhouse, Clay got out and slammed the door. Scott followed, gathered his things, and headed for the house.

Clay called from the bunkhouse door. "Didn't mean to hit you, son."

Scott didn't turn around. "Sleep it off." At the house, he slammed the front door behind him and headed to the stairs.

"Thought I heard you come in," Trish said as she entered the hallway. "Did you have fun?"

Scott stopped on the second step, looked at her, and shrugged.

"What happened to your cheek?"

"I tripped and fell."

"Let's put some ice on it." Trish headed for the kitchen.

"Just let it go, Mom." Scott bounded up the stairs.

CHAPTER 24

Trish started to follow Scott, then thought better. Whatever happened, he didn't want to talk about it. She didn't for a minute think Scott had fallen. Clay had hit him. Her temper flared, and she headed for the door to confront Clay.

She was halfway to the bunkhouse when she stopped. Scott would not appreciate her interfering. As much as she wanted to tell Clay what she thought of him, she knew better. Making Clay mad would only exasperate things. Returning to the house, she decided it was time to let the kids know about the divorce. The sooner she was free of Clay, the better.

An hour later, Clay knocked on the door. When Trish answered, he muscled his way into the house.

"I'm done sleeping in the bunkhouse," he said. "We're married and it's time we acted like it." He grabbed Trish and tried to kiss her.

The smell of alcohol on his breath repulsed her. With every ounce of strength she had, she shoved him away. "Get out of this house. *Now.*"

"I'm not going to sleep in the bunkhouse one more night with smelly Mexicans. Not in this lifetime. I've been thinking," he stabbed a finger toward her, "so here's what we're gonna do. In a few weeks we'll put this place up for sale. It's good ground and a good house. Someone will grab it up. Then we'll pack everything up and head to Texas. I can get a job in the oil fields." He weaved a little and then righted himself. "The superior sports programs in Texas schools will give Scott a better chance at a good scholarship for college."

"You're delusional, Clay," Trish spat, "and drunk. I'm not interested in our marriage or you."

He tried to smile but it came out a grimace. "You're pissed. I get that, but we have an obligation to the kids to stick together."

"In a pig's eye! I don't love you, Clay. I have no interest in you or your bonehead ideas."

He backhanded her and she stumbled. Tears spilled onto her cheeks. Anger welled in her. "Get out!"

"I'm not leaving, got that?" He grabbed her arm and shoved her toward the stairs.

Scott met them halfway. "Let her go, Dad."

"You stay out of this," Clay said.

Trish wrenched away from Clay's grip and Scott

stepped between them.

"You can hit me all you want, Dad, but you *never* hit Mom."

"She needs to know who's boss of this house." Clay tried to move past Scott, but Scott stood his ground.

"Go sleep it off."

"Where? The bunkhouse? The *hell* I will."

"Then I'll call the sheriff." Scott moved closer to Clay. "Your choice."

Clay glared at Scott. "You're talking back to *me*? You're not the son I remember."

"You're not the father I remember."

"Not my fault I wasn't here."

"So you've said."

Trish sank onto one of the steps, tears streaming down her face. "J-just leave, Clay, before you make things worse. If Scott doesn't call the sheriff, I will."

Clay balled his fists and stood his ground for what seemed an eternity before he turned and stalked out the door, slamming it behind him. Trish let out a sigh. Scott rushed to lock the door, and then sat on the step beside her. He put his arm around her shoulders.

"You okay?" he asked.

Trish nodded. "I'm sorry, Scott. I don't know what to say."

They sat in silence for a while. Trish mentally thanked God that Meghan was attending a church youth group and hadn't witnessed Clay's abuse. It was bad enough Scott had to see the mean side of Clay.

"Was Dad like this before?"

Trish sighed. "He never hit me, but he used to say nasty things about me when he'd had too much to drink." She reached up and touched Scott's face. "Did he do this to you?"

Scott nodded. "I told him he couldn't have any more beer, and that I was driving home. He didn't like that."

"I'm so sorry." She slipped her arm around Scott and gave him a quick hug. "Come on." She stood. "I think we both need an ice pack."

~

Clay grabbed the cooler of beer from the back of his truck and stomped into the bunkhouse. Trish and Scott had no right to treat him that way. Especially Scott. What happened to kids respecting their parents? Trish had ruined Scott. Trish and that lawyer. Clay was sure he had something to do with Scott's behavior.

Clay twisted the cap from a bottle and took a long drink. He shrugged. Better enjoy it, he thought. He was low on funds and may have to cut back on buying beer. Another reason he needed Trish.

He was going to get even with Trish and her lawyer buddy. He didn't like the guy. Trish always looked happy around him. Clay watched the house at night, waiting for Trish to sneak over to Lambert's place, or Lambert to show up at Trish's. He was sure if he waited long enough, he'd catch them.

Lambert's son had been over to visit Scott. Couldn't Scott have picked a better friend than a Spic? Lambert and his kid had probably poisoned Scott's mind against him. He figured Trish and Lambert were calling each other, which would be impossible to detect. He aimed the empty bottle at the trash can and missed. The bottle skidded across the floor. He'd deal with that later.

His lack of sleep was taking a toll, but he couldn't let down his guard. He hadn't meant to hit Trish, but she infuriated him to the point he couldn't stop. Well maybe that would teach her a lesson. He was sick and tired of kowtowing to Trish. He was her husband, and she better start acting like it.

"You got any more beer, amigo?" Pablo picked up the errant bottle and threw it in the trash.

Clay glared at Pablo. "Get your own damn beer."

Pablo held up his hands. "Okay. Just trying to be friendly."

"Don't. Now get the hell out of my face."

Pablo turned and muttered under his breath. "Si, amigo."

"And I'm *not* your friend." Clay grabbed another beer from the cooler. He hated the bunkhouse, hated the spics he was living with, and hated Trish for rejecting him. Things were going to change, the sooner the better.

～

Trish handed Scott a bag of ice and a hand towel. After doing the same for herself, she sat at the table with him, holding the towel-wrapped bag to her cheek. Looking at Scott doing the same to his eye got the best of her. The laugh began deep inside her and burst out.

"Mom?"

Trish swallowed her laugh. "I'm sorry. The two of us sitting here nursing our wounds suddenly struck me funny. Maybe it's the relief that your dad left. I know I shouldn't laugh about it, but I can't help it."

Scott chuckled. "I know. I kind of had the same feeling." The grin faded from his face. "What happened to Dad? I don't remember him being like this."

Trish closed her eyes a moment, searching for the right words. When she looked at Scott, her heart dropped to her stomach. He didn't deserve a father like Clay, and yet in some ways he reminded her of Clay—the good parts, anyway.

"Your dad had a hard life when he was growing up. His father was killed in a mine accident when he was five, and his mother raised him alone. It's not easy to raise a son without a father. She did her best, but she overlooked a lot of things he did. I think that caused him to think he could get away with anything. He was a good athlete and that gave him the recognition he craved.

"After we were married and he couldn't play college sports because of his injury, he began to feel sorry for himself and blame me for everything that went wrong. Whatever I did or said didn't seem to make him feel better. He wasn't physically abusive, but he was verbally abusive. His drinking got worse. I had no idea he was gambling until the men came to collect the money he owed."

"And that's when you found out he'd used the house and

orchards to cover his debt?"

"Yes."

"You need to divorce him, Mom. He's not good for you."

Trish's eyes widened. "Do you really mean that, Scott?"

"Yes."

"That makes what I'm going to tell you easier. I had planned to tell your dad that I was filing for divorce before his accident. Things were pretty bad between us. Of course, when we thought he was dead, divorce wasn't necessary. When he came back, I decided to give him a little time with you and Meghan before I served him with the papers." She set the ice bag and towel on the table. Fingering the edge of the towel, she said, "After what happened tonight, I'm going to call Jess Atkins first thing tomorrow morning and have him serve Clay with the papers as soon as he can."

"Good." Scott set his jaw. "I don't like the way he treats us, especially you and Meghan."

"I'm sorry you had to see your dad this way. No child should have to experience what you went through today."

"I'm okay, Mom. Alex has shown me what a real dad is like. Too bad Dad didn't have a good role model."

"Your Grandpa McBride tried, but Clay resented his efforts." Trish stood. "I'm going to turn in. Do you need anything else?"

"Nah, I'm good."

Trish paused at the kitchen door. "Let me tell Meghan what happened. Maybe we'll both look better in the morning."

317

~

Trish called Jess Atkins after breakfast the next morning. She was thankful she had taken the day off from the library. Her cheek looked better, except for a small bruise.

"It's time to serve Clay with the divorce papers," she informed Jess.

"Do you want to serve the papers yourself, or would you rather someone else does it?"

"Someone else. I don't want to be anywhere near Clay when he gets the papers."

"I'll get right on it."

"Thanks, Jess."

Trish heaved a sigh of relief as she set the phone down. One more thing taken care of. Her cell phone rang. It was Alex.

"Are you all right?"

"Why do you ask?"

"Because Scott is here. I made him explain his black eye. He said Clay hit you, too. It's taking all I can muster not to come over, but I know you want us to be careful."

"I'm fine. I have a small bruise, but it doesn't hurt," she lied. It was still tender.

"Just say the word and I'll have Kale lock him up. For two cents I'd find him and clean his clock. His behavior is inexcusable."

Trish could hear the barely controlled anger in Alex's voice. "No. Stay away from him. He's not worth you getting hurt. You'll just make things worse."

"I know. Doesn't change how I feel, though." Alex paused. "Scott says he's caught his dad watching the house at night."

"Scott didn't say anything to me."

"He didn't want to worry you. He kept hoping Clay would start acting better." Alex paused. "If you didn't already know it, Scott's done with his dad. He's angry and doesn't want to see him anymore."

"Is Scott still there?"

"He and Marco are out working with Lucky." Another pause. "Clay be damned. I'm coming over."

"*No!*" Trish took a deep breath. "You'll only make things worse. I just talked to Jess, and he's going to serve Clay with divorce papers right away."

"Pack a few things for you and the kids and stay over here. You're not safe there."

"We'll be fine. Clay may have hit me, but he won't go any further. He knows he's walking on thin ice, especially if he wants to continue to see Scott. If he thinks that's possible, he'll back off."

"You have a lot more faith in him than I do."

"Everything will be fine. Don't worry."

"I worry every day you're not here with me. I'm glad you called Jess and set things in motion. It's time to get this settled. I miss you so much, Trish."

"I miss you, too, Alex. This will all be over soon, I promise."

"I know. It's just so hard waiting. You call if Clay even

hints he's going to go near you or the kids."

"I will."

Trish set the phone on the kitchen table, laid her head on her arms, and sobbed.

~

Two days later, Clay lounged outside the bunkhouse. The warm sun gave him a sense of peace for the first time in weeks. A bee buzzed him every little while, and the stately maple next to the bunkhouse provided much-needed shade. His tranquility shattered when Kale Morgan drove up in his patrol car and strode toward Clay.

"Let me guess," Clay said through clenched teeth, "Trish made a complaint against me."

Kale stood a few feet away, removed his sunglasses, and narrowed his eyes. "Now why would you say that, Clay?"

"Because she's got a mean on right now." Clay stood. "I haven't done anything wrong, so shove off."

"Trish didn't call me, but maybe I'd better talk to her."

"She'll just lie. She has it in for me. So why are you here? One of the Mexicans in trouble?"

"Nope. I'm here to clear up some questions we have about your accident. The one that killed a man named Clyde Johnson."

"Told you, I don't remember the accident."

"So you've said. In that case, you won't mind coming down to the office and answering a few questions."

"I do mind."

"I can get a warrant, but you don't want me to do that.

If you come voluntarily, that looks a lot better than if I have to force you."

Clay clenched his fists. This week was turning out to be pure hell. First his son defied him, then his wife rejected him, and the damn sheriff has questions about an accident more than five years old. He couldn't catch a break.

"How about I follow you in my pickup. Wouldn't look good if I rode in the patrol car." Better to get it over with so he could get on with winning Trish back. He was going to have to apologize to her and Scott, which really galled him.

"That would be fine. See you in a few minutes."

Clay watched Kale drive away. He was sick and tired of the world treating him like he was the bad guy. Things were going to change, no matter what it took.

CHAPTER 25

Clay entered the county sheriff's branch office, sweat forming under his shirt even though the temperature was a mild seventy-five degrees. He hated law enforcement, and the sheriff's office was the last place he wanted to be. He'd practiced his story over and over before he arrived in North Fork. Since no one had questioned him, he thought he was home free. Until today.

On the drive to town, he stewed over what Kale would ask him. He inhaled a deep breath. *Get a grip.* There wasn't evidence that would prove he'd done anything wrong. He'd survived a fiery wreck resulting in amnesia. End of story.

Kale showed Clay the way to his office and gestured to the only other chair in the room. Wiping his palms on his jeans' legs, Clay tried to relax and waited for whatever questions Deputy Morgan might ask. No way he'd volunteer any information, to Kale or anyone.

"Do you mind if I record our conversation?" Kale asked.

Clay shrugged. "'Course not."

Kale pushed a button on a desk recorder, said his name and the date. "Let it be known that Clay Ryan has given his consent to recording our conversation." He looked at Clay. "For the record, please state your name and affirm your agreement to the recording."

Clay gritted his teeth. "Clay Ryan. I give permission for this conversation to be recorded."

"Thank you. What do you remember about the wreck you were involved in five and a half years ago?" Kale asked.

"Not much." He glowered at Kale. "I have amnesia, remember?"

Kale smiled. "Just relax, Clay. Do you remember anything?"

Clay shifted in his chair. "I vaguely remember stopping to get something to eat in Rangely, but that's the last thing I remember. Didn't remember that until recently."

"You don't remember picking up a passenger?"

"Nope."

"According to the gas company, it was against policy to take on passengers."

Clay shrugged. "I guess so. Don't remember."

"Seems odd you'd give someone a ride."

"Maybe I felt sorry for him, lousy weather and all."

"So you remember the weather was bad?"

Clay swallowed. Too much information. "It was

November. Douglas Pass. I'm guessing the weather was bad or I wouldn't have wrecked the truck."

"You remember it was November?"

"No. I looked up my obituary when I got here." He smirked. "I was curious." Clay shifted slightly in his chair. He read nothing in Kale's expression.

"I understand you always carry your billfold in your back pocket," Kale said.

"Yeah, I do. So what?" *Who the hell told him that?* He took a deep breath. *Trish.*

"How is it you ended up with Clyde Johnson's I.D. instead of your own? Yours burned in the truck. Remnants of a leather billfold were found."

"How the hell do I know?"

"Did you take the billfold out of your pocket?"

Beads of sweat popped out on Clay's forehead. "I don't remember."

"Seems odd you'd do that while driving."

Clay gritted his teeth. "Maybe it was digging into my butt, so I took it out to be more comfortable."

Kale smiled. "According to the accident report, the remains of who we now know is Clyde Johnson were found on the driver's side, still buckled in."

Clay swallowed. He'd put Johnson in the driver's seat so whoever found the wreck would assume any remains were his. "Thought everything burned." He wiped his brow. "How'd they know that?"

"It's surprising what remains after a fire. Not everything was consumed. Part of the skeleton was left, and the metal part of the male buckle end was still hooked in the female buckle end by the seat. Seems odd he was in the driver's seat and buckled in."

Clay glared at Kale. "Just what are you getting at?"

"Clyde was buckled in the driver's seat and the remains of what appeared to be a backpack were found on the floorboard near the passenger seat. It appears Clyde was driving, which doesn't make sense. And you somehow managed to get out of the truck with Clyde's I.D., not yours."

Clay stood and planted his hands on Kale's desk. "I don't like what you're *not* saying. I survived the wreck. Carl—"

"Clyde. His name was Clyde."

"All right then, *Clyde* didn't. I'm sorry."

"You used his name for over five years. How is it you suddenly don't remember it?"

Clay stood and headed for the door, anger furled across his brow, his face red.

"Sit down." Kale's quiet command stopped Clay. "I'm not through."

"Well, you'd better get through," Clay threatened, "'cause if you keep at me, I'm calling a lawyer."

Kale settled back in his chair. "That won't be necessary. I'm not charging you with anything at this time."

"I should hope not." Clay relaxed a bit, but his hand remained on the doorknob.

Kale leaned forward. "Why didn't you remain at the accident scene? You didn't have anything to hide, and it seems you might have required medical treatment." Kale's look bore into Clay. "Why *did* you leave?"

"How the hell do I know? I don't remember the accident. I don't know why I left. Maybe I was going for help."

Kale continued. "Would you be willing to see a doctor? Have him give you a thorough check? Amnesia is a serious condition."

"Hell no." Clay shifted from one foot to the other and his hand gripped the doorknob tighter. "I don't need to see a doctor. I'm *fine.*"

"You don't seem very upset that someone died in the wreck."

"Hell, I don't remember the wreck, so why should I care?"

"Because Clyde Johnson was a real person, and he died instead of you. That alone should make you feel some remorse."

Kale's steely-blue eyes remained unblinking, unsettling Clay. He narrowed his eyes at Kale. "I guess he was just unlucky."

They stared at each other for a moment before Clay opened the door. "I'm outta here." He stormed from the building, feeling the need to clobber the first person who got in his way. And for the first time, he feared Kale knew exactly what had happened.

~

Kale settled back in his chair, glad he'd left an open telephone line with the state patrol office. He had wanted someone else to hear the interview. "Lieutenant Robbins, did you get all that?"

A voice came through the speaker. "I did. Thanks for leaving the line open. He certainly sounded unsettled by your questions. He's definitely not telling the truth. The fact the victim was in the driver's seat is problematic."

"No doubt about it," Kale said. "Something's fishy in Denmark, as they say. I think he deliberately staged the accident, and left Mr. Johnson in the truck on the driver's side. That way the responding officer would assume the body in the driver's seat was Clay. No reason to think otherwise."

"Agreed. Thanks for giving us a heads up on looking at the reports and photos again. Our department should have been more thorough. Assumptions were made according to the scene. No reason for the investigating officer to think it wasn't Clay Ryan. It followed that Mr. Ryan was the only one in the truck, company policy and all."

"Yeah, well, wish we had more than circumstantial evidence to make our case. Maybe if we keep after him he'll mess up."

Kale ended the call and sat back in his chair. He never liked Clay Ryan. Liked him even less now. Clay had deliberately caused another man's death to get out of his gambling debts. *Amnesia, my foot.* According to several doctors Kale had talked to, Clay didn't exhibit consistent symptoms of retrograde amnesia or any other kind for that matter. The long-term amnesia Clay professed to have was the brain-child of authors when writing fiction. It wasn't reality.

Kale fiddled with the pencil on his desk. "I'm going to get you yet, Clay Ryan. You're not getting away with murder. Not on my watch." He opened a blank document on his computer. He would read the transcription of the conversation later. At the moment, he wanted to record his own observations of Clay's behavior.

~

Clay hit the pickup's steering wheel with his open palms. Anger pushed and shoved at him. Why couldn't Kale let this go? Clay never liked the Morgan brothers. Cam had been ahead of him in school and Kale behind him. Both thought they were really special, big jocks and all, but he was better than both of them. He out-played them all through school, and he could lick either one of them any day, any time, any place, right now. He'd love to catch Kale in a dark alley somewhere.

He hit the steering wheel again. "Shit!" Too many people interfering with his life. He just wanted to take Trish and Scott away and start over. Meghan, too. He didn't have much use for her, but she was his daughter. He shrugged. She was a pretty good soccer player—for a girl. He'd give her that. Problem was, like most girls, she'd grow up to make some guy's life a living hell just like her mother. He wasn't even sure he still loved Trish after the way she had treated him since he'd returned.

"If it wasn't for Scott, I'd blow Trish off," he muttered, "but Scott won't budge without her. I'm sure of that." Maybe another accident would take care of Trish, he thought. Nah, he didn't need any more trouble right now. Besides, she still stirred a hunger in him.

Time to be mister nice guy again. He brought the engine to life. *Time to beg Trish to forgive me, as galling as the thought is.* He headed the pickup toward Trish's house, hoping she was home.

~

Trish paced the kitchen. From the living room window, she'd seen Kale Morgan stop at the bunkhouse. Clay drove away right after Kale left. *I wonder what's up?* She knew Kale had been looking into the accident. Jess Atkins assured her that the divorce papers would be served this afternoon. She hoped so. She was tired of playing games. Time for Clay to get out of her life.

She tried to concentrate on cleaning the kitchen, but she couldn't help wondering what was going on. Had Kale asked Clay to drop by the sheriff's office or had Clay gone somewhere else?

She finally gave up wondering and punched Alex's number on her cell phone. Oh, how she missed him.

"Hi," she said when he answered. "What are you doing?"

"Working on some papers for a client. Everything okay?"

"I hope so." She sighed. "Clay should be served with the divorce papers this afternoon. Guess I'm a little antsy, wondering how he's going to react."

"He's not going to like it."

"That's an understatement. I saw him leave a little while ago, right after a visit from Kale."

"Maybe it would be best if you weren't home when he returns or when he's served. Scott and Marco are at summer baseball practice, so that's good. Is Meghan home?"

"Meghan is at soccer practice. They'll be home around four."

"Why don't you come over? We have nothing to hide now that Clay's being served. Besides, you do work for me. We could confer on something, like the next spray application."

She could hear his smile over the phone. "Maybe I will. I love you, Alex."

"I love you, too."

She closed her phone. Anxious to see Alex, she fluffed her hair and straightened her blouse. Her hand was on the kitchen door handle when she heard Clay's pickup rumble to a stop. *Great.* She held her breath, hoping he would go back to the bunkhouse and stay there. She moved toward the front hall. The banging on the front door dashed her hopes.

"Open up, Trish." Clay tried the door. "I need to talk to you."

What does he want? Her back stiffened, and she held her breath. She'd kept the doors locked and bolted ever since he'd barged in and hit her.

She waited, unwilling to let him in. Alex was waiting for her, and the last thing she wanted was to talk to Clay. She touched her cheek where Clay had hit her.

"Please, Trish. I want to apologize for hitting you. I was way out of line." A moment of silence, then, "I can see your shadow on the door glass. I know you're there."

Trish gritted her teeth. *Great!* "I don't have anything to say to you."

"Come on, let me in. I won't touch you. I just want to talk."

Trish hesitated before unlocking the door. Maybe if she faced him he'd have his say and go away. She left the safety chain on and blocked the opening.

"Make it fast."

"Can't I come in?"

"Say whatever you have to say right where you are."

Clay shrugged and looked down at the wooden porch planks. "Okay. I get you're upset, but you have to believe me when I say I didn't mean to hit you or Scott. I'd had too much to drink. You know how I get. It was stupid. It won't happen again. I promise."

"It won't happen again because you're not welcome here." Trish caught a glint of anger before Clay's smile turned warm.

"Trish, honey, we need to work this out. I love you and the kids. Can't you see that?" He wiped his mouth. "I get angry because I can't be with you here in our house. It's not my fault I had amnesia. I need you to forgive me. I just want us to be a family again. I know we can."

"That ship sailed a long time ago."

"Because I was gone for five years? You can't hold that against me. I didn't remember."

"No. Long before that. I should have known better the day you had me sign papers for what I thought was a new pickup. I shouldn't have trusted you then. I definitely don't trust you now."

Clay planted his hand on the doorjamb and leaned toward her. "I know I made a lot of mistakes, but I'm willing to try to do better. I'm a new man. Remember all the good times we had taking the kids camping and fishing? We can do that again. You've got to give me a chance."

"I'm through giving you chances, Clay." She closed the door and locked it. The door shuddered as Clay slammed his fist against the frame. She waited until she saw him climb into his pickup and drive to the bunkhouse. She heaved a sigh of relief and hurried the back way toward Alex's and safety.

Alex opened the door and pulled Trish into his arms before she knocked. He kissed her like a man separated from his love for too long. She savored the warmth of his arms and lips, the smell of his aftershave, and the feeling of safety. Why had she waited so long to be close to him?

"I've missed you," he whispered against her lips. "It seems like years instead of weeks."

A tear slithered down her cheek. She never felt more loved. "I can't wait for all this to be over."

Alex guided her toward the kitchen. "Want some coffee?"

"I'd rather have something cold."

He pulled a pitcher out of the refrigerator. "How's iced tea?" he asked.

"Perfect."

He poured two glasses and set one in front of her.

She took a sip. "Clay came to the house a few minutes ago. He said he wanted to apologize." She rubbed the outside of the glass. "He sounded so contrite and sincere."

"Trish, don't let him fool you."

"I'm not. I could see anger in his eyes, although he tried hard not to show it." She swallowed another sip. "I'm afraid of him, Alex. Afraid he'll let his temper go and do something drastic." Trish shuddered.

"Did you get a restraining order with the divorce papers?"

"No." She looked at him. "Should I?"

He tightened his lips. "I think it would be a good idea." He stood. "I'll call Jess and have him draw one up."

"Do I need a reason?"

"You have a reason. He hit you and Scott. That's reason enough."

"A restraining order will force him to vacate the bunkhouse, right?" Trish closed her eyes. "He's going to be furious." She sighed. "Call Jess. I'm sick and tired of Clay and his threats."

Alex dialed Jess. When they finished talking, he pocketed his phone and smiled. "He's going to get right on it. Under the circumstances, he thought he could get a Temporary Restraining Order from Kale right away. If you need to talk to Kale, he'll call. Jess will delay serving Clay for an hour or two. If Clay so much as speaks to you, you can call the sheriff's office."

Trish closed her eyes and let out a long breath. "I hope I don't have to. I pray I don't have to." She laid her head on Alex's shoulder. He drew her close and kissed her forehead.

"I'll second that. Does Scott have his cell phone?"

"Yes. Why?"

"Call him and tell him that after he and Marco pick up Meghan, they're to come here for supper. I'll feel better if all three of you aren't home when Clay gets the papers."

Trish smiled. "You take good care of us, Alex. That's only one reason I love you so much." She kissed him, and then dug her phone out of her pocket, grateful she'd bought Scott a cell phone. While waiting for Scott to answer, she said a silent prayer of thanks for a safe haven and a man who loved her without reservation.

K.L. McKee

Chapter 26

Clay sat on his bunk, unable to relax after his meeting with Kale and his unsuccessful try at apologizing to Trish. He'd done everything he could think of to placate her and was sick of walking on eggshells. The situation required action, as his resources had gradually dwindled while he tried to reconcile with Trish.

Time to move in with Trish and enjoy the fruits of her labor.

He smiled to himself at the pun he'd made. She didn't have all the orchards she'd originally owned, which suited him fine—a lot less overhead and work. She did have a good job at the library. That would suffice until they moved to Texas.

His nerves still raw, Clay grabbed his third beer and the

cooler with two more six packs still in it. He wandered outside and sat in a lawn chair under the maple tree, where he'd been when Kale so rudely disturbed him. He set the cooler next to him. If the beer didn't make things better, he'd try the whiskey he had tucked in with the beer bottles.

Scott drove past with Lambert's kid on the passenger's side and Meghan in the back seat. Clay waved, but the kids didn't respond. "Damn kids."

He set his jaw, felt his face heat with anger, and downed the last of the beer. He'd wait until they returned from dropping off Lambert's kid, and then go to the house and talk to them. Scott deserved an apology.

~

Scott, Marco, and Meghan hit the front door of the Lambert house laughing. They stopped short at the look on Trish's face.

"Sit down, all of you. I have something I need to tell you."

They settled on the couch, while Trish and Alex sat in chairs opposite them.

"Everything okay Mom?" Scott asked.

"I wanted you and Meghan to know that I've filed for divorce from your dad. It's time. It's a decision I've considered very carefully. I don't love your dad anymore. Haven't for a long time. There's no future for us."

"'Bout time, Mom." Scott's jaw tightened.

"Yeah," Meghan said. "He doesn't treat you right."

"Both of you can still see him, but you'll have to make

arrangements to do it somewhere other than the house. I've also gotten a restraining order against him."

"I don't care about seeing him." Meghan bit her lip. "He doesn't pay attention to me anyway."

"Are you sure, honey?" Trish closed her eyes and swallowed the lump in her throat.

"Yes, Mom, I'm sure. I don't feel safe around him."

Trish gritted her teeth. How sad that Clay's daughter was afraid of him. It didn't have to be that way, but unfortunately it was. "Scott?"

"I agree with Meghan. He blew us off for five years, and he's been nasty to you and Meghan since he got back. Don't need to be around him."

"He said he had amnesia." Trish wondered why she was defending Clay. He was, however, their father.

"Yeah, well, I've looked up the newspaper reports about the accident," Scott said. "There weren't any skid marks. The paper said they thought he might have fallen asleep. It also seems kind of weird to me that he ended up with the guy's I.D. and not his." Scott looked down at his hands and then at Trish. "Guess I don't trust him."

"I'm sorry, Scott." She took a deep breath. "When did you do all this research?

"While I was waiting for you at the library." He shrugged. "Needed something to do, and I was curious."

"I wish things could be different." Trish stood and gathered Scott and Meghan to her. "You two are amazing, and I love you. Thanks for understanding."

"Does that mean you and Dad will be able to get

married?" Marco asked. He looked at his dad. Alex nodded and smiled.

"Yes it does," Trish answered.

"Sweet, cuz I think you'll be a great Mom."

Trish's eyes watered, and she hugged Marco. "Go get cleaned up, all of you. We'll have supper in an hour."

Scott and Meghan raced each other to the stairs, Marco hot on their heels.

~

Clay hadn't seen any activity at Trish's house. An hour passed, then two, and no kids. *I'll bet Trish sneaked over to Lambert's.* He fumed and guzzled another beer.

Clay grimaced as a sheriff's department SUV approached the bunkhouse and stopped. Why couldn't they leave him alone? Kale Morgan exited the vehicle, and Clay's jaw tightened. "What the hell are you doing here?" Clay growled. "Wasn't all that harassment this morning enough?"

"Not here to harass you, Clay." Kale approached and handed Clay an envelope.

"What the hell's this?"

"You've been served," Kale said and turned to go.

Clay jumped up from his chair. "Served what?"

Kale turned slightly. "Divorce papers, including a restraining order. You have twenty-four hours to clear out of the bunkhouse." Kale opened the SUV's door. "I'll be back tomorrow evening to check."

Clay threw his half-empty beer bottle at the receding SUV. He clutched the papers in his hand, the veins in his neck bulging. *That bitch.* Too many people were turning her against him. He glanced at the envelope. The return address was Jess Atkins' law office. Atkins always thought a lot of himself. Clay had heard Lambert was working with Atkins. Figured. They both reminded him of slick lawyers who could charm anybody into thinking their way. He hated lawyers.

He tore open the envelope and shuffled through the contents. "That little bitch!" he spat. He wasn't disposable. Clay wouldn't let her get away with treating him like trash. He crumpled the papers and gave them a heave, grabbed the whiskey from the cooler, and took a long swallow. He vowed to get even with Trish and Lambert. They'd pay one way or another. He headed for his pickup, hate driving him forward.

~

Trish couldn't help smiling as she glanced around the table at what would be her family. It had been a while since the five of them had shared a meal. The kids chattered about baseball and soccer practice. Scott and Marco traded jabs about their skills on the field, and Meghan bragged about how she'd stopped all attempts of her team to score a goal but one. Laughter filled the dining room and the events of the last few days were put aside.

Two growing boys had nearly devoured all the food Alex and Trish had prepared, and Meghan was no slouch when it came to putting away her share. When the evening meal was over, Scott, Marco, and Meghan cleared the table, Trish loaded Alex's dishwasher, and Alex put away what little food was left over.

Once the table was cleared, the boys asked to go to Marco's room. They couldn't wait to face off on "Mortal Kombat." Meghan begged to go with them and watch. Trish shook her head at the sound of footfalls pounding up the stairs.

Alex gathered Trish in his arms, her back to his chest. "Nice sound, isn't it?"

"Like a symphony." She sighed. "Do you think this getting along will last when everything's permanent?"

"For a while, and then they'll be normal siblings, disagreements included. One thing I'm pretty sure of, though, is that when Meghan begins to date, the boys and I are going to give the third degree to every guy that comes to take her out."

Trish turned in his arms. "Really? You think they're that protective of her?"

"I certainly am, and I don't think the boys will be any different. Didn't you hear Scott? He doesn't like the way her own father treats her." He brushed a light kiss on Trish's nose. "Scott's protective of Meghan, just like I am with you." He pulled her head against his shoulder. "Which is why I don't want you or the kids staying at your house tonight."

"Alex, I—"

"Hear me out. No telling how Clay will react when he's served the papers. The divorce is going to be bad enough, but the restraining order is liable to really set him off. I'd feel better if you and the kids stayed here for the night."

Trish started to protest again, but Alex stopped her.

"You and Meghan can sleep in my room, and I'll sleep upstairs with the boys."

"Alex, you don't have to do this. If I stay, I'll sleep on the couch, and Meghan can have one of the empty rooms upstairs."

"No argument. I have a king-size bed, room enough for both of you. Girls downstairs, boys upstairs. Looks better that way."

One look in Alex's eyes and Trish knew better than to argue. "You're not going to give in on this, are you?"

"Nope. The sooner you get some things from home and return, the better. Jess said he'd let us know when Clay had been served."

"You're right. I would feel better staying here tonight. I'll get Scott to help me get a few things, and we'll be right back."

Alex nodded. "I'm going with you."

"Alex, you don't—"

"You know how pointless it is to argue with a lawyer, right?" He grinned and brushed her hair away from her face. "Go get Scott. The sooner we get this done, the better."

Trish packed a small bag for herself and one for Meghan. Thankful it was Friday and she didn't have to work the weekend, she packed casual clothes for herself, Meghan's soccer uniform and a fresh set of clothes for her to change to after the match in the morning. It took less than fifteen minutes to pack what they needed. She noticed Clay's pickup was gone and wondered if he'd been served the papers. She met Alex at the bottom of the stairs, Scott right behind her.

"I just talked to Kale," Alex said. "Clay was served about two hours ago, and he wasn't at all happy. Thought he should warn us."

Trish looked toward the bunkhouse. "His pickup is gone. Maybe he's already moved out."

"I wouldn't count on it," Alex said. "Come on, let's go before he gets back."

~

Clay drove to his favorite place for target practice. He and Scott had been shooting together from the time Scott was six. When Scott turned nine, Clay bought him a .22 rifle and they'd spent almost an entire afternoon shooting it. Scott needed to be with him, he thought. He'd teach his son how to shoot his .45 semi-automatic pistol and his .358 revolver. Time Scott graduated to the big calibers.

He picked out a cottonwood tree trunk, envisioned Lambert standing in front of it, and began firing. By the time he ran out of ammunition, the bark was shattered and bare wood showed through. Satisfied with his accuracy, Clay stowed the guns in the console of his pickup and headed to Delta to replenish his ammo supply. Sick to death of Mexican food, he splurged on a steak dinner before heading back to North Fork.

When he arrived at the bunkhouse, he noticed Trish's darkened house. He gritted his teeth and clenched his fists. Trish and the kids were at Lambert's. He was sure of it. That really hurt, especially Scott spending time there. Trish couldn't wait to shack up with Mister Pretty Boy.

Grabbing his .45, he started toward Alex's. He stopped short when he remembered Lambert's dog. He needed a plan. Tonight he'd figure out what to do while cleaning his guns. He'd been patient enough. Things were going to change. No more messing around.

~

Chaos reigned Saturday morning at the Lambert house. Meghan had a soccer match that morning, and Marco and Scott a ballgame in the afternoon. Trish and Alex would be busy all day. They decided to eat lunch in town and fix taco salad for supper.

Trish's heart swelled with pride for this mixed family and the love they shared. She closed her eyes and fought back tears of joy as she loaded the dishwasher. She would miss the house where she grew up—lots of wonderful memories with her parents and grandparents, but lately, the memories were of anger, disappointment, and struggle. Yes, she thought, I'm ready for a new start.

"Hey mom," Scott yelled down the stairs, "don't forget to pack ice water. Lots of it. It's going to be hot today."

"Got it covered," Alex answered. "Better hurry. We need to get Meghan to the soccer field. Leaving in five minutes."

Alex gave Trish a peck on the cheek. "Doing okay?" he asked.

Trish let out a satisfied sigh. "Never been better. I'll grab the sunscreen; you get the water." At the bottom of the stairs, she hollered, "Let's go. Time's a wastin'."

Two sets of pounding feet descended the stairs and exploded through the front door. Meghan emerged from the downstairs bedroom close behind the boys. Alex and Trish followed, shaking their heads and laughing at the ruckus. As Trish settled in the front passenger seat of Alex's pickup, she said a silent prayer of thanks. Life was good.

~

Clay watched as Alex's pickup full of *his* family drove past the bunkhouse toward town. The gall of Lambert, flaunting his takeover of Clay's family. It dawned on Clay that the kids must have some games. That was the only reason all of them would leave together. Well, he wasn't going to miss out. He climbed in his pickup and followed.

He parked at the soccer field and headed for the stands. Time to show Trish and the kids that he cared about being a family. He settled several rows in front of where Trish, Lambert, and the boys sat, giving them a smile and slight nod before he sat down. He'd told Trish the afternoon before he would do better. This would show her.

It was a perfect day—blue sky, mildly warm, and the smell of fresh-cut grass lifting on the breeze. They didn't make days much better than this, Clay thought. He glanced at the cerulean sky, one of the things about western Colorado he really missed in Texas. He would miss it again when he returned to Texas with his family. Once they were settled, he might be willing to vacation in North Fork in the summer and go camping and fishing with Trish and the kids.

He relaxed and turned his attention to the field as the soccer match began. Meghan kept the opposite team's score at one, while her team scored three goals. In spite of her gender, Clay was proud of her. He had to admit she was one heck of a goalie. When the match ended, he congratulated Meghan on how well she played. She said a quick "Thanks" and headed straight for Alex and Trish, getting hugs and high fives from both of them.

Clay squelched his need to clobber Lambert. Now was not the time to let his temper get the best of him. He heard Scott say something about an afternoon baseball game, so Clay left to get some lunch.

After lunch, he parked at the baseball field and found a place only a few seats away from Trish, Alex, and Meghan. Again he looked their way, nodded and smiled, proud of himself for keeping his temper in check. Trish looked apprehensive, but he couldn't quite figure Lambert. The lawyer didn't look happy. Tough. Clay refused to budge. Lambert was going to lose this standoff.

Clay nearly ran onto the field and decked the umpire when he called Scott out on strikes. Instead, Clay yelled a few obscenities. Both Scott and Lambert's boy played a good game. They each had several hits, and Scott had a walk-off home run to win the game. Clay raced onto the field and hugged Scott.

"Way to go, son!" he yelled over the din of celebration.

Scott stepped back. "Thanks," he muttered and sprinted toward Trish and Lambert. Marco was already receiving hugs and high fives when Scott joined them. He received the same, a smile as broad as the Colorado River on his face.

Clay tamped down the rising jealousy. He had made the effort to show how much he cared about both kids, yet they'd pushed him away. Fine, he thought. Let them celebrate. He would have the last laugh. A plan began forming in his head. He headed back to the bunkhouse to pack his things. He knew how he was going to get Trish and the kids back.

CHAPTER 27

"What was that all about?" Alex asked when he and Trish were alone in his kitchen fixing supper.

"What do you mean?"

"Clay." Alex frowned. "He was overly friendly at the games today. Not sure what he was trying to do."

Trish shrugged. "Maybe he was trying to be better so he can see the kids when he wants. It was refreshing not to have any confrontation for a change."

"I don't trust him, Trish. He's volatile." Alex pulled a skillet out of the cupboard and put it on the stove. "You saw the way he yelled at the umpire." Hamburger sizzled as it hit the heating skillet. "He's up to something. I'm sure of it."

Trish stopped tearing lettuce into a salad bowl and looked at Alex. "I understand your misgivings, Alex, but we have to give him the benefit of the doubt for the kids' sake. You heard how they reacted when I told them about the divorce. If I had my way, Clay would disappear from our lives. That would make everything easier. The reality is, however, that he's still the kids' father. I can't keep him from seeing them, and they need to find common ground with him." She sighed. "I don't want them resenting me when they get older, just because I can't stand Clay."

"Maybe. I think Clay has alienated them all by himself. He just doesn't realize it. Both Scott and Meghan are old enough to legally decide if they want to see him." Alex stirred the hamburger. "You know I don't trust him. Never did."

"I know." Trish sighed. "Neither do I."

"I still think he's up to something. You and the kids should stay here again tonight."

Trish started to protest, but Alex stopped her. "I'd feel a lot better if you stayed. Let's head for the mountains tomorrow morning. I'm thinking Kebler Pass. We can do some hiking, maybe even a little fishing."

"I'd like that. I'll need to get a few things from the house."

"It'll wait until morning. Don't want you running into Clay after dark."

Trish smiled and shook her head. "How in the world was I so lucky to find you?"

"Works both ways, you know." Alex kissed her, then stepped back. "You better work your magic on seasoning the hamburger before I carry you to the bedroom and ravage you." He winked. "I'll finish the salad."

"You're incorrigible." She patted his cheek.

"Want me to show you how incorrigible I am?" He wiggled his eyebrows.

She giggled. "You don't know how much I'd like you to do that, but we have to be patient." She winked. "Marriage first."

Alex picked up the paring knife and a tomato. "My patience is beginning to wear thin, but I'll manage."

Fifteen minutes later, Trish called up the stairs. "Come and get it! Taco salad on the table. *Now.*" A chorused whoop and three sets of feet raced down the stairs in answer.

~

Light streaming through the bedroom window woke Trish from a restful sleep early on Sunday morning. Careful not to disturb Meaghan, she dressed and tiptoed to the kitchen, a lilt in her step and a smile on her face. After making a fresh pot of coffee, she wrote Alex a note and rested it against the coffeemaker.

Headed to the house to pick up a few things. Be back shortly. Love you—Trish

Lucky met her at the front door. "Good morning, girl." Trish rubbed Lucky's neck and gave her a hug. As she moved toward the driveway, Lucky followed.

Trish turned. "Lucky, stay." Lucky obeyed, but whined at being told not to follow. "I'll be right back, don't worry."

Trish strode down the road, humming and taking in the beautiful day. A robin answered her song, and mourning doves lamented nearby. The mid-June air was fresh with new growth. She sneezed. The cloudless sky beckoned her to a perfect day and an outing with family. Her heart swelled at the thought.

"Thank you, God," she whispered. "You've truly blessed me."

She didn't notice Clay's pickup parked behind the house, and it didn't register that the back door was unlocked, her mind on spending the day away from North Fork. As she climbed the stairs to get a few fresh clothes for herself and the kids, her spine tingled. Something didn't feel right, but she couldn't quite figure out what. She shrugged her shoulders. *Probably nothing. Alex's suspicions have me imagining things.* She understood his misgivings, but she chose to think the best of Clay, in spite of all that he'd done since his return. What other choice did she have if she wanted the kids to do the same?

She entered her bedroom and stopped. Her heart leapt to her throat. She turned to run, but Clay's hand closed around her arm in a vice-like grip. "Don't make me shoot you." He pressed a gun against her temple.

~

Alex rose and slipped barefooted downstairs, buttoning his shirt as he went. I'll let the kids sleep a few minutes more, he thought. They had a big day yesterday. He could smell the fresh coffee wafting from the kitchen. Sunshine streamed through the windows and sliding glass doors. Trish was obviously up. It would be nice to have a few minutes alone with her before madness and mayhem erupted. He loved the kids, but he looked forward to a little peace and quiet to start the day.

He grabbed a mug from the cupboard and noticed Trish's note. As he picked it up, a chill ran down his spine. *What is she thinking?* He had tried to impress on her his uneasiness over Clay's behavior. She should have waited for him. He grabbed his cell phone and punched in her number. No answer. Maybe she hadn't taken it. He rushed up the stairs, pulled on his tennis shoes, foregoing the socks, and tried to calm the fear rising in him.

"Boys," he called as he rapped on their door. "I'm going over to the house and help your mom get a few things for our trip today. Rise and shine so we can have breakfast and get going."

Scott peered out the door. "What time is it?"

"A little after eight. Wake Meghan. We'll be back in a few minutes."

"Okay."

Lucky barked at Alex when he opened the door. "Mornin' Lucky," Alex said. "You didn't go with Trish."

Lucky whined and cocked her head.

"That's okay. Stay. We'll be right back."

Lucky barked as Alex broke into a run toward Trish's house.

~

Trish froze at Clay's chilling words. He lowered the gun to his side as he pulled her back into the bedroom. She surveyed the room, looking for something she could use to protect herself. She blinked in disbelief at her open closet doors. All her clothes were gone. Her dresser drawers were open and empty.

"What's going on, Clay?" She tried to keep her voice even, but felt it waver as she questioned him.

"We're moving to Texas. You, me, and the kids. It's time. No more fooling around." He dropped his hand from her arm, but pointed the gun toward her again.

She backed up against the door jamb, her legs weak and trembling. His eyes glared with pure evil in contrast to the smile he pasted across his face. She swallowed bile rising in her throat.

Clay lowered the gun again and reached out. She flinched.

"I'm not going to hurt you." He brushed her hair away from her face.

"I-I don't want to move to Texas. I like it here."

"I liked it here, too. But there are too many people interfering with us getting back together." He rubbed her cheek with the back of his hand. "I understand you making friends with Lambert. You thought I was dead. But that's changed. No more shacking up with Lambert. I'm very much alive."

Trish tried to protest. "I'm not—"

"I forgive you." His eyes revealed something else. "We have some making up to do." He stepped back. "Better to do that somewhere else away from this town."

"The kids and I aren't going anywhere."

"I've packed all your clothes and the kids' clothes. I also picked out a few smaller things from the house that I know you like. Everything's in the back of the truck, ready to go. We can have the bigger stuff sent to us as soon as we sell the house." He looked past her for a moment. "Even thought about burning this old wreck down, but selling it is probably better. We'll need the money to buy a house in Texas."

Trish closed her eyes and said a quick prayer for strength. "I don't think you heard me," she said with stronger conviction. "We're not going with you. You can still see the kids, but our marriage is over."

Clay's eyes narrowed, the smile gone. "And I don't think *you* heard *me*." He pointed the gun at her forehead. "Now call Scott and tell him to get himself and Meaghan over here, ASAP. Tell him you've decided to move to Texas with me."

Trish fumbled in her pocket for her cell phone and realized she hadn't brought it with her. "I-I don't have my phone."

Clay glared and pulled a phone out of his pocket. "Use mine, then. *Just do it*," he said between clenched teeth.

Trish's hand shook as she took the phone and called Scott. "He's not answering." She hit end. "H-he may not recognize the number, or he may still be asleep," she added.

"Bull shit!" Clay grabbed Trish's arm, dragged her over to the bed and pushed her down. "Use the landline."

She reached for the phone on her bedside table and considered trying to hit Clay with it. Instead, she tried Scott's number again.

"Mom?"

"Hi, Scott." She took a deep breath. "I forgot my cell phone before I came over to the house." She tried to keep her voice even. "Your dad is here, and we've been talking." Another deep breath. "I've decided I should give us all a second chance."

"Mom, you can't—"

"Just listen, Scott. We're going to move to Texas and be a family. Get Meaghan and come over. The pickup is packed and ready to go."

"What about Alex? You two—"

"He'll find out soon enough. You know how I can be. Unpredictable."

"Unpredictable? No way. Is Dad listening in on the line?"

"No. Get dressed and come over."

"Do you want me to call the sheriff?"

"That would be good."

"Okay. See you in a minute."

"*No.*" Trish looked at Clay for fear her outburst would alert him. "Just do as you're told. We're ready to go." She pushed "end" and bit her lip. "They're on their way over."

"What was the no all about?"

"Scott was excited." She fumbled the phone trying to put it back. "The crazy kid wanted to tell Alex and Marco. I didn't think he needed to do that."

Clay smiled for the first time since Trish arrived. "Good thinking. Don't want them trying to interfere." He sat on the bed beside her and put his free arm around her. "It will all work out, Trish. You'll see. You won't be sorry."

~

"Scott, what's the matter?" Meaghan asked.

Scott held up his hand and punched three numbers into his phone. He'd felt the blood drain from his face when his mom confirmed he should call the sheriff. Three long rings with no answer. *What's taking so long?* As soon as the thought manifested, a woman's voice answered.

"911, what's your emergency?"

"We need help at Trish Ryan's house in North Fork."

"Please state the nature of your emergency."

Scott nearly exploded. "*I don't know.* Just tell Deputy Sheriff Kale Morgan that Mom said we were moving to Texas with my dad."

"I don't think that's an—"

"Just tell him! We're *not* moving. I think my dad is forcing my mom to do it. There's a restraining order against him."

"Are you at the house?"

"Just tell Deputy Morgan. He'll know."

Scott ended the call and looked at Meaghan and Marco. "Mom's in trouble. I'm going over there." He headed for the front door.

"Wait!" Marco said. "Dad just left to go there. Maybe we should stay here."

"Mom may need my help."

"Then I'm coming with you," Marco said, and they both

made for the door.

"Wait for me," Meaghan yelled.

Scott glared at her. "You stay here." He and Marco broke into a run at the same time, Lucky on their heels, and Meaghan close behind.

~

Alex reached Trish's house and slowed, hoping his gut feeling was wrong. As he approached the back door, he caught a glimpse of Clay's pickup parked at the back of the house. Fear seized him. "No, Lord, please. I lost Amy. Please, God, not Trish, too." He gritted his teeth, eased open the back door, and crept to the stairs. As his foot hit the bottom step, the board beneath him creaked. He grimaced.

"That you, Scott?" Clay called.

Damn. Alex stepped back when he heard footsteps in the upstairs hallway. He watched as Clay appeared at the top of the stairs.

The next few moments were a blur. Alex saw Clay raise his left hand and realized he held a gun. Alex dived to his right just as Clay shot.

"Alex," Trish screamed.

Alex crawled toward the kitchen. As he pulled his cell phone from his pocket, he heard Clay yell.

"Lambert, you son-of-bitch, stay out of this or I'll kill her!"

"I'm leaving," Alex yelled. "Just let her go."

"She's coming with me. You can't have her. She's still *my* wife."

Alex waited a beat. "I'm leaving, but I expect you to send Trish out unharmed." Alex retreated through the back door while calling 911. He explained the situation to the operator and stayed on the line as ordered. Finding cover behind a tree, Alex watched the house and prayed.

Siren's wailed in the distance. That was quick, Alex thought. How did they—? Three kids and Lucky raced toward the house. He pocketed his phone and intercepted the group before they got too close.

Alex raised his hands. "Hold on. Go back to the house. I called 911."

"So did I." Scott choked the words out. "We heard a shot."

Marco touched Alex's arm. "What happened?"

No sense candy-coating the facts. The kids needed to know. "Clay took a shot at me."

Tears formed in Marco's eyes. "Are you all right?"

"I'm fine, son. He missed."

Scott's voice waivered. "What about Mom?"

"She's with your dad." He placed a hand on Scott's shoulder and gathered Meaghan to his side. "I heard her yell my name, so she's okay. A sheriff's deputy has been dispatched. We'll let him sort it out. He's trained for situations like this." He could see fear and anger in three pairs of eyes.

"He'd better not hurt her or, or…" Scott didn't finish.

Alex squeezed his shoulder. "Did you say you called 911?"

Scott nodded. He quickly related the conversation

he'd had with his mom.

"I'm proud of you, Scott. You did the right thing. Now keep doing the right thing and let the authorities handle it." He tried to keep his voice even to reassure the kids, but his attempt did little to calm his own fears. "A prayer wouldn't hurt," he added.

At that moment, a sheriff's SUV arrived, lights flashing. In the next few minutes, the world exploded around Alex, although it felt like everything happened in slow motion. Seconds after Deputy Kale Morgan stepped out of his patrol SUV, the front door opened and Clay stepped out, holding Trish against him with a gun to her head.

"Mom!" Scott yelled. Alex grabbed him and held him back.

Frenzied growls and barks came from Lucky, Meaghan began crying, and Marco put his arms around her and held her head to his shoulder, shielding her from what was happening.

"Put the gun down, Clay," Kale ordered, his pistol aimed toward Clay. "You don't want to do this."

"Just get back in your vehicle and get the hell out of here, Kale," Clay yelled. "This is a family matter."

"Please, Clay, don't do this," Trish begged. "We'll help you. Just let me go." Her plea was met with silence. "Clay, I'll go with you. Just put the gun down."

"You're nothing but a lying bitch," Clay hissed. "You're going, all right. Once I'm clear I'll decide what to do with you."

Tears streamed down Trish's face. "You're not yourself,

Clay. Let us get you some help."

"Shut up!" He jabbed the gun barrel harder against her left temple. She flinched.

Alex fumed as he watched and heard the exchange. He tamped down his fear for Trish and used all his resolve to keep from taking the situation into his own hands.

"Clay, you need to put the gun down," Kale repeated. "Slowly put the gun on the ground and kick it away. You don't want to hurt anyone. That's not who you are. Let Trish go."

"How the hell do you know who I am? You and your brother never cared a lick about me in high school. And you were jealous of me after I married Trish, so just get the hell out of here!"

"You know I can't do that, Clay. I don't want to see you or Trish get hurt, but you have to cooperate."

Before Alex or Marco could react, Lucky charged toward Clay and Trish. She bit Clay on the back of the leg and held on. Clay screamed. As he lifted his leg and tried to kick Lucky away, he loosened his grip on Trish. She pushed from his grasp and ran toward Alex.

"Lucky, come!" Marco yelled.

Clay swung his gun at Trish.

"*Nooo.*" Alex rushed toward Trish and tackled her as the report of a gunshot rang out. A jolt and then a sting. Another shot rang out. A warm, wet sensation ran down Alex's arm. Kale ordered Clay to drop his gun. Alex heard two more shots, almost simultaneously.

Alex had landed on top of Trish. She lay unmoving. He

could hear the kids screaming.

"Trish." He brushed her face, silently willing her to respond. "*Say* something."

CHAPTER 28

Chaos erupted around Alex. Three screaming kids ran toward him. Lucky's barks added to the mayhem. Worry about the kids getting hurt added to his fear for Trish.

"Stay back!" Alex yelled at the kids. He rolled off Trish and cradled her in his arms. "Please, Trish, say *something*." Her eyes fluttered.

"Mom!" Scott and Meghan were at Trish's side in a flash, along with Marco and Lucky.

"Dad are you all right?" Marco searched Alex's face, his brow furrowed, eyes glistening.

He looked at Marco and forced a smile. "I'm fine. You kids don't listen very well."

"We were worried."

"You should have stayed back." Alex closed his eyes

and said a quick prayer for all of them. "Just stay low. I don't want you hurt."

Trish's eyes shot open as she sucked in a shuddering breath. Alex held her against him for a moment, silently thanking God for the breath she took. He smoothed her hair away from her face.

"Are you all right, honey? Say something."

"I-I will if y-you give me a chance."

Alex bit his lip. "Are you hurt?'

"I d-don't know. You knocked the breath out of me." She closed her eyes a moment. "My head hurts."

"That's all?" Alex asked.

"I think so."

Scott knelt and grabbed Trish's arm. "Mom, you okay?"

Meghan buried her face in her hands and cried.

Trish reached toward both of them, then dropped her hand and closed her eyes. "Fine. I'm fine."

Alex fought back tears. He checked her over to make sure a bullet hadn't hit her. To his relief, he found no blood.

"Dad, you're hurt." Marco touched Alex's arm where blood seeped through his shirt. "I'll go get help."

"Wait! I don't want you hurt, too." He hadn't heard more shots, but he didn't know for how long. "I'll be fine." Pain along with a warm, wet sensation traveled down his arm, but he didn't want to worry Marco.

"Shooting's over," Marco said. "I'm going for help." He jumped up and ran toward the ambulance and sheriff's vehicles.

Scott stood and looked toward the house. "Dad," he

whispered. Before Alex could stop him, he sprinted away.

"Where's he going?" Trish asked.

"He's headed toward your house." He looked at Trish. "It doesn't look good for Clay. I'm sorry. I'll go after Scott."

"*No.* Help me up. Scott needs me. You're bleeding." Her eyes filled with tear. "Get your arm taken care of."

Reluctantly, Alex helped Trish to her feet. She grimaced as she stood.

Meaghan moved to follow Scott to the house, but Trish caught her arm. "Stay here, Meghan. Help Alex." Trish hurried unsteadily toward Scott, leaving Alex and Meghan behind.

~

When Trish reached Scott, he was on his knees, crying and mumbling something to Clay's prone, unmoving body. Trish put her arm around Scott's shoulder and knelt beside him. Lucky had followed Trish, and she licked Scott's face.

Scott rocked back and forth on his knees. "Why, Mom?" he cried. "Why'd he do it? H-how could he do it?" Sobs racked his body.

Trish pulled him close, easing his head onto her shoulder. A sharp pain pierced her abdomen, and she waited for it to subside. Rubbing Scott's arm to comfort him, she said. "I don't know, Scott. I don't have any answers." For a moment she questioned her own lack of feelings toward Clay. She only felt numb.

Clay lay face down on the ground, his eyes open and fixed, the .45 pistol a few inches away. Lucky growled as a sheriff's deputy and a medic approached.

Trish patted Lucky. "It's okay, girl."

"Mrs. Ryan," the deputy said, "we need you and your son to move away so we can secure the scene. I'm sorry."

Trish nodded and coaxed Scott to his feet. She pushed back against the pain in her side and guided him back to where Alex and Meghan waited. Lucky refused to leave Scott's side. They arrived the same time as Marco and an EMT.

Meghan ran to Trish. "Is Dad...?"

"I'm sorry, honey." Trish, Scott, and Meghan held each other, tears flowing freely.

"Looks like the bullet just grazed you, Alex," the EMT said. "You're lucky."

"We all are," Alex said. He nodded when he recognized Jake Karlson as the EMT treating his arm. "Will you check Trish?"

Jake nodded. Trish and the kids watched as Jake finished bandaging Alex's arm. Jake ordered Trish to sit so he could check for injuries. Alex helped her down on the grass, and she winced with the movement.

After checking Trish, Jake suggested she and Alex both go to the hospital for a more thorough exam. "You'll need stitches, Alex, and Trish, I'm pretty sure you have a concussion, and maybe a broken rib or two."

Alex grimaced at Trish's diagnosis. "I'm afraid that happened when I tackled her. Sorry," he said to Trish and helped her up.

"It's all right, Alex. I'll be fine." She sucked in a short

breath, and an expression of sadness flitted across her face. She motioned to Scott and Meghan and put her arms around them. Alex and Marco gave them a few moments alone, then joined them in grief and thankfulness that they were all safe.

A deputy approached. "If I might have a few minutes with Mrs. Ryan and Mr. Lambert," he said. "I need to know what happened before we got the 911 call."

Trish nodded. "Okay." She looked around. "Where's Kale Morgan? I'd prefer to talk to him. He knows the situation, and he was the first one here." She glanced around, but didn't see Kale anywhere.

"Deputy Morgan is being loaded in the ambulance," the deputy answered. "He was shot."

"Noooooo!" Trish's knees buckled, and Alex steadied her.

"A bullet caught him in the shoulder, but he's stable. He's headed to the hospital, He should be okay." The deputy pulled out his notebook. "Now if I can get your statements."

Alex addressed the deputy. "Can you hold your questions until after we're checked out at the hospital? Jake says we both need some medical attention. Can we meet you there?"

"I think that will work, but I caution you not to talk to anyone or discuss this between you until I've gotten your statements. That means all of you." He looked at the kids as he returned his notebook to his pocket. "I'll see you at the hospital."

"Good." Alex handed Marco the keys to the pickup. "Go get the truck. Looks like Trish and I are going to the hospital."

"All of us are," responded Scott. "We're sticking together."

Alex smiled for the first time since the chaos began. "Yes, we are."

"I'm driving," Marco said. "You can't drive with an injured arm."

Alex closed his eyes and nodded. "You're probably right."

Silence permeated the truck during the thirty-minute drive to the hospital in Delta. Scott, sitting in the passenger's seat, stared out the side window most of the way. In the back seat, Meghan nestled against Trish, and Trish against Alex. Marco concentrated on the road. Alex silently prayed for Kale Morgan to recover fully from his wound, healing for Trish, Scott and Meghan—both physical and emotional—and for their future together.

~

Trish left her exam room, Meghan close behind, and found Alex in an adjoining one. "How's your arm?"

Alex shrugged. "Took a few stitches, otherwise it's fine. How's your head?"

"Well," she grimaced. "They said I have a mild concussion, but I should be all right in a few days. They gave me some Tylenol for my headache and said I may have headaches off and on for a while. I also have a bruised ribs. The doctor suggested that when I hit my head I probably didn't get any more good sense knocked into me."

"He's probably right." Alex fended off her half-hearted blow to his good arm. It felt good to relieve some of the tension.

"Looks like you're doing better," Alex said to Meghan. She hugged Trish. "Just happy you and Mom are okay." Scott and Marco entered the exam room.

"So, what's the scoop?" asked Marco.

"We're all going to live," Alex said, then wished he'd chosen better words. "I'm sorry. I didn't mean…it just came out."

"No problem," Scott said. "You're right, we're all going to live." His eyes glistened.

"Did the deputy talk to you guys?"

"He did me," Trish answered. "Didn't take long. Has he talked to you, Scott? I gave him permission."

"Yeah," Scott said. "Told him what I knew."

"He's talked to me, too. Glad to have that over with." Alex added. "Have you heard how Kale is doing?"

"He's in surgery right now," Marco said. "They wouldn't tell us anything since we're not family. I think his brother is on his way."

Alex slipped off the exam table. "Time for us to go home.

Trish hesitated. "I'd like to talk to Sarah when she gets here with Cam."

"Later, Honey. You need to rest, and we need to sit down as a family and talk about what happened." Alex looked at the three kids. "That okay with everyone?"

They all nodded.

"Then let's load up and go home. Hospitals are my least favorite place to be." Alex slipped into his bloody shirt and escorted his family out the door.

~

The warm May afternoon belied the events that had taken place earlier. Yellow crime scene tape surrounding the front of Trish's house the only evidence of the earlier drama. Clay's body was gone, as well as the ambulances and sheriff's vehicles. Alex, Trish, and the three kids gathered in Alex's living room. Trish had offered to fix sandwiches, but none of them cared to eat.

Once they were seated, Alex took hold of Trish's hand. "I think before we talk about what happened, we need to pray."

They each joined hands, bowed their heads, and waited.

"Father God," Alex prayed, "we thank You for watching over us today. We especially thank You for protecting Trish." Alex squeezed her hand and fought for composure. "We don't know why Clay did what he did, but we ask You to forgive him. And we ask You to help us forgive him, too. We are all Your children, including Clay. May You continue to be with us as we move forward with our lives, and ask that You bless us as a family. We also pray for Kale Morgan, that he will heal and be able to return to the work he does so well. We've all been given a second chance, Lord." His voice cracked, and he swallowed the lump in his throat. "Help us to make the most of our lives so that we may honor You. Thank you, Father, for Your healing grace. Amen."

Alex took a deep breath. "I know it's going to be difficult, but I think we need to talk about everything that happened, starting with Trish. If we don't talk about it, it will always be a wall between us. By getting everything out in the open, we have a much better chance at healing."

Before Trish could say anything, Meghan blurted, "I'm glad he's dead. Now he won't bother us anymore."

"Meghan, you don't mean that." Trish reached for Meghan's hand, but she pulled it away.

"I *do* mean it. He was mean, and, and nasty. He deserved to die."

"Oh, Meghan." Tears slipped down Trish's cheeks. She wiped them away. "No one deserves to die. Your dad wasn't always mean and nasty, as you put it. I think the accident we thought killed him, changed him. The man that showed up a few weeks ago was very different from the man who disappeared five years ago."

"Mom's right, Meghan. Dad used to have fun with us. Don't you remember him taking us camping and fishing? He used to play games with us, too. You beat him all the time playing *Sorry*."

"I think he let me win."

"Exactly. Dad wasn't so bad. Mom's right, though." Scott's voice softened. "He changed."

The rest of the afternoon centered on what happened when Trish went to her house. They tried to sort out why Clay had become angry and obsessed, and came to the conclusion that his gambling, drinking, and causing another man's death had probably pushed him over the edge. Several boxes of Kleenex were emptied until all conversation was exhausted and a solemn quiet descended on each one.

"Let's get something to eat," Alex suggested. All nodded in agreement.

While they ate a simple meal of sandwiches, chips, and sodas, Trish voiced her reluctance to return to the crime scene. "I don't want to go back home tonight. All our clothes are in Clay's truck behind the house. We have what we need here for now, if that's okay with Alex and Marco."

"It's more than okay," Alex answered. "We'll keep the same sleeping arrangements until you're comfortable going back to the house, or we're married." He winked.

Trish smiled. Scott and Marco grinned. Meghan giggled.

After the remnants of the meal were cleaned up, Trish called Sarah to check on Kale. "He's out of surgery and doing well," Trish reported when she ended the call. "The bullet shattered some of the bone, so he'll need more surgery on his shoulder and lots of recovery and rehab, but he's going to be all right."

~

Monday morning after breakfast, Alex suggested that as soon as the crime scene tape was removed, he and the boys would get Clay's pickup unloaded and the items back into Trish's house. They'd also pack enough clothes to have at Alex's for a few days.

"You know you're going to have to return to the house

at some time. It's up to you when, but moving things back into the house will help," he said.

"I know." Trish took a deep breath. "I just dread going back over there. I keep seeing…" She buried her face in her hands and sobbed.

Alex moved to her side and gathered her in his arms. Trish let out a small groan, and Alex dropped his arms.

She sniffed and pulled a tissue from her pocket. "I'm sorry, but my ribs are still sore."

Alex cradled her face in his hands. "Forgive me. I hate seeing you hurt in any way. You and the kids didn't deserve any of this."

"Oh, Alex, you and Marco didn't deserve this, either."

Alex looked at the three kids, and then back at Trish. "We're a family. We stick together. It may be a while before it's official, but we're still a family. Nothing can change that, in my estimation, anyway. I hope you still feel the same."

Trish graced him with a smile. "Of course I do."

Scott slipped from his chair and put his arm around his mother's shoulders. "We all feel that way, Mom, right guys?" He eyed Meghan and Marco. They smiled and nodded.

Alex's arm ached, and he knew Trish's ribs and head hurt, but he decided a day away would give them all a chance to put some distance between them and yesterday's traumatic events.

"Let's put together a lunch and take a drive over Grand Mesa. Get away for a while. What do you say?" Alex asked.

All chimed in immediately with enthusiastic yeses.

"We might even stop by my folks. Let them *see* we're okay, not just hear it from us."

As they went to work putting food together for the trip, Alex thought about Amy and Alex Jr. and how far he and Marco had come since their deaths. Amy would approve, he thought. Surveying his new family, he smiled, thankful for second chances. After yesterday, he knew they could weather anything together.

About the author:

K. L. (Karen Lea) McKee has had a passion for writing since she was a young girl. After raising two rambunctious boys and earning her B.A. in English from Regis University, she renewed her desire to write faith-based stories.

Karen worked in the Reference Center of her local library for twenty-nine years, retiring to pursue writing full time. She is a member of Rocky Mountain Fiction Writers and several local writing groups.

She and her husband reside in Western Colorado, known for its fruit orchards, wineries, majestic mountains, spectacular canyons, and strikingly beautiful desert terrain. She enjoys knitting, music, the beautiful Western Colorado outdoors, and spending time with her family.

Karen was raised in the small town of Paonia, Colorado, known for its fruit orchards, cattle ranches, small farms, and coal mining. She appreciates the hard work and sacrifice needed for each of these occupations. She also understands what it's like growing up in a small town.

Other books by K. L. McKee:

Miracle, a novella

In Name Only

Worth Waiting For—Book 1 North Fork Series

Stolen Heart—Book 2 North Fork Series—Finalist in the 2020 Colorado Humanities Book Award for Romance

You may contact the author at klmckee@gmail.com